CHASING SOMEDAY

HOME IN YOU SERIES
BOOK FOUR

Crystal Walton

Impact Editions, LLC
Chesapeake, VA

Impact Editions, LLC
www.crystal-walton.com

This is a work of fiction. Names, characters, places, and incidents are a product of the author's imagination. Locales and public names are sometimes used for atmospheric purposes. Any resemblance to actual people, living or dead, or to businesses, companies, events, institutions, or locales is completely coincidental.

Book Layout ©2013 BookDesignTemplates.com

Cover Design ©2021 Blue Water Books

Author Photo by Charity Mack

Name: Walton, Crystal, 1980-
Title: Chasing Someday / Crystal Walton.
Identifiers: LCCN 2018911229 (pbk) | ISBN 978-1-7328162-0-6 (pbk)
BISAC: 1. FICTION / Clean & Wholesome Romance 2. FICTION / Contemporary Inspirational Romance

Library of Congress Control Number: 2018911229

CHAPTER ONE

If Only

Of all the ways Chase Thompson could prove how crazy he was about his best friend, this—right here—had to be top of the list. Or maybe it just proved he was plain crazy. Shaking his head, he balanced his travel mug on one knee and Livy's giant purse on the other.

Two women strolled into the dressing area, carrying nearly as many outfits as Livy had brought in with her a good twenty minutes ago. The blonde flaunted a grin his way while the brunette eyed the purse in his lap. "Waiting on a room?"

He coughed through a gulp of potpourri-tainted coffee. "No, I'm not here to... This isn't what it..." Looked like? Just a regular ole guy with a fancy handbag, sitting cross-legged on a stupid overstuffed pillow in the middle of a women's boutique. Yep, nothing embarrassing about that at all.

Chase wiped the streak of coffee running down his chin. Because clearly, he was on a roll stripping himself of all dignity. Grasping at what little remained, he adjusted his cowboy hat and hiked his boot across his knee.

Big mistake.

Everything in his lap sprawled onto the floor. He swept up the cup with only a dribble escaping, shoved things no guy should be touching back into Livy's bag, and hopped to his feet faster than a thrown cowboy dodging flying hooves.

Trying to play it off, he lifted his mug at them. What was he doing? Giving them a toast? Smooth. He swung the purse behind his back. "This isn't mine. I'm holding it for a friend. A girl friend." He slanted a glance to Livy's dressing room. "I don't mean my girlfriend. Just a friend... who's a girl." A girl who now owed him hazard pay for pure mortification.

"Well, tell your *friend* she has nice taste."

As soon as their giggles trailed into their dressing rooms, Chase rolled his eyes at himself. No wonder Livy had kept him relegated to the friend zone all this time.

He moseyed toward her room. "I hope you're enjoying this."

"Didn't say a word," she peeped from behind the door.

She didn't have to. He could practically hear her laughing in her head from here.

"You know," he whispered. "You could've asked my sister to come with you today."

"She just got back from her honeymoon."

"Exactly. She probably needs some girl time... shopping torture... whatever y'all call this."

Livy handed him a pile of clothes above the door. "Oh, stop your whining. You know you love it."

She disappeared below the door again, and Chase simply stood there with a bundle of frilly outfits draped over the purse. Yep, it was definitely love.

Truth be told, he could complain about being here all he wanted, but he'd be tempted to try on one of these dresses himself if it meant getting to spend time with her.

He'd never expected to run into his college roommate's sister again. Might've dreamed he would one day. But for her to have moved to his hometown? Whether by fate or chance, he wasn't about to let her slip away this time.

The lock unlatched, and Livy stepped out in a navy-blue dress that caressed the tops of her calves as she twirled. "Besides, who else can I trust for an honest opinion?"

There went her purse again, right down his arm. He caught it with even less grace than he had the first time.

Her face scrunched at his reaction. "That bad?"

"No, it's... You look..." What was with his lack of vocabulary today? He scratched his jaw in search of the right adjective, but one little tilt of her head sent his whole world sideways.

"You can tell me the truth."

If only.

"Oh no." She grimaced. "It's worse than I thought. You're getting that little V between your brows. The lighting in the dressing room must really be off. I thought the dress looked okay, but I know better than to trust a mirror." Examining her outfit, she fiddled with the rope belt. "It's my hips, isn't it? They're too pointy?"

Her blue eyes shot up. "Not that you need to comment on my hips. That would be totally awkward. It's just that I want to find the perfect dress to wear tomorrow, and you're a guy, so you'd know if another guy would like it, right? I mean, I realize not all guys think alike, and maybe what you think is flattering, Jed thinks is completely boring, and—"

"Livy." Chase cupped her shoulders to stop her adorable rambling. "You're gorgeous. It doesn't matter what you wear."

The rose in her cheeks deepened the way it always did when she received a compliment, but it didn't take long for her eyes to dim again. "If you were the lead singer of Driveshaft, you might feel differently. You know how many girls he meets at a single show?"

Chase begged his lip not to curl in response to the effect this guy had on her. "There's only one you, Liv. If Pretty Boy doesn't see that, it's his loss." One of these days, Chase would get that through to her.

"He has a name, you know."

Yeah, one Chase choked on every time he tried to spit it out. "Justin Bieber?"

Livy swatted him in the bicep.

"Hunter Hayes?"

"Stop." Fighting the smile he loved, she shoved him.

He kept her hand on his chest as the two girls from earlier came out of their dressing rooms. Chase looked from them to Livy and back, feeling vindicated.

For all of five seconds.

Whatever Livy's sly grin meant, it couldn't be good.

She motioned to the dresses still slung over his arm. "Want me to look for those in a larger size for you? The dressing room's free now."

The blonde returned his raised brow as she passed, and all Chase could do was tip his hat.

"Real funny," he said once they were alone again.

She gave a maddeningly cute shrug. "I learned from the best."

Back in the dressing room, she left the door open this time and studied her reflection. "You sure the dress is okay? Jed canceled the last three times. Now that he's finally going to be back in town, I want everything to be lovely."

As if she couldn't get any more attractive, the faint British accent she'd picked up during her modeling stint in London sent him over the edge sometimes. Almost enough to neutralize how much it killed him to watch her let that loser string her along.

"Considering the guy has family here, you'd think he'd make an effort to come home more often."

Livy came back out and cocked her head at him. "Says the guy who travels all over the States for a living."

Was she seriously comparing them? "It's not the same thing." Taking care of his family was the whole reason he took his job to begin with.

"I know." Her eyes softened. "But as someone who's on the road a lot, I'd think you'd have a little more empathy for him."

Not likely.

She squeezed his arm without looking away, and that was it. Resolve demolished.

"All right, fine. I admit I can relate to the strain of being on the road." He curled her long blond braid over her shoulder. "But I always come home." For his family, yes, but for her too. If Jed were half the man she deserved, he'd get a clue and do the same.

"I know." A feisty grin crept up her cheeks. "Which is why you make the perfect purse carrier." She retreated to the safety of her dressing room. "Kidding," she teased through a laugh that said otherwise. "You know I love you, Chase."

As her best friend, maybe. He swallowed the sting with another sip of the coffee she'd made him this morning. That reminded him...

Dishing out a nonchalant tone, he picked at the edge of his mug. "You know, I passed Mrs. Finch's old café earlier today. The space is still for sale."

"Don't start."

"C'mon, Liv. Don't tell me you wouldn't open your own coffee shop if you had the chance."

She draped the navy-blue dress over the door. "That's the point. There is no chance."

"Only because you're stubborn."

"Realistic," she countered.

"Trepid."

The dressing room door swung open. "Trepid?"

Apparently, his vocabulary choices were only getting worse. Chase lifted his cowboy hat and ran his fingers through his hair. "Well, not when you look at me like a bull about to charge out of the chute."

The adorable tight lines around her eyes sent the corner of his mouth quirking.

"A bull? Really?"

He rubbed his stubbly jaw. "Maybe not my best analogy."

"You think?" She crossed her arms. "You just equated me to a drooling mammoth with horns and a ring in his nose."

Chase bit his lip to curb a laugh. "I was referring to his confidence." Cocking his head, he squinted at her. "But now that you mention it..."

She shoved him again, and his laugh tumbled out.

"Hey, you started it with that dressing room crack." He handed her the purse and a teasing smile. "I'm serious about the confidence, though. Just think of starting a business like you would tackling a runway."

"That was ages ago," she mumbled.

"Still, you can't tell me it didn't take faith and guts to work those shoots." He dipped his head toward hers. "That girl's still in you. We just gotta bring her out again."

Her face stiffened. "No, we don't." She backed away and turned, voice soft and broken. "You're lucky you didn't know that girl."

"Doubt that." Chase waited for her to turn instead of pressing it.

As close as they'd gotten since she moved to Littleton last summer, she still stonewalled him when it came to her modeling days. Whatever her past held, she obviously wasn't ready to trust him with it.

A song played from inside her purse. She sifted through the rearranged contents in search of her cell. Chase didn't need to see the name on the screen. Her heartbreaking smile made it clear Pretty Boy had graced her with a call.

He backed off to give her some space and almost bumped into a mom entering the dressing area with a little boy carrying a Matchbox car. *Now* someone was talking his language.

"That's one good-looking '68 Chevy you got there." Chase squatted to the kid's level. "You know, I learned to drive in a truck just like that when I wasn't too much older than you."

The woman offered him a kind smile when her son's face lit up. But as easily as Chase could get caught up in talking cars with anyone, no distraction could override the unmistakable disappointment in Livy's voice. He'd heard it too many times to miss.

"No, don't worry about it." Even with her back turned, the quiver still reached him. "I know you're busy... Next week is fine." She traced a hand down the stunning dress draped over the dressing room door. "No, I didn't have anything special planned. Really, it's no big deal."

Lying to the loser was one thing. But lying to herself could only last so long before brokenness became irreparable.

She ended the call without moving, and Chase practically had to cement his boots to the floor to keep from getting up and wrapping his arms around her.

The kid's slur of questions about his toy blended into the background until Livy finally turned around. Her rehearsed smile fell the minute her gaze met the boy's. She looked from him to Chase, still kneeling beside him, and up to the mom. After a silent moment that seemed to scream a dozen things he couldn't decipher, Livy pointed to the exit. "Excuse me."

Chase grabbed his coffee and rustled the boy's hair. "Take care of that Chevy. You'll be driving one before you know it."

He caught up to Livy in front of the exit. "Liv."

"It's fine." She turned, her stoic mask ready to shatter as easily as her heart.

"It's not fine."

She wanted a date, and instead, she got another rejection. No wonder her confidence hung by a thread.

"You know what you need?" he said before he thought better of it.

"Besides another coffee?" She aimed a finger at him. "And don't you dare say a realtor."

He'd save that conversation for another time. He shook his head. "Practice."

"Practice."

Unable to fend off a grin, Chase lolled an arm across her shoulders. "A little coaching. A few practice dates. If you want to win over a guy, you need a guy's inside guidance. Isn't that basically what you were saying earlier?" Possibilities swirled.

She slipped out from under his arm and studied him. "You're serious."

"Why not? A little confidence booster will be good for you."

When she didn't budge from her guarded stare, Chase splayed his arms out. "Hey, you're looking at a guy who just carried your purse around all morning without losing his manhood. That's gotta earn me some kind of credentials." He nudged her with his shoulder. "C'mon, it'll be fun. What do you say? Deal?"

Her glossed lips made a slow hike to the side. "You're not gonna spit in your hand, are you?"

He laughed. "You're something else."

"Something crazy maybe."

Crazy beautiful. If there was even half a shot this plan wouldn't backfire on him, he'd be the crazy one not to run with it.

Chase edged a step closer. "So, is that a yes?"

Her lashes fanned downward, the simple movement ungluing him. He might not have lost his manhood today, but there was no doubt he'd already lost his heart. It beat faster the longer Livy waited to answer.

She looked up, lowered her pinky from her mouth.

His cell blared from his pocket before she could respond, and Chase almost chucked the stupid thing across the store. He glanced at the name on the screen. Perfect timing as usual. "Yeah, hey, Ma, can I call you back in a few?"

"Chase, baby, are you nearby?"

"Not far. Why?" His pulse skipped in her pause. "Ma, what's going on?"

"Sugar, I'm afraid your dad and I have some bad news."

CHAPTER TWO

Decoy

Livy's heels wobbled over the grainy sidewalk. "Chase, slow down."

He turned a few feet ahead, his smile betrayed by a brown-eyed storm of compassion and concern.

July's heat drilled into Livy's neck, his expression into her chest. The lines etched around his eyes from years spent outside creased the way they always did when he was worried about someone he loved. Especially his dad. After having to watch dementia swallow his father's memory moment by moment, no one could blame him.

"There's nothing to worry about." As usual, he knew exactly what she was thinking. He crossed the few paces between them. "I have some things to look into today. That's all."

Livy studied him. "Promise?"

"Promise." He picked off a thread left on her shoulder from an outfit she'd tried on earlier. "And I think you should definitely still get that last dress."

"Oh, you do, huh?"

"Well, I happen to know a guy who'd love to hang out with you tonight." His almost-unnoticeable freckles danced around his eyes. "And since you're ready to get a jumpstart on those practice dates..."

There he went sidetracking her from being upset about Jed backing out on her again. Livy shook her head but couldn't help loving him for it. "I didn't even say yes to that yet."

"But you want to." Chase angled his head under hers. "Admit it."

She pulled out the hair band around her post-dressing-room messy side braid. "Why do you want to do this, anyway? You hate Jed."

"I don't *hate* him." Head down, he rubbed a callous on his hand. "And I never said you were the only one who needed practice. Maybe I'm getting something out of it too."

As if the king of self-sacrifice had a selfish bone in his body. "Really. And what exactly would that be?"

A vulnerable grin flirted with the whiskers around his lips. "There might be someone I want to win over myself."

Her hair unfurled. "Chase! How do I not know about this?"

He laughed. "I haven't told anyone yet."

Not even her? They talked about everything. Well, mostly. Okay, fine, she kept some things from him, too, but her secrets were different. Emotions more tangled than her hair wound around her the longer she spun the hair band on her wrist. "Is it someone you just met?"

"Actually…" He took his hat off to wipe his forehead and fit it back on. "It's someone I've known for a long time."

Eyes still narrowed, Livy tapped her arm, waiting. "Oh, come on. You know you gotta give me more than that."

He tugged his ear. "Maybe when we're done with the coaching." He moseyed that ridiculously smooth smile of his closer. "C'mon, Liv, say yes."

Why she bothered resisting, she had no clue. "Fine, but lose the smirk. Gloating isn't attractive."

He adjusted his hat. "You sure about that?"

She rolled her eyes. "Positive, cowboy."

"Guess the proof will be in the results, won't it, ma'am?"

Livy would've taken on his southern charm if there were a point in fighting a losing battle, but they'd been friends long enough to know she couldn't outwit him. Just like they'd been friends long enough to know when he was deflecting from hurts he didn't want her to see.

Sobering, she took his hand. "Seriously, though, Chase. You know whatever's going on with your dad is more important, right?"

He looked down. "I'm taking care of it."

"That doesn't mean you can't have someone there to help you." Even if he'd been looking out for her as a favor to her brother, he'd still been there for her countless times when she needed a friend. She more than owed him the same.

His gaze lingered on her hand in his. "I appreciate that, but I've got it. Besides, you have things to look into yourself." With that, he turned her around by the shoulders to face the window of the old café they'd conveniently ended up directly in front of.

She spun back around. "Chase—"

"No arguments." He waved a finger at her.

"But you're—"

"Helpful."

Livy crossed her arms. "Insufferable."

"Isn't that Jane Austen code for charming?"

She huffed. "If by charming you mean having mastered the ability to drive me crazy, then yes. And how do you even know what words Jane Austen used?"

"Like I said—charming." His laugh swept around her with the late summer breeze. "Better get used to it, Miss Hensley. You'll be seeing a lot of it during our dates."

"*Practice* dates," she corrected.

He tipped his hat in concession. "Meet you at your place later this afternoon?"

This afternoon? Shoot. The whole morning had thrown her off. She'd almost forgotten what day it was. "Um, actually, I can't. I have something I need to do later."

"Something like what?"

"Something like *something*." Livy twisted her earring, rubbed her neck below her ear, and curled her now-frizzy hair over her shoulder.

Brow slanting, Chase appraised her fidgety hand. "Can you be a little more evasive?"

A lot of good it did. She strove to mimic his carefree stature. "Maybe you're not the only one who has things to take care of." Evasive, maybe, but true.

The sticky breeze rushed another twinge of guilt over her. He hadn't prodded her about her secret outings these last several months. And maybe she depended on his grace more than she should. But it had to be this way.

A host of thoughts passed Chase's eyes before he finally nodded. "Fair enough." Gracious as always, he let her off the hook. "But for now..." He turned her toward the window again. "You just stand here and dream."

All the rebuttals racing to mind petered out with one look inside. Livy pressed a palm to the glass, already swept back into the tug-of-war that hadn't stopped pulling at her since Mrs. Finch announced she was retiring and closing her family's café for good. On one hand, the town was losing an icon that'd been around for generations. On the other, the closing opened new opportunities... and awakened dangerous dreams.

"There's something almost tragic about seeing it empty like this, isn't there?" She turned to find Chase looking lost in his own war.

"The furniture's gone, but the memories aren't." He leaned a brawny shoulder against the window. "You know my dad played his first gig here. He didn't stop begging Mrs. Finch's mom to institute an open mic night 'til she finally caved." Chase's eyes laughed as they flickered to Livy's. "Patience and persistence."

"So, *that's* where you get it from."

Laughing some more, he peered back into the dusty shop. "You gotta admire a guy who knows what he wants. He walked right up to my mom after finishing his set and asked her on their first date. A week later, he asked her to marry him."

Livy almost dropped her purse. "A week?"

"They'd been friends all through school." Chase's gaze wandered back to hers. "Sometimes, you just know when it's right."

And sometimes, his eyes held such faith in love, Livy had to look away before he saw how much hers didn't.

"You okay?"

"Yeah, of course." Their banter her favorite decoy, Livy gave him a playful nudge. "I was just wondering how come I've never heard this story before. You know how many times we've been to this café?" Her hands found her hips. "What else have you been holding back?"

Visibly fumbling for a response, Mr. Smooth scratched his stubbly cheek with the bottom of his travel mug.

"Are you blushing?"

"No."

She tugged him back around when he pulled away. "Oh my word, you totally are."

"Actually, I'm leaving. And *you're* staying to flesh out all those ideas already swirling in that creative mind of yours." He kissed her cheek, dished out an aggravatingly clever wink, and pivoted her toward the window once again. "I'll swing by later tonight."

"But I—"

"Later." His grin expanded with each shuffle backward.

Extra insufferable. "You're lucky that cowboy charm works for you, Chase Thompson," she called.

If his dad was anything like him back then, his mom had never stood a fighting chance at turning him down.

With one final tip of his hat, Chase ambled down the street, leaving her standing between her best friend and an available storefront perfect for her dream coffee shop.

Just as he'd intended, the longer Livy stared inside, the more her reflection blended into a room begging imagination to fill the empty space: Low-hanging lantern lights, a brick fireplace, gorgeous barn doors, stenciled wall art—things she couldn't begin to afford.

She sighed. Truthfully, even if she had the money, a start-up business required things Chase's big heart wanted to believe she had in her. But he didn't know—

"Potential," someone said from behind her.

Flinching, Livy turned toward a middle-aged woman in a dress suit and trendy glasses. "I'm sorry?"

The woman nodded to the shop. "I can tell by the way you're admiring it that you see the possibilities."

Livy's gaze cascaded over the white walls and open floor plan. "Guess it's kind of hard not to when you're staring at a blank slate."

"No, I assure you. Not everyone can envision something out of nothing." She silenced a call from her cell and slid it into her purse. "So, what's your offer?"

"I'm sorry?" Did she know any other phrase today? Livy shifted her own purse in a useless attempt at looking unnerved.

"A girl with your obvious vision can surely see more for this location than a chain pizza joint."

"Is that what it's going to be?"

"Unless you want to do something about it." She rifled through her bag again. "Don't get me wrong, I like a slice as much as the next person. But here? On Main Street?" Scrunching her nose, she pulled out a leather business card holder. "It should be something with a little more style. From the looks of it, I'd say you'd agree." She handed her a card. "Evelyn Marshall. I'm paid to recognize these things."

Livy scanned the details on the sleek design. An investor, *from the looks of it.* "You give out loans?"

"Among other things." Evelyn's brows slanted above her square glasses. "Including free advice. So, take it from me, this little piece of retail is worth scooping up. Interested?"

"In buying the property?" She had to be joking. "Who wouldn't be? I mean, look at it."

Another peek inside, and the ideas Chase knew were already swirling multiplied before she could stop them. "Rustic outfitting, modern finishes. You wouldn't believe what my friend Ti could do to those naked walls—*bare. Bare* walls. Ti's an artist. Not anything weird. She'd just, you know, paint."

Cringing from head to toe, she inched around to face the worthless breeze and dodged Evelyn's eye contact. "It's crazy hot out, isn't it? Even in a dress, I'm sweating. Nice suit by the way. I've always loved the business chic look. Though, I'm not sure I could pull off a blazer in the summer. Whoever ends up buying the place should really consider installing an awning for some shade." An awning. Wow. Because she was transporting them back to the fifties?

Evelyn's perfectly matted lips curved with amusement. "Or a patio... with umbrellas."

Like any *normal* café. Right. "And tables of course."

"Of course."

Oh, Chase was seriously going to get it for leading her here today. Wait, did he set this little run-in up?

Evelyn flashed another entertained smile, paused midturn, and motioned to the business card Livy still had in her hand. "Be sure to give the investment some thought." Halfway past the next storefront, she peered behind her. "I'll be waiting to hear from you."

And I'll still be dying of embarrassment. Once Evelyn faded out of sight, Livy landed her forehead against the shop's window. Nothing like a great first impression to scream business owner material. Either the woman was as gracious as Chase, or she trusted his estimation of her more than she should. Same way he did.

She released a long exhale. He probably wasn't that far off about the trepid thing, but no amount of practice would turn her into the girl he wanted her to be.

Tucking the business card into her purse, Livy left the view of the old café behind her and headed to her Fiat.

Her boss's name lit up her cell as she reached the driver's side. Only one reason he would be calling—one of her coworkers had bailed on their shift tonight. Livy dug her keys out and took the call. "Hey, Lance."

"Livy, babe, tell me you're up for earning some extra cash tonight."

She nailed that one all right. "Actually, I already have plans." Granted, they weren't the ones she'd expected to have, but in all honesty, she'd probably have more fun with Chase than with Jed anyway.

"A girl like you? Of course you do. But we're talking Friday night. The after-hours crowd. C'mon, you're seeing dollar signs as we speak. Am I right?"

Frustratingly so. She couldn't deny needing the money. She cast a backward glance to the *For Sale* sign one last time. Too bad she couldn't pay back a loan in dreams. "Fine."

"That's my girl."

Ugh. She hated when he called her that. She sifted through her keys and unlocked the door. "See you at six." At least with a little extra cash, she might finally be able to get her dishwasher fixed.

Practical. That's what she needed to be. True, she wasn't satisfied with her situation right now any more than Chase apparently was, but making it through meant keeping her head out of the clouds and her feet on the path already paved for her.

As soon as she hung up, her phone chimed again. Her eyes darted to the time screaming at her for already being fifteen minutes late to her mentoring appointment.

She swiped to answer. "Sorry, Jackson. The morning got away from me. I just need to swing home to change, and then I'll be over."

"Sophie needs you here now."

The girl Livy had been mentoring the last several months wasn't a stranger to trouble, but the urgency in the group home director's voice this time sent Livy's stomach lurching. "Why? What happened?"

In the background, muffled chatter followed a beep that sounded like it could've come from a police radio, and Livy's stomach plummeted even farther. "Jackson? Tell me she's okay."

CHAPTER THREE

Messy

In his backyard, Chase finished changing the spark plugs and straightened from under the hood of his old Chevy Nova. Guzzling half his cup of sweet tea, he ran his arm across his damp forehead. A lot of good it did. Even if it weren't blazing hot out, his conversation with Dad's health insurance company had left him boiling enough to burn the grease off his hands.

How could they just up and change Dad's coverage like that? New plan year or not, this wasn't just some nominal adjustment. These were people's lifelines they were messing with—prescriptions they depended on. They had to know most people couldn't afford the astronomical costs pharmaceutical companies had the gall to charge.

Condensation dripped down his cup of tea, his questions running into each other. What did they expect Dad to do now? Mortgage his home to pay for his monthly meds? Did they even care what this meant for him?

Chase shoved his wrench off the engine. It clattered into the dirt with nowhere near the impact of the sucker punch striking his rib cage. Hunched over, he braced both blackened hands against the front of the car and blew out one hard breath after the other until he calmed. Getting mad was pointless. He needed a game plan.

"Chase Thompson?" a man called from behind him.

Chase grabbed a rag as he turned and squinted into the sun. "Can I help you?"

An older gentleman in a white, short-sleeved, button-down and pressed polyester pants strolled up from the driveway. He stopped a few feet away and checked out the car from different angles. "That's a mighty fine-looking Chevy Nova you've got there. A '69?"

"A '70."

The man released a low whistle at the car's sleek profile. "She's a beauty."

Chase had been working on her for the last twelve years, part by part. She wasn't fully restored yet, but he had to admit, the admiration felt well-earned.

He slipped his hat off, raked his hair back, and tucked the hat on again. "It's a work in progress."

"I'd say you're nearly finished." After circling the entire car, he met Chase at the front bumper and extended a hand. "Earl Schwab. I'm looking for a body man who knows his way around the classics. From what I've seen, you're the man for the job."

What he'd seen?

He released Chase's hand and admired the Green Mist paint glistening in the sunlight. "Looks like I was right."

Chase rubbed his neck. "Maybe about the body man part." Restoring classics was just a hobby—something to help him clear his head when he needed it. Not that it was helping much today. He eased the hood shut and squatted to close his toolbox.

"I'd beg to differ." Earl eyed the smooth curves Chase had fixed on the body. "Ever think of selling her? I guarantee she'd be worth a pretty penny."

Chase's head snapped up. Sell? Without answering, he rose and traced his fingers along the shiny clearcoat he'd sprayed on the front fenders last week. Maybe it was stupid to be so attached to a lifeless hunk of metal, but it was more than that to him. It held memories, milestones—parts of himself he'd poured into it through the years.

"I'll take that as a no." Earl's deep chuckle drew Chase out of his reverie. "Can't fault a guy for asking."

Truth enough in that. His shoulders relaxed as he picked at a stubborn grease stain on his thumb. "Sorry."

"I don't blame you, son. I wouldn't want to let a gem like this go either." He pulled a worn leather wallet out of his back pocket, flipped it open, and slid out a business card. "But what would you think about working with a dozen more like her every day?"

Chase took one look at the card and almost dropped it. "You're asking me to come work for Gateway Classic Cars? *The* Gateway Classic Cars?" He had to be missing something. Why would the world's largest classic and exotic car sales company be interested in a random body man from a Podunk town in North Carolina?

"Technically, you'd be a contractor for them, but yes, essentially." Earl traded his wallet for a handkerchief and wiped the corners of his mouth. "They expect exceptional work for their shows, which is why we only recruit exceptional workers."

A spark of excitement dulled the frustration Chase had been wrestling since getting Mom's call earlier. Until he saw the Illinois address on the card.

Earl must've read his expression. "From what I hear, your job takes you to the Midwest pretty often. If you're already there, think of all the headaches you could save in travel costs."

Chase lowered the card to his side. This guy had certainly done his research on him. "You're not just passing through Littleton by chance, are you?"

"No such thing as chance, son." Earl snagged a pen from his front pocket, scribbled something on the back of another business card, and held it out. "Only opportunities."

At the sight of the salary figure, Chase leaned into the car's chrome bumper. "But you don't even know—"

"Talent when I see it? After thirty years in this business, I'd say I've learned a thing or two." Earl's aged eyes held the same confounding mix of wisdom and mischief Dad's used to hold. "Professional sports teams aren't the only ones who send out scouts. I've been following your work ever since last August's Chrome and Caffeine show. That '59 Impala you worked on was something else."

Old man Gentry's car? Chase had helped restore it more out of fun than anything. He never expected his name to follow it.

Earl withdrew his keys and motioned to the cards at Chase's side. "Give me a call when you've thought it over."

Or when his muscles worked again. Still leaning into the Nova for balance, Chase stared at the business card and an unexpected opportunity with potential to be a real game changer.

As Earl strolled back down the driveway, he nodded hello to Chase's sister coming in the opposite direction. When did she get back?

As soon as Quinn reached the backyard, she tossed Chase a wry grin. "Making new friends while I've been gone?"

"You've been gone?" He shoved the business cards in his pocket before she could see them and slid a grin back at her. "Hadn't noticed."

"Liar." She hooked her skinny arms around his torso and curled into a side hug he'd missed giving her these last two weeks. In all honesty, ever since she moved back to Littleton a year ago, she'd been a regular pillar in his life.

He rustled the top of her hair, and she pinched his side while pushing away.

"You gained friends but didn't lose your obnoxiousness."

Eyes rolling, he opened his Swiss Army knife to clean the grease out from under his nails. "He's a business acquaintance." A new one anyway. "Just offered me a job in Illinois."

Quinn almost snorted. "Disappointing for him."

When Chase didn't respond, she squared in front of him until she blocked the sun's glare with her own. "You turned him down, didn't you? Please tell me you turned him down."

"I didn't tell him anything."

"Chase." She stole his knife. "You can't just up and leave. What about you and Livy? You guys are getting so close."

If it weren't for wanting to hope she was right, he would've dismissed that factor altogether, but this was bigger than his own desires.

Her arms slid to her sides. "Wait. You two are still close, right? Did you mess it up while we were gone? You did, didn't you? Okay, spill it. What happened?"

"Thanks for the vote of confidence." Chase laughed despite the nagging concern about his dating coach idea backfiring on him. Just because he hadn't messed things up yet didn't mean he wasn't about to. He brushed off the thought with a bead of sweat running down his temple. "Livy and I are fine, Quinn. Stop worrying."

Still eyeing him, she adjusted the pencil holding up her hair. "Then what's with those lines on your forehead? You really want to tell me nothing's eating at you?"

He looked away. What was with his brow making him an open book?

"Is it this job offer?"

"No." Maybe. Chase hunched against his Nova again, wishing all the times he'd poured out his thoughts while working on her could transfer words of wisdom back to him.

Traveling periodically throughout the year was one thing. Even with Dad's state of mind, his parents had been able to manage okay while Chase was out of town for a week or so at a time. But to move 900 miles away from them permanently?

He tossed his hat over his toolbox and ran both hands down his face. The card with the salary on it practically burned a hole in his pocket with its attraction. He'd been scouring for a way to come up with the money his parents would need every month now. Maybe this was it.

Quinn pinned a scrutinizing look on him. "What aren't you telling me?"

"Nothing." He swiped his knife back. "Hey, did you swing by Mom and Dad's today?" With any luck, she didn't know about Dad's insurance predicament yet. Sheltering her from that burden until he could find a solution was almost as important to him as actually finding one.

Dread passed her eyes. "No. Why? What happened?"

"Why does something always have to happen?" He rested a hand on each of her shoulders. "Relax, Drama Queen. Everything's fine. I just wondered if Mom needed help shelling those peas we picked Wednesday." That was partly true anyway.

Quinn pulled her cell from her pocket, and Chase scrambled to keep his voice even.

"Who are you calling?" Mom would spill everything in a hot second if he didn't talk her out of it first.

"Livy." Quinn's tone matched a feisty grin that all but said she had his little scheme figured out. "Nice job trying to sidetrack me, by the way, but you're not getting out of my question about you two. If you won't tell me where things stand, I'll just have to ask her."

He wrangled the phone from her hands and ended the call before Livy could pick up. "And you talk about *me* being obnoxious. There's nothing to tell."

"Right. Which is clearly why you don't want me to call her." Her stubborn smile widened. "I'm waiting."

For Pete's sake. "Fine. I'm working on it, all right?"

"On what exactly?"

He swatted a mosquito away. As sweltering as it was, the stagnant heat didn't make him nearly as uncomfortable as talking about this with Quinn did. "On a... strategy."

"A strategy," she deadpanned. "This isn't Minecraft, Chase. Just tell her how you feel."

"Like the way you were so quick to be honest with Cooper about your feelings?" He dished back her tight expression.

"Don't make me get Mama involved."

He almost dropped his knife. "Don't even start—"

"Hey, you started it when you showed up with Livy for that cookout last summer."

"Um, technically, *you* showed up with her."

"While *you* made googly eyes at her the whole time."

Googly eyes? He fought a grin. What were they? Eight again? He tucked his knife into his pocket. Two could play this game. "I might not *of* fallen so hard if the girl didn't make a killer *expresso*. But that's a whole *'nother* story."

His grammar loving sister shuddered at the mispronunciations. "I know you did not just say that."

"Oh, no, I *pacifically* meant to say that." He picked up his hat and dusted off the brim. "For all *intensive* purposes, it's kinda the same thing, right?"

"Chase, I mean it. You better stop or—"

"Quinn?" Mom said from behind them.

They both turned toward her, standing halfway down the driveway with what had to be a peach cobbler in her hands and a shocked look on her face. "Well, sugar, why didn't you tell me you and Cooper were back from your honeymoon? I would've made a second cobbler."

Strolling toward them, Mom bobbed her brows at Quinn's blank expression. "Forget I asked, sweetie. You may be back from your trip, but that doesn't mean the honeymoon's over. I get it." She threw her a sassy wink that raced a shade of red clear up Quinn's forehead. "No need to be embarrassed, dear. Your daddy and I—"

"O-kay. You can stop right there. Really. I haven't had enough coffee yet to deal with..." She closed her eyes. "That."

Oh, the pricelessness.

Quinn caught Chase's amusement, and her utter mortification quickly transitioned into something far more dangerous. Payback.

"Speaking of being embarrassed." A devilish grin overrode her expression as she took Mom's arm, clearly about to shift the conversation to him and Livy instead.

Chase looked between his sister and mom, both with secrets he was desperate for them to keep from each other. Who knew what either of them would say. But one thing was for sure. No matter how this went down, it was bound to get messy.

CHAPTER FOUR

Truth

At the group home, Livy stroked Sophie's long brown hair while the girl she'd come to care for so much gave in to the emotion she rarely let anyone see. Part anger, part helplessness, the tears escaping weren't so different from the ones Livy kept to herself.

"Jackson doesn't get it." Sophie lifted her head off Livy's lap and scooted to the edge of her bed. "Can't you talk to him for me? You're the only one who understands."

She strode to a laminated bookshelf in the corner of her room, snatched a picture frame off one of the bowed shelves, and swooned over the photo of her supposed boyfriend as if he could solve all her problems.

Meeting Luke once was enough to know his type. Smooth, mysterious, full of enticing promises. Not only did guys like him make you feel like the center of the world when they were with you, they knew how to crush that world when they left. And they always left.

Livy's chest tightened at the thought. Sophie'd had enough people in her life leave her.

"Jackson just wants to see you matched with parents you'll be happy with. And I really think you will be with the Millers." It killed her to watch Sophie sabotage her home visits with them by running away every time. "They're good people, Soph."

"Good at pretending maybe." She flicked a glance to an old guitar case covered in stickers propped against the bookshelf. "Everyone has secrets, Livy." Her voice dropped. "The minute you doubt that is the minute you'll get burned."

"Soph…" Livy cleared her throat, hating how much her own secrets could burn her too. "I've seen the way the Millers are when they're with you. They genuinely want you to be a part of their family."

"I don't need a family." Sophie wheeled around with the picture to her chest. "Why can't I have your life? You're out on your own, dating a rock star. No one says anything to you about your choices."

She obviously hadn't met Chase.

"Okay, first of all, I'm not a minor." Giving Sophie a pointed look, Livy moved from the bed to her side and convinced her fingers to release the picture. "And I'm not dating a rock star. Jed and I are…" Well, she didn't know exactly what they were, but in a steady relationship wasn't what came to mind. Even Chase's skills couldn't change that. She smiled to herself. Jane Austen code, indeed.

"Whatever you two are, it's gotta be good enough to give you that giddy smile."

What? Snapping out of it, Livy scrambled to lose the grin. The only good thing right now was Chase not being around to witness the ridiculous blush creeping up her cheeks. He'd never let her live it down. "I'm not... *giddy*."

"Sure you aren't."

Livy aimed the frame at her. "Hey, no diverting. We're not talking about Jed and me. We're talking about *you* running off with a guy who *thinks* he's a rock star."

"There's nothing wrong with chasing dreams. My mom did it," Sophie mumbled while picking at the brackets on the guitar case. "And look at Jed. He's from Littleton, and he made it. Why can't we? Luke has it all planned out."

I bet he does. "You need to be careful, Soph." Making up reasons why her mom left her would only hurt worse when Luke ended up bailing too.

Blowing her off, Sophie toyed with the bracelet Livy had given her for her birthday last month. "Is this the part where you insert Jackson's guys-only-have-one-thing-on-their-mind speech? If so, spare us both. Jackson played out that song a long time ago." She looked up at Livy. "And it's a little harder to swallow from someone who already has the perfect life."

Perfect? Was that seriously what she thought?

Livy dropped her gaze to the carpet for two breaths before returning the frame to the shelf. Beside it, a picture of the two of them at an art festival this past spring wedged the knife in a little deeper. She could hang dozens of memories in this room—all from times Livy had tried to be a steady friend for her, maybe even a mentor—and it wouldn't change how misdirected her admiration of Livy was.

She ran a thumb along the corner of the frame enclosing a smile built on lies. "My life's far from perfect, girl. Trust me."

"Better than mine." With a huff to punctuate her point, Sophie flopped backward onto her bed and tucked a fuzzy, star-shaped pillow behind her arms. "At least no one's trying to force you into slavery."

Slavery? As usual, amusement over Sophie's dramatic side collided with compassion over her scarred spirit.

"I mean, I get wanting to adopt babies—*maybe*. But a teenager?" Sophie picked at the indigo polish on her short nails. "C'mon. You don't have to be in the system to know that's a little sketchy. If they don't want to adopt me for manual labor, I guarantee it's for something worse."

"Soph." Livy sat beside her on the edge of the bed. "I know some of your foster families ruined your trust in people, but I promise there are lots of good parents out there wanting to adopt out of love." There had to be. "*Including* the Millers." She leaned over to meet her gaze. "If I were an adoptive parent, I'd take you in a second. No ulterior motive other than wanting the best for you."

A gaze as frayed as the thread Sophie was twirling around her finger wandered up from her pillow. "You could be, you know," she half whispered. "One of those parents, I mean." The slightest glint of hope chased away the guarded sorrow that rarely left her eyes. "You'd be the coolest mom. Any kid would die to have you choose them."

Livy tensed at the innocent words spearing into scar tissue without warning. Sophie didn't know what she was saying.

Didn't know the mistakes Livy had made that proved her wrong.

She stared a hole into the mattress and shifted her legs half a dozen times. But it didn't matter. No amount of stalling would summon the words she didn't have to give. As soon as her gaze intersected with the yearning still looking back at her, the shame that'd already been building chafed against regret until it finally launched her off the bed.

Sophie sat up on her elbows. "Where are you going?"

Anywhere but here. Any place she could hide, forget. "I have to go."

"Wait."

But she couldn't. Couldn't stay, couldn't turn around. If she did, there'd be no hiding the truth. Pausing only for a second in the doorway, she swallowed the tears churning in her throat. "I'm sorry."

"Liv—"

She hustled down the stairs, circled the banister, and almost ran into Jackson as he came out of his office.

"Oh, hey. Did you convince her—?"

"I can't." It was all she could get out before closing the front door behind her.

Thick and humid, the air outside finally slowed her down enough to realize losing her composure only made things worse. She needed to pull herself together, and fast.

Livy paced the dirt driveway, alternating between facing her Fiat and the house until her heels finally jerked to a stop. She smoothed out her dress. It'd be fine. She'd just go back in and make up an excuse.

And say what exactly? As practiced as she was at fast talking, even she didn't have a chance at pulling that off. She backed against the car door instead. Self-doubt burned into her with the hot metal pressing against her skin. What was she really trying to accomplish by volunteering here?

Answers she didn't want to explore steered her to her cell and an impulse she'd probably regret later. Her thumb stopped over Chase's name, but the drive of what she really craved right now kept her scrolling to Jed's number instead. With each unanswered ring, she twisted her bottom lip between her fingers. One way, the other.

"Jed McCormick."

She let go of her lip and lifted off the car. "Hey, it's Livy." Obviously. His phone had caller ID like everyone else's. *Stupid.* She cringed but kept right on talking. "Sorry, I know you're busy tonight. Which, by the way, ended up working out anyway. I have to cover a coworker's shift. Oh, speaking of that, next time you're here, you should really tell my punk boss to stop calling me his girl. It drives me crazy. He—"

She froze. "Um, not that I'm *your* girl either. I just thought he might back off if he saw we were together. Not together, like, exclusive. It's not like we're really even dating. Are we?" Oh, sweet heavens. Her spastic sputtering had no bounds.

"Pretend I didn't ask that. I don't expect you to be looking for a big commitment or anything. I mean, if you *were,* that'd be cool. I could be the committed type too. You know, if I found the right person."

When Jed didn't respond, she snapped her hair tie against her wrist to slap some blasted sense into herself. She should be committed all right. Straight into a psych ward. Where did she think she was going with this? And here, now? Really?

Livy sank onto the hood of her Fiat and deeper into the hole she just couldn't stop digging. "I'm shutting up now." She brought her fist to her forehead. "Sorry. I'm not always this flustered." *Liar.* "It's just something a friend brought up today. It got me thinking—"

"I'll be right there," Jed called away from the phone. "Livy, I—"

"Have to go. I get it. No worries." Sparing her any more humiliation was probably a good thing. "You told me you were busy today. Forget I called."

"Your calls are hard to forget. Just like everything about you." His smooth tone curled around her. "Can't wait to see you next week."

"Really?" And just like that, the reaction Sophie's words had triggered melted away, and the warmth in her cheeks transitioned from embarrassment to that indefinable feeling she longed for more than she should. "Me too," she practically sighed. "Wish we could make it work sooner than next week."

"How soon are you talking?"

She chewed her pinky. "In the next five minutes would be good." She could use the escape.

His sideways smile sang through the line. "You keep sounding that cute when you ask, and you'll make it hard to say no."

Livy soaked in the compliment until a girl calling his name in the background jolted her from it.

"In a sec," he said away from the phone. He cleared his throat, lowered his voice. "I wish I could tweak my schedule, Livy, but you know how this industry goes. I'll be in town next week."

Same way he was supposed to be in town last week. "Yeah, of course. I'll see you—"

The call ended before she could finish.

"Later," she said anyway.

She dropped the phone into her purse, pushed off the hood, and rolled her eyes at her reflection in the window. Spastic *and* pathetic. She slumped into the driver's seat and gripped the wheel. Turning to Jed was a mistake. She'd known it before she'd even scrolled to his number, but he wasn't the only one who had a hard time turning things down.

Staring straight into the truth about herself, Livy peered up at Sophie's window and turned the keys in the ignition. The perfect life? If she only knew.

CHAPTER FIVE

Gamble

Chase parked his Silverado in front of Livy's rental house, wondering if he should've called first. He usually gave her distance when she got evasive about her mystery dates or appointments or whatever it was she didn't want him to know about. But with so much weighing on his mind, he wanted to see her.

All right, he *needed* to see her. He tossed his hat on the passenger seat. If Quinn could see him now, he'd never hear the end of it. It really didn't matter that she didn't bring it up in front of Mom earlier. No doubt, the woman already knew he had feelings for Livy. Heck, *everyone* probably knew.

Except for the one person he couldn't figure out how to admit it to.

Maybe Quinn was right. If he was going to harp on Livy about having confidence, he needed to take his own advice and shoot straight with her about how he felt. What did he have to lose?

A bark drew his focus toward Livy sailing around the corner of her house, running after her neighbor's Jack Russell-Terrier mix.

"Bandit!" Splattered in mud from head to toe, Livy stopped along the walkway to her front door with her hands braced against her knees. "You better not come back here looking for a treat after that stunt, buddy."

Chase laughed. He couldn't help it. Her empty threat might've held more weight if she didn't let that crazy dog get away with murder every time he escaped into her yard.

She stood there—arms laced, face caught in a tug-of-war between annoyance and undeniable affection. Topped off with those mud polka dots freckling her cheeks, she couldn't have looked any cuter.

Her line of sight skimmed over the cab of his truck and stopped. Catching his gaze, she pulled her blond braid over one shoulder and smiled softly. Sunlight filtered through the neighboring trees and draped her in a spotlight he couldn't look away from.

His stomach tightened. What did he have to lose? Everything. But they had even more to gain. He just had to prove it to her.

Chase polished off the last swig of his sweet tea, returned the cup to the cup holder, and grabbed his hat. He met her by the porch steps. "Do I want to ask what Bandit got into today?"

Livy wiped the mud spots off her arms. "I swear that dog should be on Ritalin or something. You should see the number of holes he halfway dug in my backyard. It's, like, as soon as he starts one, another spot steals his attention. And heaven forbid a squirrel should land in the yard. Just stick with one task and finish it already."

She swiped the side of her hand across her forehead, smearing dirt smudges over her tan skin. Chase bit back a grin, and her scrunched-up expression tightened even more. "Don't you dare say it."

He splayed his hands out. "I didn't say a word."

"But you're thinking it." Livy unwound an extra hair band from her wrist and circled it around her fingers. "I'm not like Bandit. I can finish something I start when I want to."

"Mm-hmm."

She aimed the hair band at him like a slingshot. "Like this." She let go and made a run for it to the backyard.

Chase caught the hair tie against his chest and darted after her. Around the back corner, he skidded to a stop in front of a garden-hose-turned-weapon waiting for him. He raised his palms.

"Mm-hmm," she mimicked. "See, told you I'd finish it."

Only, she had no idea what she was starting. He swaggered over. "That's really cute."

"What's cute?"

Right in front of her, Chase lowered his arms. "That you think this is over." He stole the sprayer and caught her at the waist. "You need to rinse this mud off, right?"

Half laughing, half squealing, she squirmed to break free. "Bandit!"

In the corner of the yard, the dog's ears perked up. He took one look at them, charged without hesitation, and knocked them both to the grass. The nozzle hit the ground and turned into a fountain raining over all three of them.

Torn between deciding whose face to lick the most and trying to catch every drop with his tongue, ADHD Dog of the Year sprinted in spastic circles, stopping only a second or two for each task.

Chase finally grabbed him by the collar. "Sit."

Amazingly, the dog obeyed. Sort of. With his vigorous tail flapping and his antsy hind legs inching him forward, sitting still clearly had its limits.

Livy pulled herself up by her knees and barely got her legs crossed before Bandit climbed onto her lap. She half-heartedly pushed the dog away, laughing between slobbery kisses.

Chase, on the other hand, had to muster all his strength to keep from pulling her contagious smile close. Even the cold water hitting his skin didn't remotely douse his yearning to be the one kissing her right now.

"Bandit!" Her neighbor, Mrs. Finch, stood between their two yards with her knobby fists on her hips. "Aye yai yai. Look at the mess you've made."

Bandit aimed one feisty ear at her voice, took off in a sprint, and ran circles around her small frame.

"Silly mutt," she mumbled through a smile as hooked as Livy's was. "So sorry, sweet pea. I went to check the mail and must not have latched the door all the way."

"It's fine, Mrs. Finch." Livy surveyed the yard-turned-minefield. "Nothing I can't patch up."

With what? A dump truck?

A gunshot popped from inside the woods, barks shuddering through the leaves.

Livy flinched toward Bandit despite how often they heard Mr. Hood out hunting. Chase didn't blame her for being on edge. Her crochety old neighbor had made it clear more than once how he felt about Bandit getting into his yard.

Mrs. Finch muttered something that was probably the closest the sweet woman ever got to bad mouthing anyone. She rubbed Bandit's brown and white face. "If you're not careful, you're gonna run off one of these days and not make it back, you big fur ball."

She reached for his collar with a shaky hand, and Livy's face fell. She'd been worried about Mrs. Finch's failing health ever since it had driven her to close her family's café.

Chase hopped to his feet and crossed the yard to her side. "Here, let me help you get him inside, ma'am."

"Oh, thank you, young man, but I've got the little rascal." Brow raised with all kinds of mischief, she leaned in and whispered, "You just keep on after Miss Livy now, and don't you worry." She winked. "She'll come around."

Great. Apparently, everyone truly *did* know how he felt about her.

Mrs. Finch patted his warm cheek, turned, and led Bandit to her back porch at her own determined pace—an example he should be following right about now.

Quinn's advice to tell Livy the truth echoed louder than that gunshot had. Chase leveled his shoulders. No time for second guessing himself. But when he turned, Livy was hustling toward her neighbor's house.

"Mrs. Finch, wait." She caught up to her on the steps and took out her phone.

Chase didn't need to hear the conversation. Watching Livy wander back over, chewing her bottom lip, filled in the blanks.

"You got Tessa's number, didn't you?"

"Maybe." Livy raised both shoulders. "C'mon, Chase. If I were her daughter, I would've jumped at the chance to inherit their family's café. Maybe I can talk her into reconsidering."

"You can't blame Tessa for choosing to do something different with her life."

"I know." Livy turned her phone in mindless circles. "It just feels like losing a legacy, you know? For all of us."

Knowing her, the story about his dad's first gig there was weighing on her mind. He slid his hat off and toyed with the inside. "You may not be Mrs. Finch's biological daughter, but if I were a betting man, I'd wager she'd be awful proud of you for building a new legacy there. Something you can pass on to your own kids someday."

Fraught with something bordering panic, Livy broke away from him and the connection he'd meant to create.

"Did I say something—?"

"No," she answered way too fast. "I just hate that Mrs. Finch is alone. That's all."

It was obviously more than that, but he didn't push back. "She's not alone."

Livy made a face. "Bandit doesn't count."

He tucked his hat back on, his gaze unwavering. "I wasn't talking about Bandit."

Her lashes dipped at his comment. She peered toward Mrs. Finch's back porch again, the slow smile lighting her cheeks fading. Straining to deflect, she glanced at the sprayer on the ground and pitched a brow at him. "Weren't we in the middle of *finishing* something?"

That was for sure. What exactly, he didn't know. But if picking up where they'd left off before Mrs. Finch came over was what she needed, he'd play along. Chase moseyed closer. "As a matter of fact..."

A moment of hesitation stretched between them. He would've been strategizing what move to make next if he weren't caught up in the heady feeling of being this close to her. He searched for his voice and the words he still didn't know how to say. If he could just come up with—

"You two are adorable." Quinn rounded the back corner of the house with Cooper and their son, Brayden. A plastic bag hanging from her wrist swung in perfect synchronization with her gloat-worthy tone.

Livy batted an uncomfortable look away from Chase, turned off the hose, and faced his sister instead. "You want to talk about adorable? Let me see that cute munchkin of yours."

Quinn eased Brayden down her leg to the grass, and he made a two-year-old beeline for Livy. She scooped him up in a twirl and landed a kiss on his chubby cheek. "How's my favorite buddy doing?"

He buried his face in her neck. "Me hold you, Aunt Livy. Me hold you."

"Aw." She squeezed tighter. "I hold you back, kiddo." The same pained look from a moment ago flashed across her eyes for a second before she tucked it away again—hidden beside so many things Chase wished she trusted him with.

Cooper kissed Quinn on the temple and strode over to give Livy a hug hello.

From the look on his sister's face, Chase should be taking pointers from her ultra-smooth husband. Honestly, she was probably right. The guy didn't become a self-made millionaire and land the perfect family by chance. He fought for it. Just like Chase should be doing.

He dug the tip of his boot in one of Bandit's holes, his thoughts sinking back to his conversation with Earl.

Quinn lifted the bag around her wrist. "We came to drop off some cupcakes." She raised her shoulders in feigned innocence. "And maybe to check if you have any coffee made."

Livy turned. "Like you have to ask." She passed Brayden off to Cooper and gave Quinn a quick welcome-home hug on her way to the back door. "Give me two seconds."

Chase eyed his sister. "Coffee. Really? You couldn't make your own at home?"

"Not that tastes like Liv's."

He couldn't argue with that.

Quinn elbowed him. "I don't know what you're worried about. Looks to me like your *strategy's* coming along just fine without my intervention."

He was going to regret ever telling her about that, wasn't he?

Livy came out with two travel mugs and handed one to Quinn, who offered the bag she'd brought in return as if they were conducting a business deal.

"Girl, if you keep bringing me desserts, I'm gonna have to start buying jeans with elastic waistbands."

"I can take that off your hands." Chase reached for the bag of sweets.

Livy swiped it away. "Hey, just 'cause I don't *need* them doesn't mean I don't *want* them."

Girls. He laughed at the pair of them, each coddling their comfort vices. They'd make the perfect business team. Livy on the coffee, Quinn on the pastries—both doing something they loved.

When Chase turned to Cooper for a little assistance, he held up his hands. "Don't look at me, hoss. I just got married, remember? I'd like to keep it that way." He drew Quinn into his arms.

His dimples sank in, and Chase nearly chucked. Nothing against Coop. He was great with Quinn and Brayden. It didn't even intimidate Chase that Livy used to date him. Past relationships were meant to stay in the past. He knew that better than anyone.

Sparing himself from an unwanted trip down memory lane, he prodded his sister toward the side of the house. He needed to get Livy alone if he was going to tell her the truth before he lost the nerve. "Mom would be so proud you're proving the honeymoon isn't over yet."

She popped him in the stomach, but not before Cooper's amusement radar kicked up. "Do I want to ask?"

"About a comment from my mom?" Quinn snorted. "I think you know the answer to that."

"Why don't you two go talk about—" Chase stopped at the sight of Livy's teenage neighbor Wesley Bumgarner crossing the lawn.

Just what they needed. One more person added to the revolving door of interruptions.

Wes held out a bow and arrow while brandishing a graphic T-shirt with a green-masked superhero on it. "No invite to the party?"

Livy stopped beside Chase. "No party. We were just—"

"Prepping the competition. I feel ya." He strutted the rest of the way in his Converse high tops, sizing Chase up and down. "Luckily for you, Boots, I always accept a challenge from a worthy opponent."

Mouth half open, Chase shifted a glance from DC Comics Poster Boy to Livy. "Did he just—?"

"Give you a supervillain name?" Livy hid a grin behind her hair. "Yeah, that definitely just happened."

Chase dropped his gaze to the cowboy boots he would never look at the same again. He pressed his tongue to the side of his mouth but couldn't keep his laugh as quiet as Livy's. She swatted him in the chest, and that was it. He had to steal Quinn's coffee to rein it in.

"Have you seen my basement, bro? It's sweeter than Star Labs." Wesley balanced his bow on the grass and squared his scrawny shoulders as if he'd just struck a blow to him. "So, go ahead and laugh it up. I couldn't care less."

Before anyone could give him a hard time about his obsession with *The Flash*, Quinn walked straight up to Wesley and flung her arms around him. "Do you know how many people get that phrase wrong?" She hugged his neck as if they were lifelong kindred spirits. "Thank you."

Wide-eyed, the kid dropped his weapons and circled his hands around her back. "My pleasure."

"Okay." Cooper went to rescue his wife. "I think he gets it, babe." He unwrapped her arms and mouthed, "long day," to Chase and Livy.

"Wesley James?" his mom called from next door. "Did you clean Mr. Wiggles' litter box?"

All shades of red now, he strove to look menacing while backing away. He pointed his bow at Chase. "To be continued, Boots."

Chase tipped his hat at him. Anything else, and he would've lost it all over again. Returning his attention to Quinn made it hard enough to keep a straight face.

"Shut up." She turned him around and pushed him to the side of the house. While Cooper went to start the car, Quinn held Brayden out to Chase. "Give Uncle Chase hugs goodbye. We need to get to the library before it closes."

Brayden reached for the brim of his hat as Chase kissed his sticky cheek. "Me try."

He planted the hat on his nephew's head, savored the adorable image of it falling over his eyes, and squeezed the mess out of him. "Love you, big guy."

"Wuv you too."

Quinn took Brayden back and tossed Chase his hat. "Tell Uncle Staller we'll be sure to check out a book for him called *How to Man Up*."

"Up. Up," Brayden sang.

Chase glared at her. "It'll be right next to the one called *How to Stop Being Mischeeveeous.*"

Like clockwork, Quinn twitched at the mispronunciation. "I hate you."

"Wuv you too," he said in Brayden's voice.

She yielded to a smile but obviously wasn't ready to let him off the hook. She motioned to the backyard with her eyes and mouthed, "Tell her already."

"If you'd leave already, I could."

Once she finally disappeared around the front of the house, Chase fit his hat on and headed for the conversation he'd put off long enough.

He stopped beside the empty patio furniture and the two mugs of coffee Livy must've set out for them. Truthfully, another minute alone wouldn't hurt. He sank into one of the cushy chairs and breathed in the summer afternoon.

Aside from the random holes making the yard look like a game of whac-a-mole, the place held its normal tranquility. Livy had a way with creating ambiance—one of the many reasons people would flock to a café she had free creative reign to design. If it took Chase forever, that was one dream he wouldn't let her give up on.

The back door creaked opened, and Livy joined him on the patio. She handed him a cupcake. "Didn't say I wouldn't share."

"How very gracious of you." He lifted his mug. "You do realize if someone drives out of their way just for a cup of your coffee, it's worth charging for, right?"

She held out her half-eaten cupcake. "Hence, the treat."

"You know what I mean, Liv." When she didn't respond, he let it go. For now. They had other things to talk about.

He set his hat on the end table between them and switched his mug from hand to hand. "So, how was your appointment?" he rambled off instead of saying what he should've.

"What appointment?"

"Your *evasive* plans earlier," he reminded her.

"No appointments." Avoiding his gaze and the topic, she gobbled the rest of her cupcake. "It's good to have Quinn and Cooper home again, isn't it? Did you tell her about the dating coach thing?"

Chase almost choked on his coffee. He sat forward, held the mug away from his lap, and wiped his chin. "Um, not exactly." This could go south fast. "Take it from me, you don't want her involved."

"I might need all the help I can get." Livy balanced her mug on the chair arm. "I didn't want to admit it, but I think you're right. I need help." She jutted a finger at him. "And don't even think about inserting the hundred areas I need help in. I'm talking about dating." Pinching the bridge of her nose, she let out a sigh. "I'm pathetic. Truly. You should've heard me on the phone with Jed earlier. So mortifying."

"You're not pathetic, Liv. You're..." Everything he wanted to tell her swelled in his throat.

"Daft, I know."

"That's not what I was going to say." He scooted to the edge of his seat and ran his palms over his knees. "There's actually something I wanted to talk to you about. I—"

"Wait. Before you go telling me I can do better than Jed, I want you to know how much I appreciate you helping me anyway. Seriously." She stretched a hand over his. "I don't know what I'd do without this. Our friendship, I mean. Not having to worry about trying to impress someone." She hunched back in her chair and craned her neck to the open sky. "You have no idea how nice it is to have that kind of friendship without all the pressure and pretenses that go along with dating."

If she used the word friendship one more time...

Chase transferred his tension-filled grip from his knee back to his mug. Better for the hot ceramic to burn him than the truth. Though, in all honesty, she was right. Partly, anyway. "You should have that same kind of relationship with the guy you're dating too, you know."

"In theory." She squinted at him under the sun. "It's hard for me to get to that place with guys."

"What if you're already there and just don't know it?"

Question and uncertainty poured through eyes as tumultuous as the lake in a storm. Her lips parted but then stopped.

Her cell vibrated on the end table, Jed's name flashing on the screen. She blinked from Chase to the phone and back. "I should probably take this."

Resigning, he nodded and slouched in his chair as she meandered toward the oak trees bordering her yard. He squeezed his forehead while watching her come to life on the phone... with another dude.

Chase shoved his wet hair off his forehead. She wasn't the pathetic one. How many different ways did she need to tell him they were just friends before he accepted it?

He swiped his hat, lurched out of the chair, and reached in his pocket for his keys but grazed Earl's business card instead. He pulled it out and stared at the number.

"Sorry about that," Livy said on her way back over.

"It's fine." He slipped the card into his pocket before she noticed. "I was just leaving."

"Oh, okay."

An awkward pause stretched between them. The kind they rarely ever shared.

Chase peered at the clouds as if they'd sky write something to say.

No dice.

"You could swing by Long Shots later if you want." She lifted a shoulder. "I don't get off 'til twelve, but we could grab some wings on my break."

Chase fiddled with his keys. "Bars aren't really my scene."

"I know," she said softly. Chin down, Livy traced a fingernail along the outline of her cell phone. "You sure you don't want to stay a little longer then?" A slow smile hiked to the left. "I might even share one more cupcake."

Between her hopeful tone and impish expression, Chase caved. Who was he kidding? He couldn't give up fighting for her. Heck, he could barely say goodbye to her half the time. He needed to stop letting Jed get to him. The guy wasn't even around. Chase was. He always would be. Which was exactly what he needed to show her. But coming right out and telling her how he felt clearly wasn't an option. Not yet. Even if it took longer, he'd have to stick to his original plan.

Matching her playful demeanor, Chase adjusted his hat. "Make it two, and I'll think about it."

She rolled her eyes. "Don't push your luck, cowboy."

Apparently, that's what he did best.

Livy slipped in and out of her house with two more cupcakes in tow. She plopped one in his hand, eyed the other, and twirled with it back to her chair. Chase laughed. Little did she know how much natural talent she already had for making a guy turn to putty.

"So, about our arrangement..." He returned to his chair and peeled the lining off the cupcake. "If we're going to do these practice dates," he said through a bite. "I need to know what Pretty Boy's into."

She nibbled on a chocolate morsel, ignoring the name calling. "Music, obviously. Coffee..."

They looked at each other. "Obviously," they said in unison.

"Um." She picked at the cupcake top. "Anything outdoorsy, I think. He's always talking about these camping trips the band goes on together."

Chase stuffed the rest of the cupcake in his mouth to block his laugh. "That one might be a little tough."

"Hey, I go camping. Okay, *went* camping. Once. And vowed I'd never go again." Laughing, she flicked the balled-up wrapper at him. "Stop."

"I didn't—"

"Say a word. Yeah, I know." She dusted the crumbs off her hands. "Only with those enigmatic eyes of yours."

"Enigmatic?" He slanted a brow, and her cheeks turned ten different shades of pink.

Looking out to the woods, she ran her fingers down her mug handle, down her braid, and finally folded them in her lap. If her toes weren't tapping fast enough to drill a hole through the concrete, she might've pulled off the unfazed look.

What else did she think about him?

She hopped up when he rose. "You're leaving?"

"I have dates to plan, remember? These things take time." And patience. Both of which he was willing to invest to win her heart. "But…" He uncurled a strand of mud-speckled hair from behind her ear. "It's never too soon to start practicing."

The vein on her neck gave a little flutter, and he had to summon all his energy to stay smooth. "If I were saying good-bye to a girl I liked, I'd kiss her on the cheek."

Livy tilted her head. "You *always* kiss me on the cheek, Chase."

"Maybe." He leaned in and let his lips linger against her skin more softly than he ever had. "But not like this," he whispered.

When he drew back and saw her flustered reaction, there was no point hiding his own spiked heart rate. "Like I said, you're not the only one who needs practice." With a dip of his hat and a wink to match, he turned to leave before he gave too much away. He might not have all the details of his plan etched out yet, but unlike Bandit, Chase knew how to finish what he started.

At the corner of the house, he peered back toward the blush still claiming Livy's cheeks. A gamble or not, things were definitely about to get interesting.

CHAPTER SIX

Disillusioned

Livy lowered her hand from her warm cheek and eyed Bandit's half-dug holes, oh so tempted to bury herself in one. After seeing how worked up a little kiss on the cheek from her best friend got her, Chase had to be barking mad if he still thought he could teach her how to play it cool with Jed.

Sunlight pierced the clouds and glared over the only image sadder than the idea of her trying to romance a rock star—an empty coffee mug.

On her way to make another cup, she stopped in the living room and toed off her shoes beside two pairs she'd meant to put away days ago—along with the basket full of clean clothes she'd plopped in the chair yesterday. And wow, that stack of half cut-up magazines on the couch arm had been there even longer than the pile of unfinished notes on top of it.

Her shoulders fell. She really never finished things, did she?

Livy picked up one of the cut-out pictures of a café design from the magazine stack. Once again, Chase had called her out on things she didn't want to admit. She traced the outline of the rustic barn doors in the photo, knowing that was as close to untouchable dreams as she'd ever get. If nothing else, she should at least organize this mess. Maybe they could tackle that on one of their practice dates.

Yeah, because looking like a teenager on prom night after that silly kiss hadn't already tattooed LAME on her forehead. Though, in all fairness, that wasn't one of Chase's usual kisses. It was… well, a heck of a lot sexier than organizing scrap paper.

Livy feathered her fingers over her cheek again. He was good. She'd give him that. And he knew it. She shook her head. As if he weren't already enjoying hamming up this coaching thing for all it was worth, she had to go and stoke his fire today. Lovely. Forget the mug, she evidently needed to down the coffee straight out of the French press—*all* of it.

With a glance at a framed picture of them from Cooper and Quinn's wedding, she smiled in spite of herself. Whoever Mystery Girl was, she didn't have a prayer of not falling for him.

A twinge of disappointment struck her heart at the same time the coffee-cup-shaped wall clock struck another second closer to six o'clock. No time to dwell. Livy wheeled around the kitchen doorway and stepped smack into a puddle of water soaking into the furled linoleum.

"Are you kidding me?" She lifted her now-soaked sock and grimaced. Piece of junk dishwasher. Rather than kick the annoying thing as usual, she traded her mug for a dish towel, sopped up the mess, and chucked the wet cloth into the sink.

She filled a travel mug to the brim. Standing on her dry foot, she backed against the counter and clasped on a hoop earring she'd left there earlier. But no matter how hard she tried to stay distracted, the day kept replaying a blatant reminder of what a hot mess she was.

Her gaze roamed from the clock to her cell. Casting reservation aside, she snagged her phone. If her boss wanted her head to be straight tonight, he'd have to deal with her being a few minutes late.

Livy scrolled through her contacts, needing someone to process with. She held the phone with her shoulder and fastened on her other earring.

"Hey, chica," Ti answered. "I was literally just thinking of you and that hunk of a cowboy of yours. Tell me you two have gotten over yourselves and hooked up already."

Then again, maybe her outspoken friend wasn't the best person to call right now. "There's nothing to get over. I'm involved with Jed." Sort of. "And Chase is interested in..." It still bugged her that he hadn't filled her in on the details yet. "... Someone other than me. When are you gonna let that one go?"

A thick pause hung on the line, and Livy could picture Ti's exact expression—one she was glad was two hundred and fifty miles away at the moment.

"Girl, it's a good thing I'm coming out there for Quinn and Cooper's end-of-summer party."

Livy hurried down a sip of coffee. "Party? When?" Why didn't she know about this yet?

"End. Of. Summer."

Leave it to Ti to be a smart aleck. "Thanks for clarifying."

"Thanks for being excited about my coming."

"Of course I'm excited," she backpedaled. "But only if you leave your matchmaking agenda in Ocracoke with Grandma Jo and Mr. Fiazza."

"No promises," she said with a notable lilt.

"Ti..."

"Okay, fine. Dropping it. So, if you don't want to talk about your cowboy, what's up?"

Livy let the cowboy part go. Ti would always be Ti. No getting around it.

Still trying to untangle the web of thoughts the day had spun together, she headed into her bedroom and rifled through the pile of clothes on her bed.

"You still there?"

"Yeah, just thinking." Livy slumped onto the edge of the mattress with a pair of black leggings and a white shirt in her hands. "I guess it *is* kind of about Chase. Indirectly anyway. Well, more like it's about what he doesn't know it's about."

"Liv."

"Sorry. It's Sophie. The way she views my life compared to hers. It's... heartbreaking. You should've seen her face when she said I'd be the kind of mom any kid would want."

"She's a smart girl."

"She's disillusioned." Livy put her cell on speakerphone and tossed it on the bed so she could change. "My life is far from the make-believe version she idolizes."

"You've been taking her under your wing for how many months now? Of course she admires you. You can't give away that sweet heart of yours and not expect people to want to give you theirs in return."

Livy buttoned the last two buttons on her shirt and took her cell off speaker. "I'm not going there to earn something."

"Maybe not from them."

"What's that supposed to mean?"

"Girl, listen to me. What you're doing there—it's making a huge impact on those kids' lives. And I'm not for a second saying I think you should stop going. But just remember, you have nothing to atone for."

Wrong. She had everything to atone for.

Livy sank onto the bed again. "If she ever found out I..." She'd lose her too.

Ti's voice softened. "Chase doesn't know either, does he?"

"He can't." Ever.

"Why? Because then you'd actually have someone there to walk through all this with?"

The faith his eyes held every time he brought up the café compressed around her as she strode back down the narrow hall. "Because he believes in me."

"Um... kinda my point."

"And you're missing mine." If he knew the kind of girl she was in London, he wouldn't look at her the same. Livy stared at the spotless white ceiling, wishing her past were even half as untainted. "You don't understand. He grew up in a home people like us dreamed about. Was taught to put his faith and family first no matter what. They're everything to him. I'm telling you. Just the thought of someone abandoning a family member burns his britches like nothing I've ever seen." She couldn't bear his disappointment in her if he knew that was exactly what she'd done. "He's my best friend, Ti. I don't want anything to change between us."

"Back up a sec. Did you just say, 'burns his britches?' Dear Lord, stay put. I'm coming to rescue you right now."

Livy cracked a smile. "Chase's parents must be rubbing off on me."

"Already in with the in-laws. Nice."

"They're not…" Why bother? She could already hear Ti's comeback prepping through the line. Livy picked at the polish chipping on the corner of her pinky nail. "This isn't about them. It's not even just about Chase. It's about—"

"Tanner, I know."

Livy rarely ever said her son's name. Too much loss, too much remorse.

The look on Sophie's face earlier dragged her heart into a sandpit of doubt. "What if I made the wrong decision, Ti? What if Sophie's right, and he's in a home with parents who mistreat him or…" She couldn't finish the thought.

The Bradleys had seemed like good people when she'd met them during the selection process before having Tanner, but like Sophie said, everyone wore masks.

"Maybe it's time you found out."

Livy's foot slid down the wall. "Sorry, you mean try to meet him?" It had been four years. Even if that was possible, how could she ever expect him to want to see her after knowing she'd given him up? "We didn't agree to visitation rights. I'm not sure I can change that now."

"You won't know if you don't ask. Contact the adoption agency you worked with."

"I don't know if that's—"

"*And* tell Chase," Ti tacked on with extra New York flair.

Yeah, not happening. He didn't even know she'd been going to the group home. Some things she had to do on her own, just like he did.

Her coffee cup clock ticked another minute away. "I need to get to work."

"And you say *I'm* the Queen of Deflection?" Her smile almost audible through the line, Ti let her pause drive the insinuation home. As usual. "I'll let you off the hook this time, but only if you tell Chase the truth. He loves you, Liv."

"We're not—"

"—even if it's just as a friend. Which I highly doubt, but whatever."

And Ti's bluntness strikes again.

"I'm hanging up now." She should know getting Ti off that bandwagon was a lost cause. "Love you, girl."

Livy crammed the conversation in a back drawer of her mind as soon as she ended the call and hustled to the kitchen. Careful to dodge any potential leaks this time, she grabbed her keys and coffee. She should've been racing out the door. Instead, she hesitated with her cell in hand. Something she couldn't explain drove her fingers across the screen until the adoption agency's webpage stared up at her. Waiting. Her thumbs hovered over the keypad.

"Maybe it's time you found out."

She gripped the phone. What if she wasn't ready for the answer?

Livy set another three cold drinks in front of the guys at one of her tables and pinned the tray to her side. "Anything else I can get for you?"

The extra skeevy one with more grease in his hair than his picked-over onion rings roved a glance up and down her profile. "I'm not seeing the kind of dessert I want on the menu," he slurred while reaching for her waist. "But I bet we could find a way to remedy that."

Barf. Livy jerked free from his grimy hand. "I'll be sure to have my manager stop by to discuss that with you." They didn't need to know Lance would probably give him props for the lewd comment. Even if baseless, hopefully the threat would cause them to back off.

She feigned confident strides to the kitchen, where once behind the revolving door, her shoulders slumped. Fifteen more minutes. She just had to get through the last fifteen minutes of her shift, and then she could walk out of there with her tips and an iota of pride left if she was lucky.

Between the dishwasher's constant hiss and the sizzling pops from the cooks' area, the kitchen all but laughed at her. Pride? Right. She'd moved here from Ocracoke last summer for a fresh start, but nothing had changed. She was still living in a rented space in need of repairs she couldn't afford. Was still waitressing lousy hours for lousy pay. Even worse, now she worked in a bar where she had to put up with guys like Grease Ball at table five.

And Ti wanted her to meet her son? No way. Not like this.

The door swung open from the opposite side and slammed into her elbow. Grasping it, Livy held her breath to keep a shriek of pain from escaping.

"Ooh. Sorry, babe." Lance slithered in and eyed the pocket on her apron, probably assessing how much cash she'd accumulated in tips tonight. "Told ya the after-hours crowd would be worth it."

A bell dinged from the counter.

"Yeah, they're a real treat." Livy picked up an order of mudslides, balanced the two plates on her tray, and buried the sting in her elbow. "Thanks for thinking of me."

"You know I always put my girl first."

Without responding, she carried the desserts to her last table of the night. Drunken cat calls from table five rose over the pool balls clanking together in the corner, but Livy didn't so much as give them the satisfaction of casting a glance their way.

"Fifteen more minutes," she said under her breath.

Once the clock finally freed her, she balled up her apron and headed to the parking lot. The night's cool air breezed across her cheeks in a sigh of relief. It had been one long day. Her bed was calling. Shoot, even her living room floor was calling. Whichever she made it to first would suffice.

Halfway across the dimly lit lot, she pulled out her keys.

"We never got to discuss that dessert." Grease Boy stumbled around a blue pickup with a feeble grasp on his own keys. He staggered over, his buddies closing in behind him. "What do you say, sweetheart?" Looking her up and down, he reached for her braid. "You have a little spice under that sweet coating, don't you?"

"Don't touch me." Livy shoved him away, but the guy on the left grabbed her arm.

"Where you going so fast? The fun's just getting started."

Heart pumping, she searched the sparse parking lot, knowing she was on her own in this part of town. She cut a glance to her purse and the cell tucked inside. She'd only have a split second to—

"Uh-uh." Grease Boy caught her fingers and brought them to his lips. "I don't like to share."

She struggled against the tight grasp on her wrist. "Let go of me."

"Now," a deep voice said from behind them.

The single streetlight cast shadows across the guy's broad shoulders. Livy released a hard breath when he came into view. Chase. Why he'd changed his mind about coming didn't matter, only that he was here.

"Well, if it isn't Chase Thompson." Grease Boy strutted forward. "I thought you would've learned by now not to butt in where you don't belong."

He knew these low lives?

Chase's jaw twitched, but he kept his cool. "Why don't you and your buddies sleep it off, huh? There's no need for things to get ugly."

"Yet, here you are again, making things..." He cocked his chin. "Ugly."

The tension pulsing on Chase's neck seemed to throb all the way down to his balled fists. "Back off, Jeremy."

"This seems oddly familiar, doesn't it?" Practically in Chase's face, he slid a smug look over him. "You, trying to rescue a girl who's just looking for a good time."

Seething at his implication, Livy fought to break the other guy's hold on her arm. "That's not what I—"

"Easy, sweetheart." Jeremy's smirk zinged from Livy back to Chase. "This isn't your boyfriend's first rodeo. He knows full well how you girls like to play it."

That did it. Chase grabbed the jerk by the shirt. "I'm warning you, man. Walk away."

"Now, you know I can't do that." A smarmy gaze full of intentions ran down Livy's body. "Not when we were about to start dessert."

One second. He'd hardly finished turning before Chase decked him. The crack to his jaw echoed across the empty parking lot and shuddered off the brick walls.

Jeremy held up a hand when his friends hobbled forward. He spat blood on the pavement and wiped his chin, dilated eyes fired with foolish pride. "It's on now, Thompson." He swung a wobbly right cross in the air.

Dodging the blow, Chase rammed a shoulder into his torso and bulldozed him into the other two guys, barely sober enough to stay on their feet. All three stumbled into a group of metal trash cans and landed on a heap of garbage.

Chase grabbed Livy's hand and steered her to his truck. "Get in."

"But my car—"

"We'll come back for it." He snapped the door behind her, hopped in his side, and gunned out of the lot. With a quick glance in his rearview mirror, he jerked the truck onto a side road. "You shouldn't be going out in that parking lot alone."

Another whip to the left sent Livy barring a hand against the dashboard. "Yeah, well, my boss isn't exactly the kind of guy who walks a girl to her car."

Chase wrenched the gearshift into second and his sharp tone up a notch. "Then maybe it's time to find a new job."

She glared across the console. "You don't think I want one?"

"If you did, maybe you'd actually look into the café prospect instead of blowing it off at every turn."

Like she needed him to remind her of that right now. She faced the passenger window, refusing to fall apart in front of him.

The truck swerved toward the curb and came to a stop. Chase threw the gearshift into park but didn't release the wheel. "I'm sorry. I didn't mean that." His shoulders followed a slow release of breath. "Jeremy got me riled up, is all."

They obviously shared history—a heated one. Livy twisted toward him. "What did he mean about this being familiar? Was there another—?"

"Lesson I should've learned from? Yeah." He scrubbed a hand down his face.

Was that what he thought this was? She swallowed the stupid tears trekking to the surface. "I don't know what happened in the past with some other girl, but I swear I didn't do anything to make those guys think I wanted to be there."

Chase turned toward her then, and the heartache on his face plowed through every other emotion. "I know. This was about me, not you."

No, it was about the kind of girl guys expected to work in a place like Long Shots. The kind of girl she used to be.

"Either way, thank you for coming." Adrenaline waning, she squeezed her eyes shut. "I don't know what I would've done if you hadn't..."

"Hey." He smoothed a thumb across her cheek, his tender touch a mirror of his voice. "I'd never let that happen."

The warmth of his promise wrapped around her like arms of safety she could trust, sink into. Nodding, she searched his eyes, wondering what had driven him out there tonight. "I thought bars weren't your scene."

He returned his hand to the wheel and stretched out his neck. "With people like Jeremy hanging around, they're not."

No arguments there. Livy wasn't particularly fond of them either, but something gave her the feeling he carried more of a reason to avoid the scene than she did.

"Yet you changed your mind."

He rubbed a knuckle across his brow. "You have a way of getting me to do that."

She wasn't about to ask whether that was good or bad. "Well, whatever the reason, I'm grateful I was an exception tonight."

Head down and voice even lower, his chin grazed his collar. "You've always been the exception, Liv." Passing headlights caught the flicker of a soft smile as his gaze found hers again.

Though she could rarely decipher the world of meaning hidden in those intricate shades of brown, the friendship and belief he held for her never seemed to falter. It filled the dark cab, absorbing the minutes until Chase finally cleared his throat and reached for the gearshift.

"We should get going."

"Right. Yeah." Back home to her dark, empty house. Fantastic.

She turned toward the passenger window and the chance to regain her composure. But no matter how long she stared at the blur of houses streaming alongside them, they couldn't color over a day she wanted to erase. All but this—sitting here in the comfort of being with Chase.

As if hearing her thoughts, he stretched a hand across the console and found hers. Strong, compassionate. Her eyes closed at the warm touch. More than ever, she was certain what she told Ti was right. She couldn't lose this. No matter what else it cost her.

CHAPTER SEVEN

Overrated

A step ahead of Chase, Livy dragged her feet up to her front door, not ready to be alone. The possibility of what could've happened with those guys pressed in the minute she shut her eyes. Open, the darkness inside her house closed in even more. She had to go in. Still, Livy reached for the porch rail and any plausible excuse she could give for Chase to stay without letting on how shaken she was.

Right. What was she going to do? Ask him to start their practice dates now—in the middle of the night? Even Cinderella couldn't pull off romance after midnight.

She glanced at the window, torn between missing and hating the way Jack used to wait up for her by the door when they were teens. If he hadn't asked Chase to fill his big brother shoes while she lived here, she would've been on her own tonight. She knew that. Yet as grateful as she was, it irked her any time she gave him a reason to feel justified for putting Chase in that position to begin with.

She should just shake it off, let him go home and get some sleep. It'd be fine. Breathing in, she whirled around, and Chase almost bumped right into her.

"Oh, sorry." She set a hand to his chest to gain her balance. Not that it mattered. The second he steadied her by the arm, Livy backed her heels into the porch step.

"You all right?"

"Fine." She fiddled with her keys as if one would magically unlock the sanity she'd clearly lost back in the parking lot. What was wrong with her?

Chase angled in front of her. "You sure?"

"I'm good. Yeah." She turned for the door and stopped at the shadows flickering across the window panes. *Then again...* "Stay." The word flew out as fast as she whipped back around.

When his forehead crinkled, her cheeks simmered against the night's cool breeze.

Livy twirled her bracelets, wishing they could rewind time. "I don't mean *stay*, stay. Like spend the night with me or anything. Just hang out until we fall asleep—until *I* fall asleep. Alone. Just me and my pillows. Well, and the piles of laundry on my bed." She tensed. "Not that I'm inviting you to go to bed with me. 'Cause that would be..." As inappropriate as this entire conversation? "... Super awkward. You, wading through my laundry, I mean. Girl clothes and all that." *Tell me I didn't just say that.*

The freckles around his eyes all but laughed at her. "Girl clothes, huh?"

Unbelievable. She pulled in the corner of her lip before she dug herself any deeper.

As if that ever worked. Ten seconds of silence was evidently more than she could handle. "Not *those* kinds of clothes. I've never been one to wear... *that*. I love style—don't get me wrong—but some things are way overrated. Sometimes a girl just wants comfort. Besides, it's not like cotton can't be sexy, right?"

A flash up to Chase's raised brow, and Livy almost died right there. "Don't answer that. In fact, don't say anything." She swept her braid off her increasingly sticky neck. "We should probably go in—away from any laundry or beds. I'll just crash on the couch tonight. You know, in the living room." *Oh my word.* No limits. Her mouth seriously knew no limits.

His grin hitched sideways. "Is that where the couch is?"

She covered her face. "You're not going to let me forget I actually said all of that, are you?"

"Not a chance."

She pushed back her bangs and left her hand on her warm forehead. "One of these days I'll stop saying the most awkward things imaginable."

"I hope not. It's one of your most endearing qualities."

"Is endearing another word for spastic? Because that's definitely more fitting." As thankful as she was for Chase's protection tonight, even he couldn't rescue her from herself.

The thought sparked flashes from Long Shots' dark parking lot again, and just like that, her detour into humiliation territory nosedived right back to the collision of emotions she hadn't recovered from yet.

Without looking up from a crack in the first step, Livy toyed with the button on her sleeve. "In all seriousness, Chase, I'm really sorry about all this. You, coming out to the bar and having to deal with those guys. I'm sure being my knight in shining armor wasn't exactly what you signed up for when my brother asked you to look out for me."

"I might've hoped it would be." A grin rivaling the swag in his stride edged toward her.

Livy nudged his arm. Apparently, his charm had fewer restraints than her runaway thoughts. Even the porch light's yellow glow was drawn to the warmth in his eyes. But not for the first time, she couldn't have been more thankful for his gift for taking her mind off things.

With a gaze as gentle as his touch, Chase took the keys from her and nodded to the door. "C'mon. Let's get you to sleep." His mouth quirked. "On the couch."

Or in a time machine. Oh, how many things she'd go back and erase from ever leaving her mouth if she could.

Livy stopped in the entryway. "Would you mind if we pretended earlier didn't happen? I don't want to think about it right now." Or ever again. Repressing a shudder at the feel of that creep's breath on her face, she hung her purse on the decorative wall hooks and started for the kitchen and the perfect escape. "There's no way I can sleep yet. Want some coffee? I'm making decaf."

"Does it come with a cupcake?" He wandered back down the hall from where he must've been making sure the rest of the house was secure. Chase Thompson, ever the protector… and her favorite distraction.

"Cupcakes? Psh. You know those are long gone, pal. How 'bout some popcorn?"

He poked his head around the kitchen doorway. "Only if I can help."

"Sure." Livy poured coffee beans into the grinder. "But hands off my coffee press."

Passing her, he lifted his palms. "Wouldn't dream of interfering with an artist's work."

"Mm-hmm." She flicked a coffee bean at him as he opened the pantry door. "Make sure you grab two bags. I may not have many talents, but demolishing an entire bag of popcorn in one sitting is definitely one of them."

Chase withdrew only one bag from the box, brow raised in challenge, but must've thought better of it. Wise man.

While he heated the popcorn in the microwave, Livy added the milk and spices she'd warmed to the coffee and topped two mugs with whipped cream and a chocolate-drizzled design. She stood over them, contemplating. Something was missing.

Chase reached for one.

"Wait." She added mint leaves for garnish, plunked in a cookie straw, and handed him the mug with a satisfied smile. "In lieu of your cupcake."

He admired her artwork. "And you don't have any talents?"

"It's just coffee."

"I couldn't come up with something that looked like this, much less find a way to make decaf taste this amazing."

The investor's comments about her vision rushed in on the tails of his compliment. Livy scooped some whipped cream off the top of her drink, flipped the spoon upside down in her mouth, and tapped it against her lip. She eyed him, debating on how to play this.

"Did you know a chain pizza joint may be moving into Mrs. Finch's old café?"

He lounged back against the counter on his elbows. "Where'd you hear that?"

"Oh, I just *happened* to run into a lady from an investment firm today."

Chase feigned surprise. "You don't say."

"Mm-hmm." She'd go along with his game. Stalling at his piqued interest, she relished another scoop of chocolate-covered cream. "And she might've suggested I should make a counter offer on the property."

As if his sugar rush weren't already testing the limits of his cheekbones, pure satisfaction claimed his whole face. "Is that right?"

"Don't go getting over excited. It's just a possibility—a far off, highly improbable possibility."

His darn smile moseyed toward her. "But it *is* a possibility?"

Livy curled both hands around her warm mug and breathed in the spiced scent of hope she'd long ago tucked away. He'd said she had a way of changing his mind. Maybe it was time she changed her own. Even if tonight's run-in with those guys hadn't happened, she couldn't stay in the same dead-end situation if she wanted to prove to her son that she'd changed since having him.

Her own café. Could she really make it happen?

A thick breeze sweeping off the woods sailed through the window with the weighty force of doubt.

Livy set her mug down and faced the counter. "Do you think I'm crazy for even considering this?"

A soft touch glided across the tops of her shoulders. "I think you'd be crazy not to."

Unswerving confidence met her when she turned. "Why is it so easy for you to believe in that dream?"

"It's not the dream I believe in, Liv." A slow blink brought Chase's eyes up from a spot of mechanical grease along his thumb. "It's you."

When he looked at her like that, she wanted to believe in what he saw too. Wanted to grab hold of his faith.

She broke the connection. "I should probably get that popcorn." Livy slipped past him in search of two large bowls from a bottom cabinet and, with any luck, the chance to change the subject.

Thankfully, he let it slide.

In the living room, she plopped onto the carpet, took another sip of her coffee, and cozied into one of the husband pillows backed against the bottom of the couch.

Chase followed a moment later. Only two seconds passed before he nodded behind them. "So, the couch really *is* in the living room?"

He laughed at her sad attempt at punching his arm. Thanks to her uncanny luck, he bumped into the laundry basket she still hadn't taken back to her bedroom.

She glared from the now-considered incriminating girl clothes to the grin climbing his cheek. "Don't even think about it."

"Too late." He held his mug away from his lap before it ended up spilling faster than his laughter when she swatted him with a throw pillow.

Why did she set herself up for these things?

Still laughing, Chase tried to get comfortable stretched out against the other raggedy husband pillow she'd gotten in high school during her phase of sprawling decorating ideas across her bedroom floor.

The stack of cut-up magazines on the couch arm smirked at her. Okay, maybe she hadn't entirely grown out of that phase yet. Or at all.

She had to chuckle. "You really are a trooper, Chase. You know that? Not many people would put up with my utter weirdness."

"Weird?" A puff of stuffing flew out of a tear in one of the arms of the hot pink pillow. "I always prefer to crash on the floor instead of a soft couch right behind me at one in the morning. Besides, normal is..." He tossed a piece of popcorn in his mouth. "... overrated."

"You've been dying to use that one, haven't you?"

He hid the answer behind his mug and then raised it in a toast. "To weirdness."

Giving in to those blasted freckles, Livy clinked her mug with his and settled into the pillow and the ease of being herself. Who needed a soft couch when her best friend always knew how to make her feel the most comfortable?

"I know it's been a long day for both of us," she said. "But are you ready to tell me what's going on with your dad now?"

The labored breath whooshing out of him deflated the lightheartedness he'd just worked so hard to create.

"Sorry, I shouldn't have—"

"No, it's fine. It's just some stuff with my dad's insurance." He stared into his coffee. "Unless we figure out a way around the cuts to his coverage, he's gonna lose his prescription." His knuckles whitened around the mug handle. "Along with Nurse Murphy's home visits."

Livy's heart blanched. Nurse Murphy was practically family to them. Between her help and the right medication, Mr. Thompson had been more lucid these past eight months than he had in years.

Angling toward Chase, she pulled a leg to her stomach and tucked her foot under her thigh. "Isn't there anything we can do?"

"I'm working on it." He set his bowl of popcorn aside and rubbed his neck.

The way he carried others' burdens made her heart ache even more. "Maybe we could look into alternative medicine. Or what about Coop? If you asked him, I know he'd absolutely give you the money to—"

"Not an option." Back stiff and unyielding, Chase adjusted his jeans at the knees. "It's my family to take care of."

"It's Quinn's too." Why was he being so hardnosed about this? "There's nothing wrong with asking—"

"Can we just drop it?"

She raised her hands. "Fine."

After her coffee clock ticked a painful minute away, Chase heaved a long exhale. "I'm sorry. Just ignore me. You're right. It's been a long day." He wrapped an arm around her shoulders, brought her close, and kissed the side of her head. "Thank you for wanting to help. It means a lot."

"You're my best friend." She settled into his side. "I'll always be here for you. You know that."

When he didn't respond, she started to sit up. "Chase?"

He kept her in place and rested his cheek over her hair. "I know," he whispered.

A trace of sadness shadowed his voice. She couldn't place the source, only that it was there. While she let it go, he held her a little tighter. Another quiet minute lapsed. And this time, as she nestled close to her best friend, Livy couldn't help envying Cinderella a little more than she should've. Even if princes were overrated.

Chase must've felt her inward laugh. "See?" The sudden shift in his tone obliterated the sadness that had dulled it just a few moments earlier. "This dating practice isn't so hard. You're completely at ease in a guy's arms without even realizing it."

Little did he know... "First of all, our practice dates haven't started yet. And you're not a regular guy. You're... you."

"I'll try not to take offense to that."

"You know what I mean." She poked his side, sat up, and grabbed her bowl. "Who else can I feel comfortable enough smashing a whole tub of popcorn in front of?" She stuffed a handful in her mouth. "Attractive, right?" she mumbled.

Laughing, he brushed a kernel from the corner of her lips with his thumb. "Once again, you don't even realize it."

"Realize what?"

He scratched the back of his hair as though debating on answering. "We're going to get you feeling every bit as confident as you should, Liv. But trust me." His eyes lifted her way, soft, sincere. "You already have every reason to be."

Maybe when he looked at her like that.

She swept her gaze to the floor, and Chase cleared his throat.

"It's too bad this won't work."

Livy darted her head up. "What won't?"

"This—snacks, coffee, husband pillows," he added with a grin. "This is perfect date material for *you and me*, but for a guy with Jed's kind of money?" He scrunched his nose. "Pretty Boy's gonna want to be sitting with you in some high-rise condo, ordering the fanciest take-out possible. Not on the floor eating microwave popcorn." Ankles crossed, he tossed another piece into his mouth. "You ready for that kind of lifestyle? 'Cause I can switch up my coaching strategy. Slip in some oyster shell cracking lessons."

Livy might've laughed at his obnoxious wink if her stomach weren't turning at the thought of slimy seafood. "I'd rather eat Cheerios."

"Cheerios."

"Cereal for dinner." She splayed a hand to her side. "Don't act like you haven't done that a thousand times."

The quirk in his lips alone made a full confession. "So, all a guy needs to do to impress you on a date is bring you Cheerios?"

"Add a banana and some candlelight, and I'll never look back." She dished out an impression of one of his usual sultry grins but could only pull off his charm for five whole seconds. Laughing instead, she picked at the kernels left in her bowl. "I don't need a guy to try to impress me. That's the point."

"Does Jed know that? 'Cause that might be a challenge for a guy who tries to impress people for a living."

Livy ignored the masked edge that always snuck into his tone when Jed came up. Chin down, she rubbed the salt off her fingertips. "It's not exactly easy for me to talk about stuff like that with guys."

"You're talking to me about it right now." He dipped his head to steal her gaze. "Isn't that the way it should be?"

With him? Sure. "Didn't we just go over this?"

"The whole, I'm not a regular guy thing. Right." He chugged the last of his coffee. When he looked up again, his eyes held a glint of something she couldn't place. "Okay, you know what? You need practice talking to a guy you're interested in, so let's do this. I'm Jed. Tell me how I make you feel when you're with me."

"What?" She waved him off. "No."

"C'mon." Chase turned her toward him, so they were face to face, moved her bowl, and took her hands. "Don't overthink it. Just say whatever you're thinking."

Locked on to his eyes, the only think she was thinking was how bad at acting she was.

"Liv."

"Okay. Fine." Wriggling up her shoulders, she swept her braid back and cleared her throat. "*Jed, when I'm with you, you make me feel... special.*" There. Done.

Chase blinked at her. "Special. That's all you've got?"

"What's wrong with special?"

"It's..." He made a face. "Lame."

Trying not to laugh, she swatted him in the arm. "I can't believe you just called my feelings lame. I'm trying to get vulnerable here."

"That wasn't vulnerable. That was safe."

"Oh really?" She swiped her bowl back. "Let's see you do it then, coach."

Two point zero seconds. That's all it took for Livy to regret asking. Already in character, all Chase had to do was steer his focus to her hand in his, and she was glued to whatever he was about to say. Add in the familiar little V forming between his brows, and her heart was done.

His thumb grazed across her knuckles. "Sometimes, I have these days when everything in my life feels upside down, and I just want to run away from it all. The noise, the questions. The pressure." A slow exhale brought his eyes back to hers. "But then I see you. All the noise shuts down. I hear your voice, and..." He took off his hat. "I can finally breathe again."

If she could've done the same, she would've spoken. Or at least cut off the tears starting to blur him with a dream that felt too real. But she couldn't look away, couldn't find a response. "Chase, I—"

Barks erupted from the backyard.

They both peered toward the window and back at each other. "Bandit," they said at the same time. No telling what trouble that dog had gotten in to now. Though, for once, Livy was grateful for the interruption.

Outside, the cool grass at the edge of her patio blew against her toes. "Bandit, come here, buddy."

Instead of running to her like usual or chasing every little sound, he hovered between their two properties as if an invisible leash tethered him to his house and barked louder.

Chase came up alongside her. "What's he doing?"

"I don't know." Livy ran her hands along her arms. Something wasn't right. One look at the concern shadowing Chase's face confirmed he sensed it too.

Cautious strides led them across the lawn together. Bandit took off to his back stoop, stopping only seconds at a time to make sure they followed him. Barely sitting still, he whined each time the open screen door rattled in the damp breeze blowing off the woods.

Livy cast another apprehensive glance Chase's way while reaching for the handle.

He set a hand over hers. "Let me go in first."

The dog squeezed through before Chase fully opened the door.

"Bandit, hold on."

Why she expected this to be one time he'd actually listen, she had no idea. He disappeared into the dark house, leaving a trail of whimpers like breadcrumbs.

Inside, the wind howling against the shutters swept an eerie stillness across the kitchen and goose bumps across Livy's skin. When she grabbed Chase's arm on instinct, he motioned for her to wait there while he checked it out.

Like that was happening. She practically ran into him to catch up. But once at the edge of the living room's orange carpet, everything froze—her feet, her voice. She grasped Chase's arm tighter this time. Tender and protective, he covered her fingers with his, but even a knight's shining armor couldn't shield her heart from the piercing shadows.

Another whimper brought Bandit into focus. From the center of the room, his eyes glowed in the dark above a silhouette of what could only mean one thing.

Livy's hand soared to her mouth. *Mrs. Finch.*

CHAPTER EIGHT

Shaken

Despite Chase's tight grip around Bandit's collar, the farther the ambulance's taillights drifted down the road, the harder he struggled to run after it. Poor dog. He might not know his tail from a hole in the ground half the time, but no one could question his affection for his owner.

Beside him, a sniffle echoed Bandit's heartbroken whine. Chase drew Livy to his side. "Hey, she's going to be fine. The EMT said he sees these kinds of falls all the time. And knowing Mrs. Finch, she'll be back on her feet by the end of the week."

The last glimpse of the ambulance faded into darkness. "You're a lousy liar, Chase Thompson." She nuzzled deeper under his shoulder. "But I love you for it."

And he loved the way she found such ease leaning into him. If his embrace could ward off all the doubts she carried, he'd hold her 'til the sun came up.

She pushed her bangs off her face. "Can anything else happen tonight?"

With her in his arms, he sure hoped so. Sometimes, the urge to kiss her came on with such fervency, he could hardly restrain himself. But the timing still wasn't right. He knew that. Hated it but knew it.

"C'mon." He prodded her and Bandit back to her house. "Nothing else is happening tonight except sleep."

Livy let out an exhausted moan. "Is it bad that I feel like I already *am* sleeping?"

Not as bad as it was for him. Wide awake, and he couldn't stop himself from dreaming.

His cell rang as he opened the door for her. Same area code as Earl's, but Chase didn't recognize the number.

Livy leaned over. "Who's calling you at this hour?"

He silenced the call and tucked the phone back into his pocket. "Someone from Chicago. Probably the wrong number." If it had anything to do with Earl's job offer, he didn't want to get into it right then.

Inside, Bandit lunged straight for the couch, sniffed every crevice, and finally curled into the corner. He plopped his chin over his front paws and wheezed an elongated sigh worthy of the clock's 2:00 a.m. chime.

Chase laughed. "Looks like you might have a sleep companion after all."

And now, here he was, envious of a dog. The lows just kept getting lower.

Yawning, Livy crashed beside Bandit on the couch. "There's room for you, too, if you want to stay a little longer."

Her rustled bangs poked out in several directions, making her look tousled and adorable and... Wow, he needed to leave.

Chase rubbed his knuckles along his overgrown whiskers. "I should go." Before he couldn't. It was past late. Past the limits of his resistance. He gathered their empty bowls and coffee mugs from the floor.

"Leave them." Livy bundled a throw pillow under her arms. "I'll wash them in the morning. The dishwasher's broken."

The mug handles dangled on his fingers. "Again? I thought your landlord fixed it."

"He did. Twice." She pulled her hair tie out and fingered through her braid, long waves spilling down her shoulders. "Either whatever YouTube video he watched failed him, or that stupid dishwasher has it out for me. I haven't decided which."

Earl's job offer tingled in the back of his mind. Moving might be a way to take care of his parents, but what about being here for Liv when she needed him too?

"What's wrong?"

Chase barricaded the unanswered questions behind a smile. "Nothing. I'll come by tomorrow to fix the dishwasher." He carried the mugs into the kitchen. "No arguments."

She followed, begrudgingly cutting off whatever rebuttal she was about to make and leaned against the doorjamb. "Anyone ever tell you you're pushy?"

"Another thing you love about me."

"You mean, another thing I put up with."

"Free of charge." He set the mugs in the sink and sauntered toward her. "But you better save some of that tolerance for our next date."

Her arms strayed to her sides. "What date?"

"The surprise one." Chase stopped in the doorway with her and brushed a wavy strand of hair off the nape of her neck. "Get some sleep. We have lots of practice ahead of us."

"Who needs practice?" Livy straightened against the trim. "My charm-resisting skills are already in perfect condition."

His gaze not wavering, he leaned in to kiss her cheek. He brushed a thumb beneath her ear, his voice against her skin. "We'll see about that." When her breath fluttered, he stretched back and met a blue-eyed maze of emotions he prayed for the wisdom to navigate. A little extra strength wouldn't hurt either. Tenacity, patience—anything to help him pull himself away before he ended up kissing her too soon. Because right then—this close, this connected—even his breathing betrayed the need to wait. "I should go."

Her back stayed glued against the frame, her eyes on his. "You already said that."

Right. So, why weren't his feet listening? And heaven help him if his heart beat any louder. He swallowed. Hard. His fingers tightened around the trim.

From the living room, Bandit whined like he was dreaming.

At least Chase wasn't the only one. He hooked a thumb behind him. "I'm leaving now." He kicked himself all the way to the door, only stopping long enough to flash her a half-composed wave goodnight.

Livy caught the screen just before it closed. "Wait." Outside, the porch light caught a look in her eyes that could bring him to his knees if he wasn't careful. "Thanks for tonight. For everything, really." She rubbed one bare foot over the other. "I appreciate you staying and keeping me distracted. I needed the company."

"Pleasure's mine." Always would be.

Taking out his keys might've kept him in place if the wind singing through her messy hair hadn't drawn him right back up the two steps he'd already made it down.

Maybe he wasn't a rock star or a knight or even a regular guy. But as long as he could be what she needed, he'd never stop trying.

With a fortifying inhale, he tamed her flyaway bangs. "Lock up behind me and call if you need anything."

"I will." Her lips curved. "But now that I have a watchdog, what's there to be worried about, right?"

A snore with an impressive amount of bass barreled out from the living room with the obvious answer.

They both cracked up. "Uh-huh. You just make sure you keep your cell on."

She nodded through a yawn. "Night, Chase."

"Night." Still not leaving, his defiant feet brought him a step closer and his pulse a beat faster.

Until another classic snore rumbled from inside like a warning bell.

He laughed to himself. It wouldn't be a bad idea to take Bandit on all their dates. Chase evidently needed help running interference. Resigned to wait, he pressed a shadow of the kiss he wanted to give Livy to her cheek instead. "See you tomorrow."

"Night, Chase."

He rubbed a thumb down the corner of his mouth, fighting a grin. "You already said that."

She let go of the hair tie on her wrist and shoved his arm. "Get out of here before the sun comes up, will ya?" One last gaze swept toward him as she turned for the door.

Once the deadbolt sounded, Chase crossed the lawn to his truck, half relieved he'd hung on to his resolve one more night, half afraid it wouldn't matter in the end.

He tossed his hat onto the passenger seat and rubbed his eyes. He couldn't get ahead of himself and push her away. Not this time.

The thought sent Jeremy's twangy voice jabbing into wounds that should've healed by now. "*This seems oddly familiar, doesn't it? You, trying to rescue a girl who's just looking for a good time.*"

Despite how tightly Chase clenched the wheel, he couldn't cut off memories of the summer Kaley had broken up with him. Jeremy was right. She hadn't wanted to be rescued. Not even from choices that hurt them both.

His cell rang in his pocket. He wrangled it out, thankful for the interruption until he saw the number on the screen. Whatever had his mom awake in the middle of the night couldn't be good. "Hey, what are you doing up at this hour?"

"Your dad. He's..." She gasped at something crashing in the background.

Chase's pulse beat a disjointed rhythm of concern and exhaustion. "Ma?"

"I don't know what's gotten into him." Her voice quivered through the line. "He was fine earlier, but then he—"

"You give me those keys right now before I call the cops," Dad yelled.

In all his years, Chase had rarely heard him raise his voice. The unrecognizable tone sent his heart through the floorboard. Losing parts of his dad to dementia over time had been hard enough, but this felt different. Dangerous almost.

Chase checked the rearview mirror and gunned away from the curb. "Hang on, Ma. I'll be right there."

His tires screeched to a stop in front of his parents' house sooner than they probably should have. Part worried, part overtired, he hustled out of the truck without grabbing his keys and stopped mid yard at the scene in front of him.

Mom stood at the bottom of the porch stairs with a robe strapped across her body and a frantic look in her eyes.

"Just relax, George." Nurse Murphy's familiar voice came from the driveway where she and Dad were standing, both looking like they'd rolled out of bed only moments before. With her hands up, she blocked him from the driver's side of his old Chevy. "Everything's okay. What do you say we go back inside?"

Dad's curved shoulders heaved. He jutted a frustrated hand behind him toward Mom. "Tell this woman to give me my keys. I have to get home. I have to—"

"You're already home, George." Nurse Murphy's gentle tone soothed and calmed as it always did. "There's nowhere to go. You're safe right here with the people who care about you."

Dad swung a distressed glance from her to the house, to Mom, and back. "No." He shook his head, eyes shrouded in a distant, foggy sheen. "I need to leave. Need to get back to…" His words trailed as if searching for something already forgotten.

"It's all right." Nurse Murphy took a cautious step toward him. "Why don't you let Paula bring you on inside so you can go back to bed."

"Paula." The slightest quiver in Dad's voice nearly broke Chase right there on the lawn. "But I…" He shuffled in an unsteady turn, squinted at Mom as though straining to place her, and shook his head again. He brought both hands to his face and rubbed his forehead. "I don't understand."

Close now, Nurse Murphy rested a gentle hand on his arm. "I know, but there's no need to be afraid. We're here to help—"

"No." He jerked away. "I don't need help. I need to go home." Belligerent strides propelled him up the walkway straight for the keys clutched in Mom's hands.

On instinct, Chase reached her first and hedged her behind him, ready to do whatever it took to protect her—even things he'd never in a million years picture himself having to do. "Enough, Pops."

His father stopped a foot away. Though cloaked in shadows, the look on his face still stripped the authority in Chase's voice down to a tremor. Instead of an angry, volatile stranger, a lost and disoriented version of the hero who'd taught Chase how to be strong now slumped in front of him. His vacant stare took Chase in under the porch light until his frustration gradually gave way to broken layers of cognizance. "Chase?"

His whispered name, wrought with the ache of confusion, splintered through Chase's chest. "Yeah, Pops. It's me." He squeezed his dad's shoulder. "You're gonna be all right. I promise we'll work things out." No matter what it took. "Let's get you inside." When he resisted, Chase firmed up his grasp. "I know things feel a little off right now, but I need you to trust me, okay?"

In a strange, reverse parenting role, he extended his father the same assurance he'd lent to Chase enough times to be the bedrock of his identity. Watching a disease draw that assurance from him like a leach draining him of his soul almost crushed the last of Chase's strength.

How could his mind deteriorate so quickly? It didn't make sense, didn't seem fair.

Mom set a hand to his shoulder from behind, somehow knowing.

Chase drew in a breath and steadied the shoulders she counted on. For her, he wouldn't crumble.

Nurse Murphy came alongside them and clasped Dad's hand. He gave her the faintest nod of perception, and Mom and Chase both ushered an exhale of relief as they led him up the porch steps to the house that had been his home for better or worse.

Inside, Mom and Nurse Murphy helped Dad return to bed while Chase waited in the hallway. He backed against the wall and massaged his temples.

Nurse Murphy gave his arm a gentle pat on her way past him. "He's gonna be fine."

Chase nodded. But when Mom came out of the room with eyes wearier than he'd ever seen them, he wasn't so sure.

"Thanks for coming, sugar." She squeezed his hand. "Your daddy's a strong man. We'll get through this. Don't you worry."

But he *was* worried. How couldn't he be after seeing his dad turn into someone else tonight? He straightened off the wall. "I didn't expect the lapse in meds to affect him this fast."

She tucked one side of her pink robe into the other, her gaze bouncing across all angles of the hallway with whatever she wasn't saying.

"Ma."

She huffed. "Oh, all right, but it's nothing to get your knickers worked in a knot over."

Could've fooled him.

"He's been without his prescription for five weeks."

Five weeks?

Mom read the look on his face and raised a hand. "Didn't I just say not to get worked up?"

The woman could truly leave him dumbfounded sometimes. "You've known about this for five weeks, and you just told me today? Why would you keep this from me?"

"You mean, the same way you're keeping it from Quinn?" She arched a knowing brow at him. "Mm-hmm. I know you're trying to shelter her from this, sweetie." She patted his cheek. "You're just like your daddy. Always trying to protect those you love."

"Considering you haven't told Quinn yet either, I guess it runs in the family."

Mom's stern look melted into a half smile. "I reckon you're probably right about that, sugar." She cast a glance to the closed bedroom door, likely picturing the faded reflection of the man she'd married thirty-seven years ago.

The momentary lift in her demeanor faltered under the reality of what faced them. Still staring at the back of the door, she released a long breath. "When the pharmacist told me the new cost, I just stood there speechless like I was half a brick short of a load." She closed her eyes. "Heaven only knows what the poor boy must've thought of me."

"I'm sure he understood."

Mom tsked. "Unlike those insurance folks. Ooh, those scoundrels really burn my biscuits." She balled her fists so tight, the little firecracker in her belly nearly singed the gray roots on top of her head. "Every time I call, they wanna talk me to death in circles. All this corporate policy nonsense. Don't you go peeing down my back and try to tell me it's raining. I ain't a fool." She pulled her robe belt tight and kept on mumbling. "So aggravating, they could make a preacher cuss."

Though the moment might not have called for it, Chase couldn't help chuckling at the little five-foot-two cannon in front of him. Whichever insurance rep took Mom's next call had better have a stress ball nearby.

He laughed again until the sound of Dad saying something in his sleep trailed under the door and filled the hallway with a sense of gravity no amount of humor could lift.

It pressed against his sternum. The questions, the fears. But nothing pierced deeper than the unrelenting voice of inadequacy. Eyes closed, he willed it away. There had to be something he could do, some way to come through for his family.

The softest cry sounded in front of him, and Chase reached for his mom's weathered hand. "Ma?"

The firecracker that had ignited a moment before now smoldered in the ashes of the same helplessness nearly suffocating Chase.

Mom squeezed his hand, a practiced southern smile failing to drive away her tears. "I'm sorry, honey. I didn't want to have to involve you kids in all this. But now..." Her voice cracked, and so did his heart.

He cleared the knot in his throat. "Like I told Dad, we'll work things out."

"What if we can't?"

He'd never seen her unshakable faith waver. Had never once seen her expose the doubts he admired her for not having. Yet as he stood in the hallway, watching that faith seep through a sieve of questions she had every right to voice, all Chase could do was bring her close and hope this would be one time she couldn't sense what little faith he had of his own.

"I'll take care of it." Amid a hundred other uncertainties, not failing Dad was the only thing he was sure of. He rested his chin over her head. "I have some money saved up." Not enough to be a long-term solution, but at least enough to hold them over 'til he found one.

"Honey, no." Mom pushed back from him. "You're already helping us out with the mortgage. We're not draining your savings too. I won't have it, Chase. You need that for your future."

"A future I wouldn't have without sacrifices you and Dad made for *us* growing up." The line of picture frames on the wall mirrored the memories. Head down, he rubbed a callous under his ring finger. Sacrificing to take care of them, providing for his family at any cost—more than just a legacy, Dad's life was a model Chase would spend his life striving to emulate.

"That's what parents do, sugar." Mom tucked herself under his arm again. "When you're a father yourself, you'll understand it's not as much of a sacrifice as you think." She patted his stomach. "Keep your money, sweetheart. We'll find another way."

Not wanting to argue, he kissed the top of her hair, held her tight an extra moment, and led her down the hall to the living room where they found Nurse Murphy still waiting.

She pushed up from the couch. "I'd like to stay the night, if that's okay."

A teary smile answered for Mom before she spoke the words. "Of course you can, sweetie. Let me just fetch you some fresh linens."

Chase stopped Nurse Murphy on her way after Mom. "Does she know?" he whispered. The changes to their insurance didn't just mean losing a nurse. It meant losing a friend they counted on.

Her tired eyes drooped. "Not yet. I've worked it out to stay on 'til the end of the month. After that, I'm not sure what else..."

"It's okay." Chase peered down the hall and lowered his voice. "Don't tell her yet. We'll figure something out." Once again, he offered a smile from his overdrawn assurance. He tipped his chin and slipped outside to the porch to clear his head.

Nothing but the hum of crickets and his heartbeat filled the late hour. He backed against the porch rail to face the sky and let one more breath pass before pulling out his phone and the card Earl had given him. He punched in the numbers and waited.

As expected for this time of night, his voice mail clicked on right away. Chase pushed off the rail and ran a hand over his mouth. "Earl, hey, it's Chase Thompson. Listen, I was mulling over your offer, and..." He peeked behind him to the light in his parents' bedroom turning off. "I think we should talk."

CHAPTER NINE

Delirious

Livy studied her backyard from four different angles, satisfied with her work. Well, minus the filled-in holes she'd tried to blend in with the rest of the yard, but it wasn't like Evelyn would be paying much attention to that part anyway. The patio was the selling point—the circular brick firepit it'd taken her forever to build, the old bistro furniture set she'd gotten secondhand and restored, the artistically placed ferns. Even in daylight, the lantern lights would add the perfect touch.

Ti would be proud. Heck, Livy was glowing herself. Style and design. She'd always enjoyed it. Had always thrived on the artistry of bringing projects to life. With any luck, the little haven she'd created would give Evelyn a taste of what she could do with the vacant corner shop if given the chance.

Wouldn't it?

A zinnia-scented breeze whispered for her to relax. The venue was set. As long as she ensured the coffee was ready to wow her, everything would be fine.

Back in the kitchen, Livy opened a fresh bag of dark roast Arabica coffee beans, poured them into her grinder, and breathed in the perfect choice for today. Bold but with a clean and smooth taste. With a little added magic from the recipes she'd tested out over the years, the first drink she planned to offer Evelyn was sure to impress.

She tapped her nail against the teakettle, uncertainty nagging at her. Maybe she should start with a different drink. Something simple, not too innovative. It was one thing to impress and another to look like she was *trying* to impress.

Her stomach joined the grinder's noisy churning. Ugh. What was she thinking? She'd met a random investor for all of three minutes yesterday, and now she was inviting her over for an impromptu interview?

Sure, getting out of her dead-end rut had never felt more urgent last night, but this was crazy. Even if Evelyn miraculously decided to loan her money for the café, undertaking a start-up business was so unbelievably out of her wheelhouse.

Livy planted her forehead against the cabinet door. How did she get herself into these things?

Like she had to ask. Chase was obviously rubbing off on her—his confidence, persistence. Not to mention his uncanny ability to sweep them up into this whole make-believe romance. No wonder she was a wreck today. A little breath against her hair last night, and she was ready to challenge every top-forty love song with one of their own.

Man, he was better at this pretend dating stuff than she'd counted on.

Clutching the counter, she inhaled the coffee aroma until a measure of sanity finally regained a tiny foothold in her brain. This interview must have her even more worked up than she thought. She was getting delirious. And in obvious need of coffee.

She set her mug beside the press and dug out a spoon from the drawer. Giving a trial cup a go had never been a better idea.

"One meeting. It's no big deal. Stop freaking out." She paused in the middle of the empty kitchen. "And seriously, stop talking to yourself before Evelyn finds out just how mental you are."

A whimper blended into the teakettle's slow whistle. She turned toward two sappy, brown eyes looking up at her.

"Hey, buddy. I almost forgot you were here."

Bandit pushed his snout under her hand in a shameless plea for love.

"You want to be my sidekick for this meeting today, don't you? Uh-huh. Don't act like you don't use that puppy dog charm on everyone you meet. You're as bad as Chase." Livy squatted in front of him and ruffled both ears. "If I end up blowing this whole gig, you'll at least help me recover, right?"

Bandit cocked his head at her as if considering the petition.

Not only was she talking to herself, now she was asking a dog to be her personal therapist. Brilliant. "I can't get much lower, can I?"

He covered his face with his paw and whined some more.

Well, that answered that. Lower it was.

Laughing, Livy pushed off the floor. Coffee was a better therapist anyway.

She added the boiled water and grounds to her French press, grabbed the milk from the fridge, and watched the clock. Four minutes until caffeine therapy.

Her cell vibrated on top of the microwave. She startled away from the counter, thankful she didn't already have a mug in hand, and stared at the group home's office number lighting up the screen. She held the phone between her ear and shoulder while opening the milk carton. "Hey, Jackson. I'm not late this time, I swear. We switched my days, remember?"

"Tell me you've seen Sophie today."

The concern in his voice trembled down Livy's arms. She lowered the milk. "What do you mean, have I seen her? Are you saying she—?"

"Ran away again. Yeah." He expelled a breath away from the phone. "She was here last night for check-in, but when she didn't show up for breakfast this morning... I don't know, Livy. I had this funny feeling in my gut."

Like the one seizing hers right now?

"So, I went to check on her, and sure enough, she was gone. No note. No nothing. She's not answering her phone. None of the other kids say they saw her leave or heard any cars pull up last night."

Livy steadied herself against the counter and scoured the memory of her last conversation with Sophie, searching for a clue of where she might've taken off to.

"I shouldn't have pushed her so hard about the Millers. All I did was drive her away." Another heavy sigh rattled the line. "If something happens to her—"

"Don't even go there, Jackson. It's not your fault." Already in the living room, Livy swiped her keys off the hook beside the door.

Bandit barked from the kitchen doorway and nudged an empty bowl along the floor. She'd been so preoccupied this morning picking up her car and getting things ready for Evelyn, she hadn't even fed the poor guy. She looked from him to the door and almost kept going but stopped with her hand on the knob. She couldn't leave him starving.

"Jackson, hang on a second." She jogged back to the kitchen, grabbed the bag of dog food she'd brought over from Mrs. Finch's house off the floor, and spun around with it.

In a matter of five seconds, all fifty pounds of the food fell through the bottom of the bag and scattered across the linoleum like a bucket of pebbles. Livy just stood there in the middle of it, blinking. She lifted the empty bag and gaped at the sodden paper.

A pained glance slid to the stupid dishwasher and on to a trail of water spreading from underneath the appliance to where she'd kept the dog food last night.

Unbelievable. Un-freaking-believable. She dropped the bag and clenched her keys. She couldn't deal with this right now.

She jutted her phone at Bandit. "Don't you dare eat all of this. You hear me?" Trying not to slip on bits of dog food, she scurried toward the door again. "I mean it, Bandit. Just... just hang tight 'til I can get back."

Please don't let his stomach explode.

She could only handle one crisis at a time.

Livy brought the phone to her ear. "Jackson, listen, don't worry. I think I might know where Sophie is." She just had to make it there before it was too late.

CHAPTER TEN

Time

With ten minutes shaved off a trip that should've taken forty, Livy jerked her Fiat into park and flew into the bus station.

A sea of people flooded the terminal. Livy maneuvered through the crowd, searching the throng of faces. "Sophie?" She had to be here, but each call got lost in the rumble of chatter and engines echoing off the high ceiling—unheard, unacknowledged.

Livy kept pushing until she found a security guard. "Excuse me. Have you seen a young girl? Sixteen, long brown hair. She'd be alone."

"I'm sorry, Miss. Too many people come and go through here to keep up with every patron. Is this a missing person case?"

"I…" She turned in frantic circles, nameless faces whizzing by. "I don't know. I just thought maybe she'd…" Over by the window, the profile of a girl grabbed hold of her. Livy didn't wait, didn't apologize. She tore across the terminal, leaving the guard behind without explanation.

"Sophie?"

A mix of shock and guilt looked up from her seat. "What are you doing here?"

"I could ask you the same thing." Livy knelt to the floor, took Sophie's hands, and finally breathed. "What were you thinking, Soph? You can't keep taking off every time you have a home visit scheduled with the Millers. Especially to go meet a guy who doesn't even care about you."

Hurt and defiance flashed across Sophie's strong-willed eyes. She jolted to her feet, backpack tumbling to the floor. "He does too."

Seeing how much she wanted to believe that broke Livy's heart even more. She hung her head in a quick prayer for the right words before standing. "I'm sorry. I didn't mean it to come out like that, but guys like Luke and their empty promises aren't worth running away for."

"Is that why you ran off to call Jed yesterday?" Sophie's skinny arms crisscrossed over her stomach. "I heard you outside my window."

The terminal closed in on her. "It's not the same thing," she barely got out.

"Whatever. It's your business." Sophie slung her bag over her back. "I just expected you, of all people, not to judge me for mine."

"I'm not." Was she?

"Then cover for me." The overhead speaker announced an incoming bus, and Sophie adjusted her bag strap. "C'mon, Livy. It doesn't matter how many classes the Millers have taken, or how well their home study went. You really think they're gonna be different from any other family I've been placed with? Things are never gonna change for me if I stay." She twisted the pendant she'd told everyone belonged to her mom back and forth. "This is my chance to dream."

A dream Livy couldn't bear to see shatter. Swallowing, she grabbed Sophie's elbow as she turned. "Soph, wait. Look, you're right. I can't promise the Millers will be any different from the rest, but you can't know they won't be either. Not without giving them a chance." She slid her hand to Sophie's fingers and squeezed. "And I get why you want to be with Luke. I do. I just don't want you to be afraid to hope for something more."

The words rebounded to places boarded up behind her rib cage. She blinked, waited. But no matter how many times she told herself they were talking about Sophie, her heart knew better.

The certainty in Sophie's eyes wavered until her cell rang. She lifted the phone to her ear and glanced at the schedule scrolling above the ticket counter. "Hey, Luke. My bus is almost here. I can't wait to—"

He must've cut her off. Probably with some lame excuse of why he wouldn't be there to pick her up. Livy knew the excuses inside and out. Had heard them all. Another pang of self-awareness climbed her neck.

"Understand? Are you kidding me?" The fire igniting Sophie's cheeks could've rocketed her little five-foot-one frame into the stratosphere. "Don't tell me to take it easy. Do you know what I went through to make it to this bus station?" Her gaze brushed Livy on its way back to the floor.

Thick with raw emotion, her raised voice dwindled to a broken whisper. "Yeah. Yeah, I know exactly what I mean to you. Thanks for spelling it out for me." She turned toward the window and stuffed her phone in her pocket. Her shoulders kept moving up and down. And in a terminal that never silenced, the pain in one girl's heart out rang every noise.

Livy gave her a minute before approaching. "Soph—"

"Forget it." She pivoted around, strong arming away tears she didn't want Livy to see. "I don't need an I-told-you-so speech."

"I was going to say, I'm sorry." She dipped her head under Sophie's the way Chase often did to her. "You're worth more than you think. Luke's thick skull doesn't diminish that for a second."

A series of flutters released the stubborn tears hanging on Sophie's lashes. "What if you're wrong?"

The vulnerable ache in the familiar question pulsed in Livy's chest. "I get a lot of things wrong, love. Believe me." She wrapped Sophie in a hug and rested her chin over her head. "But knowing how special you are is most definitely not one of them."

For a long minute, Sophie simply held on. Whether to hide from the embarrassment of trusting Luke, or to wait for Livy's assurance to become her own, she wasn't sure. Either way, Livy was in no rush to let go either.

The overhead speaker blared the arrival of the bus Sophie had been waiting for. Someone bumped into Livy from behind on his way to the platform, and Sophie wiped her nose while backing up. She grabbed her backpack but still didn't meet Livy's eyes.

Understanding, Livy slung an arm across her shoulders. "What do you say we get out of here, huh?" She prodded Sophie to the exit, taking the uncertain nod as her answer.

Her phone buzzed on their way through the door. "Jackson, hey. I found her."

"Thank God. I'm a block from the bus station. Got stuck in traffic. Stay put, and I'll be there to get her in a second." He paused. "Hey, the Millers are calling. Let me take this so I can reschedule Sophie's home visit."

Sophie finally looked up then, and somehow Livy knew. Things would be okay... with time.

Time. A jolt of panic pricked the pit of her stomach. The café. Her meeting with Evelyn. A glance at her phone swept a rush of heat up her body. Twenty minutes to get home? She'd never make it. Stress steamrolled into adrenaline. She couldn't mess this up.

As soon as they got Sophie situated in Jackson's car, Livy took off for her Fiat. The stuffy heat in the car billowed out in waves, dousing her in sweat on its way through all four windows. She looked back and forth from the road to her phone in search of Evelyn's number.

"Hi, you've reached Evelyn Marshall. You know the saying. Time is money. Leave me a message, and I'll make sure you're getting the most out of both."

And here she was wasting the two commodities Evelyn valued most. Fantastic.

"Evelyn, hi, it's Olivia Hensley. I'm so sorry I didn't call sooner, but something came up. An emergency, actually. But I'm on my way home now. If you get there before I do, make yourself at home on the back patio. I'll be there as soon as I can."

A glimpse of the sign for the highway passed overhead. She swerved to catch the exit. "I promise, the coffee will be worth—" Her tires bounced over a bump in the road with such force, her cell slipped from her hands and tumbled onto the passenger side floorboard.

Livy regained control of the wheel and glanced at the unreachable phone. Just stinking perfect.

If that wasn't annoying enough, now her tires felt off. Livy clutched the steering wheel tighter, the uneven oscillation unnerving her. But with a car right on her bumper, all she could do was speed up to merge into the highway traffic.

Please, let me make it home.

She stuck her hand out the window to thank the person letting her in. Something warm and wet flung up from the wheel well and smacked into her fingers. She did a double take at her now-sticky hand. Was that—?

The road dipped, and more of the sludge flew through the window and splattered across her face. Stunned, she didn't let up on the gas, didn't move. She just blinked, frozen.

Until a tiny piece of what looked like roadkill slithered down her cheek and landed on her lap. One look in the mirror broke her paralysis. Downright horrified, she flailed like a madwoman trying to get the ick off her face. Her foot slammed onto the gas pedal. The faster she went, the more gunk streamed off the wheel and flew into her hair.

She screamed. This wasn't happening. She flung the bits of roadkill off her lap like burning ashes and screamed some more. No telling what people in the cars passing her must've thought. She didn't care. She jerked her Fiat to the shoulder, bolted out, and squirmed on the side of the highway like she was auditioning for some kind of bizarre eighties tribal dance competition—complete with head banging moves to shake out her hair.

After scrubbing down her body with sanitizer wipes in every direction possible, she finally stilled long enough to catch her breath. Someone honked on their way by while someone else with their window down let out a low whistle.

She flung up a hand. "Yeah, thanks, buddy," she yelled back. "Free roadkill dances right here." *Prats.*

One more full-body shudder tremored through her in front of her car. She cleaned off her seat with her last wipe and tried not to gag while getting back in it. What a nightmare. Seriously, was she a magnet for disasters today, or what?

She snagged her cell from the floorboard. No missed calls. If luck was done laughing at her, maybe she'd get away with the consolation of Evelyn running late too.

Holding her breath in the stinky car with the windows rolled up was easier than holding on to that farfetched hope. Still, she tried. At least, until she pulled into her driveway. At the curb, an Audi she didn't recognize glowed in the sun like a glaring sign, warning her to abort mission.

But she couldn't. This was too important.

Livy hustled around the back of the house to find Evelyn getting up from one of the bistro chairs. "I'm so sorry I'm late. I had to—"

"Swing by the zoo?"

She followed her gaze to the rat's nest of grimy hair frizzing over her shoulders, and her once off-white shirt now speckled in things she didn't want to think about. Her hair, her outfit, her great first impression—completely ruined.

Okay, technically it was her second impression, but still. This meeting was supposed to showcase her as a professional. Someone qualified and worthy of entrusting an investment to. Not a carcass-smelling basket case.

"Um, I can explain. It's actually a funny story." She forced a laugh. "But do you mind if we go inside first? It'll take me a few minutes to clean up." Or maybe a few decades. "And then I'll make you some of that coffee I promised."

More patient than she deserved, Evelyn nodded and motioned for her to lead the way.

Livy directed her up the back steps. "I volunteer at a group home for kids between foster homes. One of the girls ran away this morning, and I—"

A single step inside jerked her to a stop. Blood drained from her face. Her living room, finally straightened up enough to pass off being somewhat organized, now looked like the aftermath of a detonated bomb—a furry, mischievous bomb that just happened to be sitting in the middle of pillow stuffing left from what he'd torn apart while she was gone.

"Bandit!"

Evelyn slipped around her, and it took everything in Livy not to catapult the woman out of the house in a worthless attempt to salvage any remaining dignity. Instead, she stood there with her limbs like wet noodles and mumbled, "I'm dog sitting."

"I see that."

Bandit slunk over to Evelyn as if looking for protection from Livy's impending wrath.

"Well, aren't you just a little booger." Evelyn rubbed his head, entranced by his adorably guilty puppy eyes. "You're lucky this isn't my house. Yes, you are," she cooed.

At least she was a dog person. One point in Livy's favor. Maybe.

Still shell-shocked, she somehow convinced her legs to head to the kitchen, where yet again, they stopped short. She'd been in such a hurry to leave, she'd left the milk out on the counter and the coffee over-brewing in the press. The giant, murky puddle accumulating in front of the dishwasher topped it off. Between the spilled dog food and some coffee grounds Bandit must've knocked into the water, the puddle looked like the Wicked Witch of the West had melted right there on her kitchen floor. Oh, what she'd do for a pair of ruby slippers right then.

The whole fiasco-of-a-day finally took its toll. She broke. She couldn't help it. Delirious and uncontrollable laughter spilled from her lungs.

Evelyn rounded the doorway. "Are you all right?"

"The Wicked Witch," she managed to get out between airy laughs.

"Uh-huh. Listen, I have another appointment, and you clearly have some things on your plate right now, so why don't I show myself to the door."

"No." Livy grabbed her arm and let go a second later. Totally inappropriate. Along with everything else she was doing. She collected herself. "I'm sorry. It wasn't supposed to be like this. I had everything planned, and then the entire day just sort of went off the rails."

She warned Bandit this would happen. And here she was, a walking premonition.

"Life has a way of doing that." Evelyn unfolded her sunglasses. "It's what business owners have to learn to roll with— the unexpected, the endless fires to put out. Carrying on business as usual with no one the wiser is the real trick of the trade."

A talent Livy obviously didn't have.

The lines around Evelyn's eyes softened. "Listen, Livy, I stand by what I said earlier. You have potential, no question. But starting a business will take every ounce of focus and energy you have."

She slid her sunglasses onto her head and drew her keys from her purse. "Volunteering at a group home, taking in friends' dogs—they're things that keep your life full. Nothing wrong with that." She raised a shoulder. "But if you're serious about getting a loan to open a café, you need to think about what you'll have to give up to make that happen."

Leaving the open-ended statement for Livy to mull over, Evelyn jutted her head toward the door. "I should go." She lowered her glasses, glossed lips tipping. "And you, hun, should definitely take a shower."

Or twenty.

At the entryway, Livy offered her a final look of apology for what had turned into an utter debacle and opened the door right as someone on the other side lifted his knuckles to knock.

Livy gaped through the screen, shock climbing back up her body.

"Jed?"

CHAPTER ELEVEN

Complicated

Jed picked up a tattered throw pillow from the middle of Livy's living room floor. "Wow, you really did have quite the day, didn't you?"

Livy pushed her grubby hair off her forehead, relieved Evelyn was gone at least. "And that was only half of it." She hadn't relayed the entire sequence of events, but she'd shared enough to give him the gist. Or at least to explain why she looked like something out of *Pet Cemetery*. She flung her fingers away from her hair and shuddered all over again.

Either Jed had sinus issues, or he really liked her after all, because he leaned close enough for his aftershave to make her heady. "Then I guess it's a good thing I came when I did."

At the exact moment she wanted to dive bomb into a hole in the ground? Of all days...

"I'm a mess."

"Messy isn't always a bad thing." His flirty tone backed her against the wall. Leaning even closer, he flexed a palm beside her, and she darted her gaze away from his like an awkward preteen on her first date.

Bandit peeked his head out from behind the couch, scrunched his eyebrows at her, and buried his snout under his paw.

Lovely. Even the dog was embarrassed for her.

"Um, speaking of messes, I should probably clean up the one Bandit made in the living room."

Jed slid a glance behind him and back. "I'll take care of it while you take a shower."

"You?"

He cocked a brow. "Is that so surprising?"

"Yes. No. I mean… kind of?" She lifted a shoulder. "It's just that you're, you know…" A guy who probably had maids to clean for him.

Eyes on hers, Jed grazed the side of his finger along her cheekbone. "My hands are good for more than just playing the guitar."

Too bad her lungs weren't good for anything besides preventing oxygen from reaching her brain. Otherwise, she might've been able to hide the I'm-about-to-faint expression from her face.

A nervous laugh flitted out on its own. "You're cute. I mean, *he's* cute. The dog. The dog's cute." She cringed. What was this? A children's book reading?

Another forced laugh escaped her tense diaphragm. "Cute but a handful of trouble. Obviously." She pointed to the disaster left in her living room. But when she looked back, Jed's eyes hadn't left hers.

"Trouble isn't always bad either." His breath tingled her neck with insinuation.

That was one way to stop her blabbering.

Reminders of being this close to Chase last night shadowed the flutters in her stomach now, but these were different. Hauntingly familiar.

She faced the ceiling, panic setting in. Instead of white paint, tarnished memories from London projected in front of her like a broken slideshow. She needed to move, needed to run.

"Shower," she blurted out. "I could really use that shower right about now. You?"

The corner of Jed's mouth slanted to the left, and Livy almost slunk behind the couch with Bandit.

Hardly ten minutes with the guy, and she'd managed to ask him to take a shower with her like she was casually offering him some coffee. Brilliant.

He pressed his other hand to the wall, boxing her in. "You read my mind."

Good thing he couldn't read hers.

"Sorry. I didn't mean it to come out like that." Or at all. "I actually have a shower-alone policy." She lifted a hand to her neck. "Hygiene... and all that."

"Hygiene."

From behind the couch, Bandit whined for someone to put her out of her misery.

"Yeah, I... should..." Livy motioned to the bathroom. She turned, banged her leg into the end table, and batted a picture frame in the air like a *Cirque du Soleil* artist. She squeezed her eyes shut before peeking behind her on the off-chance Jed missed that.

Right.

"I'll be back in a few minutes." Just as soon as she figured out how to come back to life after dying from humiliation.

Massaging her temples, Livy kicked herself all the way to the bathroom. Why didn't days come with a reset button?

Then again, if Chase was right about finding someone she could be herself with, Jed was certainly getting the full picture. At least he hadn't run away in horror yet.

A scrub at a time, her tension gradually waned with the water circling the shower drain. Yet despite lathering her hair four times, she couldn't fully wash away the unease still nagging at her. She'd been waiting for weeks for Jed to visit, and now he was here—to see her. This was what she wanted. So why was she clamming up?

In front of the mirror, Livy gripped the sides of the sink and faced her blurry reflection. *Deep breath, Liv.* Whatever confidence looked like, it definitely didn't include hiding out in the bathroom. She threw a robe on, twisted her wet hair into a towel, and began her makeup routine.

A knock at the front door tunneled down the hallway. She poked her head out. "Can you get that?"

Instead of a reply, another knock echoed back to her.

"Jed?"

Still nothing. Tightening her robe belt, Livy hightailed it to the door.

Of all people, Wesley stood on the porch with eyes as wide as a kid who'd just scored his first trophy. He lifted the bill of his red hat to take in the full scope of Livy's bathroom getup. "Wow, my timing's sweeter than I thought."

Livy bunched the top of her robe together at her neck. "Is there something you need, Wes?"

"A date with the prettiest girl on the block." He bobbed his bushy brows.

And once again, that darn reset button was looking more and more appealing.

She grabbed the edge of the door. "Now's really not the best time to—"

"Who's that?" He bent his Converse sneakers, standing on his toes to peer around her.

Livy looked over her shoulder at Jed coming in through the back door. "That's, um..."

"More competition." Wesley tugged his hat down in the front and back. "I see what's going on here. You need me to prove my manhood to win you over."

"Yeah, no, that's definitely not what's—"

"I'm catching your vibe, Livy." He winked. "And don't worry. I'm up for the challenge." Rolling his bony shoulders back, he rotated his neck from side to side and stretched his laced fingers out. "Nothing me and a little friendly algorithm can't handle."

"Algor...?" She lifted a hand. "Never mind."

"Livy?" Jed called as Bandit barreled into her legs from behind.

She held the dog down while he licked her hands like they still had animal smell on them. Ugh. They didn't, did they? She nonchalantly lifted them to her nose and then skimmed them to her neck when Jed tossed an arm around her shoulders.

A solid once-over traveled from the lightning bolt on Wesley's hat to his worn *The Flash* T-shirt and down to the rolled-up comic book in his hand. Jed rubbed his jaw. "I think you might've missed your exit for the Comic-con, kid."

Oh, boy.

Wesley flapped open his button-down as if exposing the emblem on his T-shirt would give him the same superhero powers. "And you obviously missed the you-better-step-off-my-girl-before-I-have-to-make-you exit."

"Your girl?" Jed sized him up again before leaning back from Livy like she was a cradle robber or something.

Seriously? She swatted him in the chest like she always did with Chase. But instead of Chase's playful tug back, Jed stared at her like *she* was the one who should've been booking a ticket to the next Comic-con.

Wesley stepped up. "Look at her like that again, punk, and we'll see whose girl she really is."

"Okay," Livy jumped in. "This conversation so isn't happening right now." Or ever. "Wes, you should really get going."

Seemingly satisfied with his chivalry, Wesley bowed and fanned his comic book out. "As you wish."

Livy squelched the urge to laugh at the *Princess Bride* reference.

Once Wesley started his trek to his house next door, Jed flashed Livy a look caught between annoyance and relief. "Was that kid for real?"

If he only knew. Livy smiled to herself. In all honesty, Wes was a sweet kid. Quirky as all get out, and definitely over the top sometimes, but harmless. His little teen crush was even kind of cute when he wasn't driving her mad.

"Don't ask." She headed back inside and scoped out the straightened-up living room.

Jed's cell phone vibrated on the end table. Livy passed by, pretending not to notice the name *Ginger* lighting up the screen. "So, what were you doing out back?"

"Letting the dog out." He wiped dirty paw prints off his jeans. "You don't believe in leashes?" Though playful, the words held the slightest note of judgment.

"Mrs. Finch pretty much lets him roam wherever."

"Doesn't mean *you* have to."

"Well, he's not my dog, so..." Why was she getting defensive?

Jed adjusted his oversized watch. "I'm just saying—"

Another knock at the door bounded into the room. Livy craned her neck back. That boy seriously never knew when to quit.

She flung the door open. "Wes, I thought I told you..."

Not Wesley. "Chase? What are you doing here?"

His warm smile streamed over her with the late afternoon sun. "Bad time?"

"No, it's, um..." She ran her terry cloth belt through her fingers in search of a plausible response.

"Oh." If his expression meant anything, he must've taken one look from Jed to her robe and drawn his own conclusion. Chase backed away from the door. "Sorry. I'll just... come by later."

She gestured for Jed to give her a minute, closed the door, and jogged after him. "Chase, hang on. It's not what you think."

He stopped in the middle of the walkway, his face devoid of readable emotions.

Shifting, Livy pulled the towel free from her hair. "I know that's the lamest line in the book, but it's true. Jed just got here a little while ago. I wouldn't have showered except, oh my word, you should've seen me."

She twisted the towel in a spiral against her stomach while pacing back and forth. "First, I got a call about..." She froze. *Shoot.* "A friend."

A tendon on his neck pulsed in and out. "A friend, who?" He tilted his head, waiting for her to expound, but she couldn't. Not about that part of her life.

"No one you know," she rambled off. "She had an issue. An emergency, really. And I had to drop everything here to take care of it. Then a stupid dead racoon or possum or heaven-only-knows-what got caught in my wheel well and flung into the car every time the bloody tires turned. It was in my hair, on my face, my shirt. It was horrifying, Chase. Horr-i-fying."

The towel whipped in the air as she wheeled around. "Then Evelyn was here, irritated I was late. And really, who could blame her?" She waved a finger at the house. "And to top it off, Bandit tore the place apart, the milk soured, and I acted like an asylum escapee, going off about the Wicked Witch of the West. I ruined everything, and now that stupid pizza chain is gonna replace Mrs. Finch's café and—"

"Whoa." Chase cupped her shoulders to calm her. "Are you sure you're all right after all that?"

"Yeah." Her chest slumped. "Maybe." But if he kept looking at her with that heartfelt concern, she'd be far from fine. She'd crumble into his arms and cling to the only place where that reset button felt within reach.

She clutched the towel instead. "A shower helped a little." Raising a shoulder, she pulled her lips to the side. "With the smell, anyway."

He leaned in, sniffed, and scrunched his nose. "You sure?"

She elbowed him, relishing their banter until the skin wrinkling between Chase's brows slowly drove his laughter away. Chin down, he rubbed at one of the stubborn callouses on his hands.

He didn't still think she showered with Jed, did he?

A wave of awkwardness rushed in on the breeze.

Livy tightened her robe. "Jed showed up by surprise."

"Liv." As usual, Chase seemed to read between the lines. "You don't owe me an explanation. This is why we're doing practice dates, remember?" His eyes offered a heartbreaking smile when he lifted her chin. "So you can be with the guy you choose."

Why was that starting to feel more complicated than it should?

The longer he held her gaze, the faster her pulse picked up. He leaned in, and her body tensed again until the tenderness of his kiss to her cheek eased her muscles, and everything felt... safe.

"I want you to be happy. You know that." His freckles resumed their usual charm as he leaned back. "Just stay clear of any oyster dinners 'til we cover that practice date."

Shaking her head, Livy gave him a shove, and he kept her hand on his chest as always.

Another breeze whirled past them. And another. His focus roamed from her hand to the house behind her and settled on the ground again. "I should go. I'll come by to fix your dishwasher another time." He let go, tipped his hat, and turned to leave.

He'd reached his Silverado before Livy finally freed her bare feet from the pavement. "Wait." She jogged to the curb. "Is that the only reason you came? To fix the dishwasher?"

Because if it wasn't... what? She'd go run off with her best friend to play more make-believe? She wasn't the seventeen-year-old hopeless romantic she was when they first met. And this was Chase she was talking about here—*her* Chase. Practically a second brother.

She straightened, positive some kind of toxin in that roadkill had soaked into her brain. Still, his pause made her heart race against all logic.

Looking toward the sky, Chase scratched his scruffy cheek. "I was going to ask you about our next practice date, but..." He opened his truck door. "Looks like you don't need it." He climbed into the driver's seat. "And hey, don't worry about the pizza shop. There's always a loophole. Just remember to step up that confidence we talked about."

When she didn't respond, he closed the door, and she simply stood there.

Confidence. Sure. She'd get right on that—as soon as she detangled the confusing knot of emotions growing thicker inside her by the day.

What was going on with her lately?

She looked from Chase's tailgate pulling away to her house where Jed was waiting. "You sure messy isn't a bad thing?"

A robin in the yard arched his head at her like it wondered who in the world she was talking to.

"I'm just talking to myself, little guy." She looked around. "And now to a bird. While standing outside in my bathrobe."

More caffeine was obviously in order.

She balled the towel in her arms as casually as she could and speed-walked back up to the porch before her neighbors saw her.

Inside, Jed sat on the couch, busy on his phone. If she could ignore the flirty grin on his face, she might've been able to ignore the nagging question of who he was texting.

The floor creaked under her feet, and he looked up from his cell. "Everything good?"

"Yep." She pointed to the phone. "You?"

Not so much as a blush. Only a shrug as he tucked his cell into his pocket and rose. "Business stuff."

Bandit's nails clacked against the floor as he stuck his head out from his hideout behind the couch. Guilty eyes pouted at her, and she couldn't decide which he regretted more: tearing apart the living room or taking on the job as her personal therapist.

Clearly, he failed at the latter.

Chuckling on the inside, Livy headed toward the one thing that never disappointed. "You want some coffee?"

"Later." Jed intercepted her and spun her toward him, his hands circling her waist. "The place is clean." He brushed one side of her wet hair over her shoulder. "You're clean." He swept the other side off and left his hand on her neck. "Why don't we relax, unwind?"

Did he think this was helping?

Standing vulnerably in only her robe, she managed a dry swallow and eked out, "We should talk." She slipped under his arm. "Definitely talk." *After* she got dressed.

His face crinkled, but she didn't wait for a reply. She fled to her bedroom to change, shuffled back before he got a word in, and plopped onto the floor in front of the couch.

"Uh, what are you doing?"

Livy looked around. "Sitting." Did it look like she was doing something else?

"You're on the floor... where the dog lays."

"Yeah, I've sort of always sat on the floor. When I was a teen, I had—"

"Forget the floor. You said on the phone you wanted us to hook up, right?" Reclined on the couch, he pulled her up by the hand. "I'm here now." He moved in. "You're here." He gripped the top of the couch above her. "We should make the most of the day."

The feel of his lips grazing her ear ushered an echo of unease through her again. She inched across the cushion. "I thought we were going to talk."

"We are talking," he hummed between kisses along her neckline.

The more unwanted memories from London resurfaced, the farther she scooted away. "Talking's good," she managed. "So, what do you like to do for fun?"

With his hands around either side of her on the couch, he stalled as if wondering whether she was serious.

"You mentioned camping." She channeled her nervous chattering to her hands and fiddled with the hem of her V-neck T-shirt. "Is that what you do to unwind?"

"The guys and I go when we can." He sat back and raked a hand through the top of his hair. "Actually..." He looked at her, and the mild look of frustration passing his face transitioning into a slow smile. "You should come with us next time. I think you'd have a good time."

An involuntary shudder slinked up her spine at the mere thought of sleeping in the woods. She could hear Chase's jokes now. "Yeah, definitely. I'm all about some... outdoorsy... stuff." Which evidently included sounding like a clueless moron.

"Perfect." He edged her into the corner of the couch. "'Cause the nights can get pretty chilly alone."

Still squirming, Livy braced a palm against the couch arm. "I can imagine. Aloneness stinks." *Aloneness?* She almost risked removing the hand barring Jed a safe distance away just so she could smack some sense into her head.

Luckily, she didn't have to.

With perfect timing, Bandit skittered out of his den of shame, hopped onto the couch, and wedged himself between them with big, expectant eyes.

Livy scratched both sides of his neck, ready to reinstate his therapist mantle. "Hey, buddy. You want to thank Jed for cleaning up your mess for you?"

When Bandit whipped his head toward Jed, a giant glob of slobber landed smack on the seat of his pants. A good thirty seconds of blank staring passed before Jed's obvious dislike of dogs sent him jumping up like she'd just spilled hot coffee on him.

Livy would've sworn Bandit smiled, and she had to pinch her lips together to keep from laughing. "Sorry about that." She reached behind her for a tissue. "Here, let me—"

"I got it." His cell buzzed. This time, she only caught half the name on the screen but enough to wonder if his entire contact list consisted of nothing but girls named after spices.

Jed yanked a tissue from the box and aimed his phone at the back door. "I need to take this."

"Yeah, of course. Go ahead."

Once he slipped out back, Livy leveled her gaze with Bandit's. "You're in big trouble, mister." His slobbery tongue lolled out from another smile, her laugh following. She ruffled his ears. "We're quite the pair, aren't we, buddy?" A *disastrous* pair. After as long as she'd been waiting for a day with Jed, she should've been ready for this. Not mucking up the whole thing.

Before another thought passed, Livy grabbed her own phone and scrolled to Chase's number.

"Hey." He answered on the first ring. "You all right?"

"Only if a walking train wreck counts as all right."

His soft laugh seeped through the line and blanketed around her. "I'm sure it's not that bad."

"You do know me, right? It's bad." She crossed the room and tried to peek through the blinds without looking like a stalker. "That coaching session you were talking about? I still need it. Trust me." Livy slipped back to the couch when Jed turned around. "You said you've already planned our first practice date, right? Can we do it next weekend?"

He hesitated.

"Seriously, Chase. I'm dying here. Dy-ing. I don't know what's wrong with me."

His pause stretched into an exhale. "There's nothing wrong with you, Liv."

"You're not here. Believe me. Even Bandit's amused."

At the mention of his name, the dog climbed up her legs and weaseled his snout past her hand to lick her face.

At least one of them knew how to give kisses without in-hibitions.

She pushed him down. "Chase? You still there?"

"Yeah," he said after a moment. "I'm here."

"So, that date you mentioned. Are we still on?"

"If it's what you think you want," he said slowly.

"It is." She sighed with relief, wishing they were already on it. "So, where are we going?"

Another pause stretched—this one holding audible amusement. "Camping."

CHAPTER TWELVE

Undone

Chase finished pitching their tent, pushed off the dirt to stand, and admired the oaks and cypress trees enclosing their camping spot for the night.

Livy swatted a mosquito away. "I still can't believe you got me out here."

That made two of them. He tried not to laugh at the way she whipped around every time she heard a noise in the woods. She fiddled with the hair tie around her braid, completely unaware of how attractive her little quirks made her.

Chase tossed his hat by the unlit fire pit. After scheduling a visit to Chicago to check out Earl's shop, he had all but talked himself out of following through with this date coaching thing. And when he saw Jed at her place last weekend, the fight between holding on and letting go had just about crippled him. Then again, something about Livy always found a way of crippling him. Hence, the reason they were here. He'd caved. Again.

A flicker of the sunset streamed over her. She looked up, a coy smile meeting his gaze. One day, he'd admit there was no option but to cave for good.

Chase sorted through his camping gear for his hatchet. "You're the one who said this was what you wanted."

"Yeah, *before* I knew you were dragging me off to the mountains."

Something scurried a few trees behind her, and she practically climbed into Bandit's lap instead of the other way around. With a noisy yawn, the dog pawed her away.

Livy rubbed his ears anyway and muttered, "Some rescue dog you are."

Proving her point, Bandit rolled onto his back and let out his notorious snore.

Flinching out of nowhere again, Livy flicked away whatever she thought was crawling on her. She glared from the can of bug spray in her hand to Chase. "Why am I starting to feel like the almost-stepmom in *The Parent Trap?*"

"Hey, don't look at me. That spray's the real deal." He wasn't trying to sabotage her camping experience. Not entirely anyway.

"Yeah, well, they must just like meeee..." A squeal launched her off the ground and into a flailing frenzy. "Get it off. Get it off." She finally stopped her river dance long enough to wave at the back of her neck. "Chase!" she squealed again when he evidently didn't move fast enough.

He reached for her shoulders before she squirmed a hole in the ground. "Relax."

That pause couldn't be good.

"Did you really just tell me to relax?"

"Would it save me if I said no?"

She swung her head around. "Get this spider off my neck, and you might live."

"Yes, ma'am." He didn't bother leveling his grin. But when his thumb grazed her neck while brushing her braid to the side, he half wished someone would level him to the ground with one of those logs. A night under the stars with the girl he had to pretend he wasn't in love with. Real smart plan.

"Do you see it?"

If he could see anything past how good the base of her shoulders felt in his hands, he might've been able to answer.

"Chase!"

"Yeah, sorry." He scrubbed a hand down his whiskers. "No spiders. You're in the clear."

"I swear something was on me." One final shiver turned her around, and his earlier amusement crept back up his face. She scrunched her eyes at him. "Glad I can be your entertainment for the evening."

"Don't worry." He grabbed the piece of firewood he'd started stripping earlier. "I'm sure when you go camping with Jed, he'll find your Mexican jumping bean dance just as..." He winked. "*Endearing.*"

"You know I officially hate that word now, don't you?"

"Yep." Enjoying it all the more, he swung his hatchet into the corner of the wood and splintered off a long strip. He had high hopes for tonight—getting her to picture what a relationship with Pretty Boy would truly look like being top of the list.

She wiped some dirt off her hands. "I might hate you too."

Chase slid a glance her way. "Then why are you smiling right now?"

"I'm not." Fighting it lasted all of five seconds. She flicked a twig at him. "You know, I'm a little disappointed in your camping prowess. I would've pegged you for being a boy scout growing up."

"What makes you think I wasn't?"

"Oh, I don't know." She strolled over and leaned above the pile of wood shavings he'd accumulated so far. "Something about this hamster bed you're making."

He rose and straightened—all but his grin. "Every fire needs a little kindling to get it started."

Livy zeroed in on the quirky look he couldn't shake. She didn't know his end goal for this dating game. If he was smart, he'd keep it that way until the right moment. But sometimes, he couldn't control the reactions she stirred.

Still dissecting his expression, Livy held out a hand. "Okay, Captain Subtle. I'll bite."

He scratched his jaw. "Um..."

"You want me to go all in with this whole camping scene since it's what Jed likes. Kindling. I get it." She motioned for his hatchet, and he handed it over without a response.

Definitely not what he'd meant, but that scrunched look of concentration on her face as she lined herself up in front of the log like a golfer was too cute to mind.

"I'm sure he won't expect you to split wood."

Livy shushed him with a wave of her hand. After another calculated positioning of her feet, she swung the hatchet dead into the center of the wood. She stared at it for a minute before aiming a finger at him. "Don't say it."

"Say what?" He squelched a laugh. Pointless. As soon as she turned and fought one, too, his tumbled out anyway.

She braced a hiking boot against the top of the log, gripped the hatchet handle with both hands, and pulled with all her might. "Just needs a little kindling," she mocked.

Even more amused, Chase came up behind her and slipped his arms down hers. "You're gonna have to give it some torque if you ever plan to get it out of there."

"A little torque?" She slanted a teasing glare over her shoulder, his face just beside hers. Her eyes seemed to appraise him and then smile. "You're a smooth one, Chase Thompson, wanting me to get this thing stuck so you could come to my rescue."

This close to her, the scent of cotton wrapped around the hints of pine stirring up in the wind. "I..."

"Hey, I can be a good pupil when I need to be." She nestled her back into his chest, her soft hair feathering against his cheek. "When I'm on the camping date, you want me to pretend I don't know when Jed's making a move, right? Just lean back and let him lead. Maybe even turn my head like this and—"

Completely tense, Chase yanked so hard, the hatchet broke free and flew out of their hands. He swung around in time to see it land in an oak tree on the opposite side of their camp site. Smooth.

If there were ever a time for proverbial crickets, it was then.

He turned slowly, knowing darn well what would be waiting for him.

A smile. A crazy sexy, impish smile. Livy tucked her hands in her jean shorts' back pockets and raised both shoulders. "Does that mean I passed that test?"

Finally regaining his composure, Chase ran his knuckle over the corner of his mouth. "That depends," he ribbed back.

"On?"

"On whether you can get that thing down now."

Livy tapped her arm, countering his confidence. "Challenge accepted." She marched right over to the tree and studied the tall oak like she was mapping out a rock-climbing venture. "Piece of cake."

Chase eyed her recently-polished nails. "Uh-huh."

She coiled her braid into a bun and palmed her cell phone against his chest. "Watch and learn, coach."

Admittedly more skilled than he thought, Livy scaled the limbs and freed the hatchet with little to no effort. It dropped to the ground beside Chase's feet, burying his pride.

He peered up to a gloating fest showering over him. Laughing, he ran a hand down the back of his hair. "It wasn't wedged in that branch as deeply as it was in the log."

"Uh-huh," she mimicked with satisfaction. She maneuvered to the bottom branch, gained a solid grip, and swung her body down.

Chase reached for her underarms to help her the rest of the way. Suspended in the air for a moment, she held his gaze before letting go of the branch. He lowered her to the ground.

And when her arms slowly came around his neck, even the night's shadows couldn't diminish her blush.

His hands slid to her waist, his breath not catching up. It was one thing to have her cheek nearly pressed to his from the side. But to have her lips right below his—to be this close, this intimate—he'd need more than an acrobatic hatchet to save him.

Her bun unfurled, his heart following.

"You're better at this than you think."

The softest smile swept her lashes toward the ground. "At tree climbing?"

"At making it impossible for your date not to fall for you."

She looked up, searched his eyes. One breath passed between them. Another. Without looking away, Livy tightened her fingers around his shirt as though afraid of losing herself if she let go. "I'm sure it's not that easy."

Chase pulled a broken leaf from her hair. "Maybe it should be." Couldn't she see that? This—them together, right here, now—was the way a relationship should be.

A well of emotions brimmed as she stood in his arms and in a choice that could be so easy if she'd let it be.

He looked down. "Liv..."

Winning the World's Worst Timing award, Bandit needled his way in between them, flaunted clueless brown eyes from one to the other, and whined to be petted. Apparently, even a dead sleep couldn't stand as a buffer against his keen sense of missing out on affection.

Chase craned his neck back and almost laughed. 2-0, Team Bandit. Chase should've been grateful for the dog's track record at running interference, but he couldn't help wishing he didn't need him to. How much longer could he do this? Torn, he looked at Livy, wanting her to know. To understand.

She caught his appraisal and dropped to her knees faster than the last glimpse of the red sun sinking behind the treetops. "Did I tell you this little stinker came to my rescue last week?" The ache in her voice wore through the playfulness trying to mask it. Talking baby talk, she ruffled Bandit's ears. "You weaseled your way right in between Jed and me on the couch, didn't you? Yes, you did."

Was that what she felt now? Relief for Bandit rescuing her?

His jaw ticked in and out. Picturing her and Jed on the couch hurt almost as much as watching her cling to Bandit for deflection from him too.

He tugged the hatchet out of the ground, his heart lodged between hope and disappointment. "I thought you wanted Jed there."

"I did, but ugh. You should've seen me. A total mess."

The leaves behind their tent rustled. Bandit whipped his head toward the sound, sniffed the air, and took off.

Livy caught her balance and rose to her feet. "I don't know what's wrong with me. He freed up a night just to come see me—was even sweet enough to clean up after Bandit—and I couldn't even handle getting close enough to him to thank him."

Thank him? The hatchet handle's grooves pressed into his fingers. "If he tried to make you feel like you owed him something…" So help him.

"You didn't hear me on the phone the other day. I'm the one who practically begged him to come like a desperate groupie." Head lowered, she twisted her bracelet. "I can't blame him for expecting more than a timid girl who clams up at the slightest touch."

Chase could blame him. For a lot of things. He turned to the woods and dragged a hand down his chin to keep from saying something he'd regret.

"I thought I'd moved past this."

The pang in her voice drew him around. "Past what?"

"Nothing." She severed eye contact. "Forget it."

A heavy exhale lowered his defensive shoulders. As much as he wanted to deck Jed square in the jaw, the ache of seeing Livy believe things she shouldn't ran deeper. "Liv, listen…"

"You don't need to say it. It doesn't matter anyway, because he didn't stay." She rolled her hiking boot over a rock and shrugged. "Business stuff."

Business stuff. Sure.

With her elbows clasped across her chest, she stared past the tree line, lost in the things he'd watched her tell herself again and again to keep from falling apart.

"But hey." A rehearsed smile tucked all traces of hurt behind it. "Leaving before dinner meant no oyster-eating fiascos, so don't worry. Whatever crazy coaching session you have planned is still on." Her broken laugh drifted into the quiet of the mountainside, and Chase had to grind his sneakers in the earth to keep from running after every fractured piece.

"*All* the sessions are. Which is why we're here, right?" She backed up, arms splayed. "Ready to start coaching, Prince Charming, or what?"

Not as ready as he was to tell her why he really brought her out here.

Bandit trotted around the corner of the tent with a stick in his mouth and an oblivious look in his eyes. He flopped beside the unlit firepit, kept one end of the stick under his paw, and chomped away on the other.

Even oblivious, the dog certainly played his part well. It was time Chase did the same, or that stack of wood he'd chopped earlier wasn't the only thing about to go up in smoke.

CHAPTER THIRTEEN

Promise

Chase eyed his pile of kindling. Patience and persistence. They just might be the death of him. Reaching for the hatchet, he glanced at the darkening sky. "We better get a fire going before we do anything else."

The goose bumps on Livy's arms agreed.

While she sat against a giant log he'd rolled up to the pit, Chase built the fire. "So." He dusted off his hands. "If I'm gonna be an effective coach, I probably need to know where you see things going with Jed." He reclined beside her. "Are we talking marriage eventually?"

Bandit yelped, and a nearly-choking Livy let go of his ear. She flashed the dog an apologetic look, tapped a fist to her chest, and coughed. "Sorry. I think I swallowed a flake of ash or something." She drew Bandit back to her side, still not answering the question.

"Should I take that as a no?"

A blank stare slanted his way. "Oh, I'm sorry. You were serious?"

He laughed. "Why not? Marriage is a natural progression in a serious relationship."

She blinked at him. "Okay, first, Jed and I aren't in a serious relationship. And second…" Her voice dwindled, stoking Chase's curiosity.

"And second, what?"

Livy drew her knees up, gave a little shrug, and mumbled, "Marriage isn't for me."

She might as well have chucked the hatchet into his chest.

"Never?" The single word came out quieter than he'd intended.

She gave another uncomfortable shrug. "Guess it's just not something I ever really saw for myself."

A piece of firewood popped right along with that lie. He exhaled with relief. "Yeah, sorry, not buying it."

"Excuse me?"

"C'mon, Liv. Don't try to tell me those *husband* pillows haven't soaked up hundreds of dreams of your wedding day."

"Maybe one or two," her tight lips eked out as if torn between loving and hating that he knew her so well.

"Uh-huh." Chase nudged his hat up. "You had the whole thing designed and everything, didn't you?"

Her toes tapped in the air like she wished they could wave off this entire conversation.

"If you want to have a successful date, you have to be willing to open up, get personal." He stretched back against the log and laced his fingers behind his head. "Just sayin'."

Her eyes constricted at him but then circled to the deep-indigo sky. "Fine. It was going to be in a barn. Happy now?"

"A barn. You?"

"I might've gone through a little country phase for a while, so a barn seemed... fitting. Wild flowers, twinkle lights in the rafters, old rustic benches. I even pictured having lilies for my bouquet, 'cause... you know, lily kind of sounds like Livy." Laughing, she covered her face. "I was such a geek as a kid."

Chase peeled her hands back and kept one in his. "It sounds kind of perfect to me."

Though she didn't look away, the hope in her eyes did. "It was just a silly dream."

"We dream for a reason." He had to believe that.

Livy must've noticed him appreciating the way her shoulder brushed up against his, because she leaned toward the fire instead.

It crackled, sending ashes of forgotten dreams into the sky and soft waves of light over her pensive smile. He took her in, this woman who had more reason to dream than most. If he accomplished nothing but helping her see that, it would all be worth it.

Chase leaned both forearms back against the log. "So, a wedding in a barn."

"I knew I shouldn't have told you."

"What? I'm just saying, it sounds like a good venue for marrying a cowboy. That's all." He tipped his hat at her to prove his point.

She flicked the front of it. "A *real* cowboy, actually."

"Ouch." He scrambled up, her words registering. "Wait. Are you saying you...?"

"Fell for a cowboy? Yeah." Laughing, Livy looped a pine needle above the silver ring on her pointer finger. "Hey, I was a fourteen-year-old girl living down the street from a ranch, and Jimmy Sterling might've been a little crush-worthy."

"Jimmy Sterling?" Seriously?

She arched a sassy brow. "Your cowboy boots got nothing on a seventeen-year-old ranch hand in all his summer-tan-skinned glory. Sorry." Another laugh carried her gaze across the fire and into memories he'd sell his boots to be a part of. "There might've been a few daydreams about dancing with him in his barn loft too." She popped Chase in the arm. "Now *that* would be a great idea for a date." Her blue eyes beamed at him. "I don't know, coach. Maybe *I* should be the one giving out the lessons."

Laughing softly, Chase drank in all that made up Olivia Hensley. "I think you already are."

A bashful blink lowered her lashes as she unwound the pine needle from around her finger. Like every other time he'd gotten close to climbing the wall between them, he had to backpedal before she built it any higher.

Keep it light, Thompson. He crossed his ankles. "So, did this *supposed* cowboy break your heart? Because I could write you a country song right now if—"

"Oh my gosh. You're seriously going to make me regret telling you that, aren't you?"

"Not as much as I regret leaving my guitar at home." He winked. "Don't worry. I'll make it up to you." He dragged his backpack over and withdrew a camping popcorn popper.

"I hope you brought another one if you actually want any too."

"Now, what kind of coach would I be without maximizing your talents?" Chase uncovered another popper along with her very own bowl.

After loading the poppers with oil and salted kernels, a gushy grin settled her in beside him. "This beats oyster-eating any day."

He chuckled. "See, camping's not so bad."

"With you maybe."

As hot as the coals had already gotten, her words warmed him more.

Keeping his tone casual, he shook the kernels back and forth. "What made you so uncomfortable with Jed the other day?"

Livy dropped her popper into the fire. It came unfastened, launching sparks and half popped kernels in all directions. She scooted back and bumped into Bandit, who didn't even budge this time.

Chase snatched the popper, spilled hot oil on his hand, and let go a second later.

"I'm so sorry." She reached for his fingers. "Did it burn you?"

"I'm fine." Or he was, anyway, before her soft hands were caressing his.

When she didn't pull her thumb away from the thin red mark forming on his skin, he dipped his head under hers. "You know you can talk to me, right? Even about Jed?"

"I know." She feathered her gaze away from his to the flames and swept a strand of hair off her cheek. "The idea of a camping date with him probably has me worked up is all. I mean, seriously," she added with the perfect amount of deflection. "Why can't he like dancing instead?"

Chase would've laughed at how much she hated camping if he weren't hung up on the last part. He'd worked hard all day in the heat, but nothing made him sweat more than the prospect of dancing. His two left feet had caused him enough embarrassment for one lifetime.

He shifted against the log. "Since when are you into dancing?"

A feisty expression glowed in the firelight. "We all have our secrets."

Though playful, her words held more meaning than she was letting on. He could sense it. Had for the last several weeks. Especially the times she'd been so evasive about the plans she'd kept from him.

Smoke waved into the stillness, thoughts drifting with the minutes passing.

When Chase didn't reply, Livy brought a hand to her elbow and stared into the coals. "I know you're wondering why I'm wasting my time on a guy like Jed."

Chase took his hat off and ran his hand along the inside. "Actually, I was wondering why Jed would waste his time on anyone but you."

The pink already coloring her fire-warmed cheeks deepened, and it took all his restraint not to reach for them with both hands.

Keeping his cool, he set his hat on the log and added another piece of wood to the pit. "Remember that first break I came home with Jack? You were sitting on your parents' front porch, upset over a boyfriend you'd caught out with one of your friends."

Livy covered her face. "I was so mortified you caught me crying."

"You were cute."

"Your friend's little sister, blubbering like a schoolgirl is not cute."

She had no idea. "Well, it was a good distraction." The memory enveloped him. "I'd just found out about my dad's dementia."

Her hands strayed to her lap. "Why didn't you say anything?"

Chase picked at the threads wearing in the knee of his jeans. "I don't know. I guess sitting on those steps, talking with you... It really helped keep my mind off things for a while."

No need for words, Livy nestled her shoulder under his. The fire danced in the quiet, the wind its partner. And once again, being with her calmed the noise inside him like nothing else could.

She traced a hand down Bandit's back. "That night seems so long ago, doesn't it?"

"It was."

Livy picked up another pine needle and tied it in a knot. "Even then, you went out of your way to comfort me when *you* were the one dealing with actual pain." She tossed the needle into the fire. "How have you put up with me this long?"

"Patience and persistence," he teased.

She nudged an elbow into his side. "Yeah, well, you're gonna need a lifetime supply of both with me around."

A lifetime with her was exactly what he wanted.

The smallest laugh seemed to tug her back into the memory. "Bradly Johnson. Why I ever wasted tears on him, I'll never know." She cringed. "And here was this cute college guy sitting beside me while I spent ten minutes looking like a ditsy blonde trying to get that silly—"

"Teal scrunchy out of your hair." He laughed.

She'd wrestled that monstrous thing with such adorable flair, he'd known right then. Less than an hour with her, and he'd already fallen.

She twisted toward him, her face a cross between humiliated and impressed. "You remember that?"

"Every day." Chase lowered his gaze from hers for just a moment before finding it again. "You've grown a lot since then." Lips tipping, he fingered the thin, brown hair tie around the end of her braid. "Including changing up your choice of hair adornments."

Livy shoved him, but he held on. To her hair and her eyes.

"I promised you that night that you'd find a guy who'd treat you the way you deserve." He brushed a thumb over a smudge of soot she'd managed to get on her cheek. "That promise still holds, Liv. Not all guys are players. Some of us have been waiting for the right girl all our lives."

From the look on her face, she caught the full meaning of "waiting." But unlike the look he got from his buddies who thought his values were old fashioned, Livy's eyes didn't hold judgment or pity. They held a sorrow he didn't understand.

She breathed in, batted away the sheen in her eyes, and curled under his arm again.

Leaves rustled all around them in place of words. Although secrets still filled the gaps between them, for the moment at least, he prayed her forgotten dreams felt a little more within reach.

"Chase?" she said after another moment.

"Hmm?"

"Will you promise me I'll never lose you?" she whispered.

All night, he'd pushed Earl's offer to move him to Illinois out of his mind. Livy didn't know he was considering the job or what that might mean. Still, her question burrowed an image of the open-ended plane ticket Earl had emailed him into his side. He exhaled, the choice still weighing on him. There had to be an option that didn't cost him someone he loved.

The fiercer the uncertainties pressed in, the tighter he held Livy to him. He didn't have answers for much. Maybe the ones he did have were wrong. But with his arm curled around her back and his cheek against her temple, Chase grasped for the faith that always eluded him. "I promise."

CHAPTER FOURTEEN

Embers

Sunlight stretched across Livy's face. A hint of barely-burning cinders curled around her as she snuggled closer against her pillow. Her eyelids flew open. Not a pillow. Chase—asleep next to her, warm and tousled and way too... boyfriend-like.

Every tendon in her body tensed as she peered around the camp site and down their almost-tethered bodies. *Please be dreaming.*

Glimpses of the skyline flickered through the treetops, fragments from last night raining to memory. Definitely not dreaming.

With a sky too majestic to shroud, moving into the tent hadn't even crossed their minds. They'd stayed up late joking around until she'd forgotten all about the mess she called life. So natural, the laughter and conversation had eventually dwindled to the lull of swaying tree branches. The warmth, she remembered. The peacefulness, the ease. But when had she decided to make Chase her personal body pillow? And why in the world was she still wrapped around him now that she'd woken up?

With any luck, he hadn't noticed she'd turned into Gumby sometime in the night. Livy uncurled a finger at a time from his side, slowly retracted her arm from across his torso, and lifted her head off his shoulder. Once in the clear, she lunged to her feet and untangled her disastrous braid.

Relax. You can explain this. You just got comfortable... really, really comfortable.

Livy dropped her forehead to her fingertips. Between the way Chase made it feel safe to dream and all that had been going on in her life lately, she could understand the other times she'd gotten caught up in the make-believe of it all. Who wouldn't? But last night had felt different... real.

All the feelings she knew she should write off rushed in on a breeze and trickled across her arms. If she was smart, she'd beg this fresh mountain air to clear the fog in her head. Instead, she slipped on Chase's flannel shirt, picked up his hat, and dusted the dirt off the bottom. Without thinking, she brought it close and breathed in the familiar scent that had lured her to sleep last night—the same scent that had escalated her heart rate under that tree.

She shouldn't have slid her arms around his neck, but the emotion in the way he'd looked at her, held her... The ground had barely kept her steady. If Bandit hadn't interrupted them...

Chase stirred, and Livy dropped his hat as if she'd been holding one of the hot coals.

Just what she needed. For him to wake up and catch her standing over him like some crazy stalker in the middle of the woods. She should've eased away, or at the very least, *looked* away. But when the raised corner of his T-shirt exposed a sliver of skin above his beltline, her arms came farther undone with each cascading glance over his built-from-hard-labor body. She stretched her hair tie so far, it flung all the way across the camp site.

She flashed a glance from the hair-tie-turned-missile to Bandit, who she swore was laughing at her on the inside. "Don't look at me like that," she whispered. "This isn't funny. It's..." *Confusing?*

Or maybe just crazy. She tiptoed around the firepit, needing to get out of there. Needing distance, shock therapy— something. She scoured the perimeter of their site. Where was she supposed to go? Up a tree?

"Morning," Chase's raspy voice called from behind her.

Without turning, Livy stopped beside a tall pine on the periphery.

"Venturing into the woods alone? I'm impressed." Movement rustled behind her. "See, nothing like a night of camping to show you how brave you are."

Or to reveal you need a straitjacket.

"Nice touch with the flannel, by the way. Guys love to see their girls in their clothes."

Their girls. She sank into the words.

Gah. What was she doing?

Willing the blood in her cheeks to drain, Livy dragged her feet around. "Yeah, sorry. Didn't mean to steal it. I needed to... go to the bathroom, and it's chilly out, so..." *So, naturally, I decided to wrap myself in your shirt?* She scratched her neck below her ear. "But don't worry, I promise I'm not gonna pee on it or anything. I took that yoga class for a while. Remember? So, I'm totally used to squats and awkward positions and stuff. I mean, how hard can it be, right?"

Speaking of awkward...

She picked at the bark she now had her focus trained on like she could dig her way to Wonderland if she clawed as fast as she rambled.

"Definitely not as hard as some things."

If he only knew.

He yawned as he rose, and Livy just stood there, taking in every inch of the rustic country boy she'd made herself promise she'd never fall for.

"Here." He tossed her a roll of toilet paper. "You don't want to forget that. Unless you'd rather use a leaf," he added with one of his blasted winks. "And you can try balancing against a tree. You know, if the yoga training doesn't pan out."

Too bad she hadn't taken a Tai Chi class instead. She'd fan-kick that grin right off his face. "Did you warn Mystery Girl how easily you amuse yourself?" She'd meant it as a playful rib, but the aftertaste stung more than it should've.

"I'm pretty sure she already knows."

Of course she did. Head down, Livy turned the toilet paper 'round and 'round enough times to motor her out of there. If only. Instead, thoughts circling ten times faster kept her rooted in place.

"You want me to come with you?"

"No," she belted out like he was on the other side of the mountain. Cheeks heating, Livy drew her hair over her shoulder and tried again at a normal decibel this time. "Thanks, but I'm good."

Good, as in practically paralyzed. *Turn around, Liv. For the love of coffee, turn around and get the heck out of here.*

When Bandit's tongue lolled out of another amused grin, she pointed the roll behind her. "I should go take care of this." *Oh my word.*

Chase brushed off the dirt from his hat—the hat he probably saw her clinging to like Linus to his blanket. Mouth pulling sideways, he looked up with those stinking sultry eyes. "Be careful out there."

"Careful. Got it." She finally pivoted, kicked herself, and trekked into the woods—away from the feelings turning her insides back to Gumby.

She gnawed on her pinky nail. This wasn't happening, *couldn't* happen. Of course she'd always known Chase's tender, southern spirit could melt any girl's heart, but any girl wasn't her. They were friends—*best* friends. She couldn't ruin the one good thing in her life.

Once far enough away, she scanned the quiet area. Nothing but a few chirps coming from the trees. Maybe here, the mountain air would finally reach her brain.

In all honesty, she actually did have to pee. She looked from the toilet paper to the pine needle-coated ivy vines on the ground. "Camping just keeps getting better and better." Sighing, she unbuttoned her shorts, squatted, and reached for the tree behind her for balance. She really shouldn't have quit that yoga class.

A squirrel popped up from the leaves a few feet away and stared like he was startled by the intrusion. That made two of them. Though, at least Livy had the decency to pretend she didn't notice him. He, on the other hand, gave a whole new meaning to bright eyed and bushy tailed.

Livy gaped back at him. "You mind?"

Apparently not, because he continued to nibble on an acorn like it was a piece of popcorn.

As if trying to pee in the middle of the woods wasn't awkward enough, now she had an audience. Fantastic.

Humming for distraction, Livy tried looking in every direction but kept coming back to the overly attentive critter. Forget it. This obviously wasn't going to work. Stupid nature.

She almost made it back up when something else rustled nearby. She glared at the squirrel. "Invited a friend?"

He took one look behind him and scurried up the nearest tree trunk.

That couldn't be good. Livy managed to get her shorts up, but not before whatever was coming toward her closed in. She backed up on her hands and feet like she was in the world's fastest crab walk relay, bumped into a bush, and dropped smack on her rear in a patch of green foliage.

Something dropped from an overhead branch and slid down the inside of her shirt. The inside! A full-body shudder burned right through her five-second delay of shock. Screeching, she scrambled to get out of what she prayed wasn't poison ivy while flailing to shake the tree poop out of her bra.

A brown-haired rabbit jerked to a stop four feet in front of her. On its hind legs, it paused only a moment before continuing to zigzag forward.

Livy covered her face until the thump whizzing by left silence in its tracks—for a minute anyway. In the distance, something else crept toward her.

Seriously? What now?

Two beady eyes zeroed in on her from under a bush. One paw crept out. The other.

Was that a...? "Fox!" Livy catapulted to her feet in less than three seconds this time. The animal had to be rabid because it didn't hesitate either. It sprang for her. She chucked the stupid roll of toilet paper at it, missing the darn thing by a good three feet.

Amazingly, it stopped anyway.

Livy raised her hands. "Easy, Mr. Fox. Why don't we stop and talk about this for a sec, huh?" Lovely. As if talking to a squirrel wasn't bad enough, now she had to go and add negotiating with a fox to the reasons she needed therapy.

It slunk closer, teeth bared.

"Then again, who has time to talk, right?"

As soon as she backed up, the fox pounced. Screaming again, she whirled around and smacked into Chase's solid upper body, Bandit at his side.

He steadied her. "Whoa."

"Fox," she managed to get out between breaths.

Bandit took off after it at the same time Chase swept her between him and the pine tree. With her arms squeezing his waist, she buried her face in his back and waited, listened.

No howls, no snarls. Only a snicker filled the now-seemingly-harmless silence.

Livy peered around Chase's brawny bicep to the still forest. "Tell me I didn't imagine that."

"That little thing's more afraid of us than we are of it."

"Speak for yourself." Having her arms still entwined around Chase's waist obviously spoke enough for her. She flung them free, and he turned, staying just as close.

Everything about him seemed heightened now—ridiculously attractive bed head, jawline even scruffier than usual, the lingering scent of fire clinging to him.

Her throat turned dry. She would've had better luck taking on a rabid fox than Chase's eyes right now. She looked out to the woods. "We should probably go after Bandit." She needed to move.

"He'll find his way back."

Livy stared at his unwavering confidence. "We're in the middle of nowhere. I think you're staking a little too much in his skills."

"Nothing to do with skills." Instead of the expected grin, Chase looked at her with a depth incapable of containing the whole of the forest. "You're like home to him." He freed the hair tucked behind her ear. "That'll always be enough to lead him back to you."

For all the thousands of oxygen-producing trees surrounding them, every single one failed to help her breathe. The past two weeks replayed through her mind—each moment, every butterfly. Even now, the yearnings she'd tried to convince herself weren't real smoldered with embers Chase had sparked the moment he sat beside her on her parents' front porch over ten years ago.

This whole time, it'd been more than acting for her, more than a game. Somewhere in the middle of learning how to win a guy's heart, she'd lost her own to the one who'd always held it.

She vanquished the tears she wasn't about to try to explain. "I really think we should go look for Bandit."

"I've got bacon cooking back at the site. Trust me, *he'll* find us."

Along with how many other animals? Turning, Livy attempted another subtle bra shake, still feeling like something was on her. "Maybe we should skip breakfast."

"You're just starting to get the hang of things here."

More like this mountain was starting to strangle her. Running water, electricity, a shot of something strong enough to burn off the feel of things crawling nearby with legs as prickly as hers had probably gotten overnight—that wasn't too much to ask for, was it?

Now hung up on the last part, she casually rubbed one leg against the other. Sweet land of razors, how did campers deal without showers?

Chase must've read her thoughts. "Seriously, Liv. I know camping isn't your thing, but as far as successful dates go, I'd say you nailed it." He took his hat off, kept his focus on it, and traced two fingers along the brim. "But if you get to this point in the date and still aren't sure if the spark is real, the best way to find out would be to ask the guy to kiss you."

His gaze roved to her lips. "Emotions can be confusing sometimes, but when you kiss someone..." He inched a step closer. "The truth's pretty hard to deny."

The rough bark pressed into her back, her heart in her throat. This close, he smelled like hard work, smoked cherrywood, and everything she shouldn't be letting herself feel. Defenseless in a totally different way than earlier, she lost herself in the pull of his soft smile and the possibility of things too costly to hope for.

Her lashes fluttered with a breath. "What if I'm not ready for that?"

The slightest crease passed his brow. "Then wait until you are."

Chin lowered, Livy balled the cuff of his flannel under her fingers. "Guys don't wait, Chase. They walk away."

The mountainside held on to his pause.

"If the guy loves you, he'll wait forever." Chase tucked his hat on, handed her the hair tie she'd torpedoed back at the site, and closed her fingers around it. "Real love doesn't abandon, Liv." Smiling sadly, he backed away from the tree, but Livy didn't move.

The guilt of giving up her son nearly broke her right there.

"Not every girl deserves a guy who'll wait for her."

The V between his brows deepened. "Why would you say that?"

Livy faced the branches above her, never hating the truth more than right then. She was wrong about not acting. She had been all along, selfishly pretending he'd always be the safe, constant man in her life. That nothing ever had to change between them.

"We come from two different worlds."

"What's that supposed to mean?"

The edge in his tone brought her eyes to his—eyes that had been spared the things she'd seen in life. "It's not important." They needed a subject change. "You're a great coach, by the way. *Really* great. A couple times last night, you even had me wondering if..." She twisted and untwisted her hair tie. "Never mind." She might've been able to turn if her legs weren't half as defiant as her runaway mouth. "I mean, you didn't bring me camping to...?"

Curiosity crinkled around his eyes. "To?"

To let her make a fool of herself? Because she apparently kept passing that test with flying colors.

"To... I don't know. It almost felt like we weren't pretending. Like it was a real date." She snapped the band to her wrist, resorting to pain to shut herself up. "But that'd be totally weird, though... wouldn't it?"

"Weird. Yeah." His awkward laugh sounded as out of place as hers did. Chase picked at a grease stain on his nail, and the harmless silence from a moment ago now felt anything but. After a moment lasting forever, a sobered gaze found hers. "Rest assured, Liv. I'd never purposely make you feel uncomfortable."

She reached for him. "That's not what I—"

"We should go." He ran a knuckle along his whiskers until his usual playfulness returned to his eyes. "Unless you want to stay and try that bathroom routine again."

"You saw that?" The mortification just kept on coming.

"Not as much as your animal friends saw."

"Shut up."

When she shoved him, he lounged an arm across her shoulders. "C'mon, Snow White. Time to get you back to civilization."

Livy leaned into his side, desperately wanting to hang on to their uncomplicated friendship. "Does that come with a venti cup of coffee?"

"Or you could try sweet tea instead. I mean, if your brother's *cute* college friend drinks it, you should probably trust his taste."

Oh, sweet mercy, she'd really said that last night, hadn't she?

She let his sardonic lilt slide. But if she didn't get coffee in her soon, she'd be sliding that goofy grin of his right off the edge of the mountain.

Back at the camp site, Livy moseyed over to where she'd left her phone by the log. She eyed the coffee maker he'd already set up and smiled. *Sweet tea, my foot.* He knew exactly what she needed. Knew her better than anyone else. And even though *she* knew better than to hang on to what she'd eventually have to let go of, when it came to Chase, her heart rarely listened. "You know, I guess we don't necessarily *have* to rush."

He raised a brow. "You sure?"

Bandit galloped back into camp, tail wagging like he was in doggy heaven.

Livy laughed. "We can at least eat some bacon first." She swept a thumb across her cell. "If we don't, Bandit might—"

A text she'd missed sometime this morning glared at her in the sunlight. *Shoot.*

CHAPTER FIFTEEN

Strings

How could things unravel so quickly?

Bandit jumped out of the back of Chase's Silverado the minute he parked in front of Livy's house. Given the way she had withdrawn into herself again, Chase was surprised she hadn't jetted out of the truck with him. This definitely wasn't how he'd envisioned their date ending.

He tapped the wheel. "You sure we're good?"

Livy pulled her attention away from the window and whatever thoughts had her miles away from him. "Hmm?"

"You've hardly said a word since we packed up the site." He slipped off his hat, frustrated with how easily the progress he thought they'd made last night had already spiraled. "If you're worried I was trying to use this trip to—"

"It's not that." Livy shook her head, still looking distant. "I'm just late for somewhere I need to be."

"I can take you."

"No."

If her brusque response meant anything, that *somewhere* was evidently a place she didn't want him to know about. Again.

He squeezed his neck. "Is this about your friend with the emergency?"

Her voice faltered. "Please don't push this, Chase."

"Push what? I don't even know what we're talking about because you keep shutting me out." He brushed a thumb over the red mark left on his hand from the popper, her secrecy burning deeper. He'd tried letting it go numerous times, but something about today broke him. "If you'd just talk to me…"

"I need to go." She unbuckled her seat belt.

Chase reached for her arm as she turned. "Liv."

Already halfway out, she kept her head down. "I'm sorry." The muggy breeze sweeping into the truck swallowed the quiet words drifting out with her.

Chase gripped the wheel to keep himself in place until her front door closed. He tugged his sweet tea from the cupholder and chugged a quarter down. If she didn't fully trust him, a relationship would never work. He'd been down that road already. Knew exactly where it led.

Old wounds sparked. Partly aggravated, partly dejected, he shoved the gearshift into drive but didn't make it more than a few blocks before slowing to a stop. In the middle of the street, he tipped his head against the headrest. What was he doing? With all of it? Livy, his parents, his job? Were any of his decisions even halfway on track?

Instead of an answer, a glimpse of Livy's Fiat zipped past his rearview mirror on the street behind him. Chase sat up, hesitated less than a second, and spun his truck around before he lost sight of her car.

His mind, on the other hand, he'd obviously already lost, or he wouldn't be tailing her right now like a PI. She'd have his head if she caught him. Even if she didn't, this wasn't him. What was he doing?

The logic yelling above the roar of his exhaust pipe would've turned him around if something about the whole thing didn't feel so off. She was scared. Of what, he wasn't sure, but her fear of telling him didn't stop him from caring enough to find out.

He kept a buffer of several car-lengths between them until she turned onto a long gravel driveway. With no other cars to hide behind, Chase stopped at the entrance, his heart pulling him in two directions. He craned his neck back again, waiting for gravity to drill the right choice through his thick skull.

Apparently, he'd need a backhoe to break through his noggin, because his hands circled the wheel to the right against his better judgment.

What had looked like a long driveway from the road now seemed a heck of a lot shorter. He reached Livy's Fiat sooner than he wanted to. And when her glare could've scorched a hole through his windshield, he almost four-wheeled his way right off the property.

Manning up instead, Chase swallowed and lumbered out. "Don't be mad."

If the way her face just contorted had anything to say about it, they were already well past mad. "Liv, just hear me—"

"I can't believe you followed me." Her crossed arms nearly squeezed her in half. "There are lines, Chase."

Ones he was continually blurring. He couldn't deny that, but this was different. Last night pressed in—the hope, the vulnerability. "What if I don't want any between us?"

"That's not your call."

"We're supposed to be friends."

"That doesn't mean every part of my life is a free-for-all."

He winced but kept striding for her. "No, it means we're honest with each other, Liv. It means I..." Right in front of her, he brushed her bangs off her lashes and breathed through the mix of emotions heaving his chest up and down. "It means I care about you."

She shut her eyes at his touch. "And asking you to respect boundaries doesn't mean I care about you any less."

"You sure about that?" A pang of hurt he couldn't hide dragged his arm to his side.

"That's not fair," she whispered.

Life never was. But if she stopped stonewalling him, at least they'd be walking through it together.

His focus strayed past her to a sign on a large house in the corner of the property. A group home? "This is where you've been coming? Why would you keep this from me?"

She turned. "Leave it, Chase."

Not this time. He cut off her path to the door. "You have a friend here? A relative?"

Livy flung her hand up, eyes a watery sea of fear she kept him from crossing. "Don't. Please."

"Don't what?" He studied her. "What are you so afraid of?"

Her lashes creased together. "Things you wouldn't understand."

The zing burned into scars lurking closer to the surface than they should've been. "Now who's not being fair?"

When she didn't budge, Chase walked away with his fingers threaded through the back of his hair. He stopped five feet away and turned. "I'm trying here, Liv. I'm really trying."

"Trying to what?"

He dug his keys from his pocket, an answer so much harder to grasp. "You know…" He searched her closed-off eyes one more time, shook his head, and opened his door. "I'm really not sure anymore." About anything. Except that following her here was clearly a mistake.

All the time they'd spent together, the openness, the connection—had it meant nothing? Halfway in the truck, he stopped with his heart more exposed than ever. "I thought we were starting to…"

"Chase." The tattered warning in her voice ground his heart into the gravel with the answer he needed to know.

He swallowed the sting, nodded a final time, and cranked the ignition.

The rocks churning under his tires nearly drowned out the sound of his cell ringing from the cupholder. He almost ignored his boss's call but brought the phone to his ear on the last ring. "Hey, Brad, can I give you a call back?"

"Only if you want to miss out on the best score we'll see this season. Looks like we've got an incoming hail storm about to hit northern Chicago."

That wasn't far from Earl's shop.

"The payout on this one should last us a solid six months." Brad spat away from the phone. "Ready for another run?"

At the end of the driveway, Chase cast a look in the mirror toward Livy standing in front of the door she continued to keep parts of her life boarded up behind. "As a matter of fact, I already have a ticket."

"You already have plans?"

"Possibilities."

"I hear that." Brad sounded like he moved whatever he was chewing to the side of his mouth. "As long as it doesn't interfere with your work, it's all good. We need you on the team, Thompson. The boys are meeting up at noon on Tuesday. I'll text you the info."

Truth be told, Chase had been half dreading the call for their next job. The nature of his business meant living on the fly. Depending on the severity of the storm, he could be gone for weeks or only a few days. With all the stuff going on at home, it'd been getting harder for him to leave. But the windfall from a job of this size could keep Nurse Murphy's home visits up for another few months. And right now, taking a breather from everything might be exactly what he needed to make the decisions still facing him.

He cast one more glance in the rearview mirror, flipped on his blinker, and turned off the street Livy had roadblocked him from being a part of. "I'll be there."

In his parents' kitchen Tuesday morning, Chase deleted the voice message he'd just listened to. Denied. In a thirty-second voice mail, the insurance company had denied Chase's petition like his parents were just faceless names on a routine calling list instead of real people whose entire lives their flippant decisions impacted. He shoved his phone off the placemat.

The sharp movement garnered a peek from Mom over by the stove.

Chase straightened out his silverware and his attitude before that pointed brow of hers could turn into a lecture. "You really didn't have to make me breakfast before I leave."

"Nonsense." She waved her wooden spoon in the air. "As if that so-called airport food could be better than my famous hash brown casserole."

"Famous, huh?"

"In this family, yes." At the table, Mom spooned the cheesy breakfast onto his plate and jutted the pan at him. "And don't you forget it neither."

Dad sneezed in the living room, and Chase's smile fell as he watched him shift uncomfortably in his recliner like an out-of-town guest. Sometimes, forgetting would be easier.

An ache in Chase's chest longed for Livy as it had ever since he'd driven away from the group home Sunday morning. But something about being here, seeing Dad like this, deepened the yearning to hear her voice even more.

He scrolled to the number he'd almost called a hundred times over the last forty-eight hours and shut the screen off again. He shouldn't have let his insecurities get the best of him.

"Those potatoes aren't gonna eat themselves, sugar."

Chase took a bite. "Sorry. Caught up in work."

"Mm-hmm." Mom grabbed a pot holder from a drawer and opened the oven. "You're caught up in something all right. But unless you want to call a blond-haired, blue-eyed girl work, then I reckon you better rephrase."

His forkful of potatoes stopped halfway to his mouth.

Mom slid a pan of muffins onto the stovetop, closed the door, and strode for the table. She folded her arms over the chairback beside him. "I may be old, sweetie, but I'm not blind."

Unlike Chase apparently was. He lowered his fork. "Livy just wants to be friends, Ma." And deserved a better one than he'd been to her lately.

A solid slap landed upside his head. "Boy, if you get any denser, you could throw yourself on the ground and miss. As surely as I love your daddy, that girl loves you."

He rubbed the back of his head. "Must be why she wants me to coach her to win over Jed McCormick instead."

"That singer from Ginny's party last year?" Mom shooed the towel at his comment like it were a fly. "That boy thinks the sun comes up just to hear him crow. Don't you worry about him, sugar. He's nowhere in your league."

Nothing like a mother's vote of confidence. Chase checked his cell, begging the clock to pave an exit route from this conversation. He cracked his neck, scooted his chair in and then out again, and ran his fork through the casserole.

A hearty laugh bellowed beside him. "Aw, now, stop your squirming. You're acting like you're fifteen again, all embarrassed about asking Kaley out."

His fork clinked into the plate.

"Ah," she practically hummed. "So, that's what this is about. Livy's not Kaley, honey."

He flicked a glance away from her. "I know."

"Then what's holding you back?"

What *wasn't*? "Her, me, life." He straightened the placemat 'til it was flush with the table's edge. "You can't always make things happen a certain way just 'cause you want them to."

"You reckon not, do ya?" Mom pushed off the back of the chair. "Is that why you're dead set on fixin' your daddy?"

Chase banged his knee under the table but managed to hold his tongue. For ten whopping seconds. "It might be a little easier if you were on board with me."

She flapped the towel over her shoulder as she turned. "We've already had this discussion, sugar. We're doing what we think is best. But you be sure to thank your sweet Livy for bringing by that list of alternative medicines she researched for us. Bless her heart. That was awful kind of her."

Chase blinked. "Livy came by?" Not that he should've been surprised she'd want to help. She had a bigger heart than she realized.

Mom planted a hand on her hip. "I can be good company, you know."

"No, no, of course." He shook his head. "I just meant..."

"You just meant you're hurt she hasn't come to see you yet." Mom jimmied one of the muffins out of the tin with a spatula. "Has it occurred to you she might be waiting for *you* to go to her?"

Chase grabbed his phone. They weren't diverting the conversation to him and Livy again. "Where's the list she brought? I can look up—"

"Sweetie, I just finished saying we're not interested."

"How can you not be willing to try?" With his fingers clenched around his cell, he aimed it toward the living room. "Do you see Dad right now? We should be exhausting every option."

She faced him. "I already told you. We prayed about it and—"

"That's not enough." He palmed his phone to the table. "Prayers aren't bringing back his memory, Ma. We're losing him. Can't you see that? I don't understand how you can be clinging to faith when—"

"Enough." She threw the balled-up dishtowel onto the counter. "I'd rather die believing without seeing, than to go through a day of this life without faith." Her resolve echoed against the hollow place where Chase's used to be.

"I'm sorry..."

She lifted a hand to stop him. Eyes softening, she walked to the doorway separating the kitchen and living room. "I'm not saying I'm against medicine, honey. You know better than that." She leaned into the jamb and looked in on the husband she was on the verge of losing. "But there are times when faith and family are what gets us through more than anything."

Family. Dad had always been the bedrock of theirs. He'd modeled the importance of sacrifice, provision. But of all his lessons, he'd never taught Chase how to watch the man he admired most in the world deteriorate without any way to prevent it.

Back at the table, Mom patted Chase's hand. "If we stop reminding each other who we are, sugar, your daddy won't be the only one who's lost right now."

A nod to the living room steered his gaze to the guitar propped against the couch and to the implication she had a way of cutting straight to. Without needing to say more, she trekked back to the rest of the muffins she'd left on the stovetop while leaving Chase to face yet another choice.

He hadn't been able to bring himself to play the guitar over the last few years. He dragged his fork through the casserole aimlessly, torn between missing the feel of the strings and fearing their familiarity. After another minute, he dropped his napkin beside his plate and pushed away from the table but didn't make it past the doorway to the living room.

"I picked up his prescription," he said mostly to himself. "Why isn't it helping?"

"Oh, I reckon it is, sweetie. But I'm afraid the lapse in taking it may mean we're starting over again. Give it some time."

Time they were running out of.

Mom slid a muffin onto a cooling rack. "And don't think we're done with that conversation, young man. I told you not to go spending your savings on us, and I meant it."

Chase didn't argue. Unless he found a way to afford Dad's prescriptions in the long run, it was a moot point anyway.

A deep breath led him toward the recliner, his boots sounding heavier against the hardwoods than they should have. Despite how much Mom's country décor filled the room to the brim with a sense of home, Dad's vacant eyes turned it into an empty shell of what it used to be.

He idled beside the ottoman and cleared his throat. "How you doing today, Pops?"

A slow blink brought his father's attention to him, but no response followed.

Chase eyed the half-touched plate of casserole on the TV stand next to the chair. "Careful," he teased. "Or we're gonna drive Mom to put her hash browns in this year's cookoff just to prove how famous they are." His laugh drifted up the fireplace unreciprocated.

"Hash browns," Dad said as if the word took a moment to register. He shifted his focus to the plate. "Mighty fine cooking here. You should try some before you leave."

"It sure is. I have some on the table."

Nodding, Dad set the plate in his lap and swirled his fork along the sides.

Chase tapped his thighs in step with the grandfather clock's steady ticking. "So... did you sleep okay last night?" he finally said.

"Oh, as well as I need to, I guess. The bed could use a new mattress, but the cooking's mighty fine." He extended the plate. "You should try some."

It never got easier to hear him repeat the same thing only moments later without any awareness of saying it before. The slight tremor in his hand somehow made it even harder.

He took the plate from Dad's shaky grasp, set it on the tray, and picked up the guitar instead. After a quick tuning check, he held the instrument out to his father. "Why don't you play something? I think you'd enjoy it."

Dad gripped the chair arms. "Oh, I don't think so." He shook his head. "I wouldn't know how."

Chase held his expression together long enough to sit on the ottoman and bring the guitar to his lap. With a slight quiver of his own, he strummed the beginning of a song Dad had taught him when he was thirteen. Memories hugged every chord—the times listening to Dad play while sitting in front of this same recliner, the evenings he'd carved out time to place his fingers over Chase's until he could do it on his own. They'd spent plenty of time together working on cars, on the property. But those nights of passing on his love of music after a long day's work had brought his hero status to a new plane. One Chase had never imagined ever seeing him fall from.

He kept his fingers and eyes on the guitar after finishing the song. A breath passed. A prayer. And when he faced his father once more, something had shifted.

A flicker of recognition chased away the vacancy crowding his gray eyes. His fingers moved along the edge of the arm rests. "I… I taught my son that song."

Chase hung his head, gain colliding with loss. "Yeah, you did. One among many songs." He stifled the beginning of tears and held out the guitar. "You're a great player."

Dad took it with visible hesitation. But once the familiar grooves on his fingertips found the strings, another wave of recognition seemed to awaken something inside him. One chord followed another. And little by little, the tremble in his aged hands gave way to the graceful flow of a seasoned guitarist whose love of music no illness could steal.

Nearly two decades might've passed since Chase used to sit on this ottoman, listening to Dad play until he fell asleep, but the admiration in that little boy's heart had never left him.

A chime from the kitchen signaled the alarm he'd set on his phone. As much as he wanted to stay and linger in this momentary lapse in time, making his flight might be the only real way to make it last.

He rose, kissed his father on the head, and clutched his shoulder. "I love you, Pops." Flying out to Illinois today was for him. For family.

Across the room, Chase stopped and looked behind him when the music stalled. On the edge of the recliner, Dad wrapped his hand around the neck of the guitar and around a spark of awareness of who Chase was. He tipped his head in a silent "thank you," and not for the first time, Chase was grateful they had never needed words between them.

He'd barely made it into the kitchen before an array of emotions rocked him. He swiped his cell off the table and tapped Livy's number. He needed to apologize and make things right before he left. Needed her to understand why he'd been on edge lately. Maybe more than anything, he needed her to help him figure out what to do.

One unanswered ring stretched into another until her voice mail cut off his hope of her picking up.

"Her place is on the way, you know," Mom said from the sink.

Chase finagled his keys from his pocket. "Whose place?"

Apparently, the pointless question didn't even warrant a response. Mom motioned to a plastic container on the table. "Take those hash browns for the road, sugar. And come give your mama a kiss goodbye before she has to tan your hide."

A laugh prodded him across the room and into a hug. "Thanks for breakfast, Ma. Don't hesitate to ask Nurse Murphy to come by if you need her, okay? I'll call when I know how long I'll be gone this time." He always hated having to leave them on their own, but this time especially rubbed him raw.

"You just worry about keeping yourself safe, you hear me?" She tapped a sudsy hand to his cheek. "My boy, the hail chaser."

"That's not exactly—"

"Mm-hmm." She dipped her rag in the sink water and wrung it out. "Just be sure you don't lose sight of what you should be chasing when you get home." An exaggerated bob of her brows held enough insinuation to wheel him the heck out of there.

On his way to the door, Chase grabbed the old margarine container she'd put his hash browns in.

"Tell Livy I said hi," she called through the screen.

Already at his Silverado, he cranked the engine in hopes of drowning out her singsong tone.

Of course not. Mom's voice might as well have been Siri's. From the minute he got on the road, it steered him straight past all reasoning until he found himself turning into Livy's neighborhood.

The ache to see her pulsed even stronger now that he was here. Cell in hand, he called her one more time as he turned onto her street. He coasted up to the curb and tapped the edge of his open-ended plane tickets against the wheel. "C'mon, Liv, pick up. Give me a chance to…"

The tickets fell to his lap. Sunlight streamed through the front window onto Livy walking in sporadic circles with her cell to her ear and a nervous smile on her face—the kind she always wore when talking to Jed.

CHAPTER SIXTEEN

Loss

The Midwest. Chase had never been a huge fan. Of the land, maybe. The pace of life. But ever since Kaley had chosen it over Littleton, something about this whole region of the country rubbed him the wrong way.

He bumped the wipers on his rental car up another notch and squinted through the sheet of rain whirling off the windshield. If the storm would let up for half a second, maybe he could see where he was going.

The wind's fierce howl swayed the car. He steadied the wheel and squinted to see a clear view of the double yellow lines. Two-lane roads weren't foreign to him, but he wouldn't mind his GPS working right about now.

He tossed the trifold map onto the passenger's seat and checked for a signal on his phone for the umpteenth time. Not that he expected one. He got spotty reception in this part of the country even on a good day. Still, his thoughts kept gravitating to Livy, wondering if she'd tried to call, if she even knew he was gone.

Against all warning, the feel of her fingers trailing down his hair when he'd helped her from the tree transported him back to a moment he'd relived a ridiculous number of times in such a short span.

Every detail of the weekend rewound through his mind, stopping again and again on Livy's closed-off eyes. He'd wanted her to feel at home in his arms, wanted to *be* her home. Instead, he'd ended up driving her away.

Jagged strips of lightning ran through the thick clouds. Images of another storm from another time flickered across the dark sky—he and Kaley's dad standing outside their house, words sharper than the cold rain beating into him. *"If you honestly thought my daughter would choose some aimless, blue-collar nobody over a chance for a real future, you're an even greater fool than I thought."*

A horn blared up ahead. Chase jerked the wheel to the right. His car fishtailed, the guardrail only inches away. He let off the gas pedal, but his pulse kept accelerating until his tires finally rolled to a stop.

Rain pounded against the hood of the car, his heart against his ribs. A breath at a time, he peeled his hands off the wheel and ran them down his face. He'd been driving over an hour. Surely, he had to be close to Earl's shop by now. He flexed his tense fingers in and out, expelled a hard breath, and stretched out his neck. *Get it together, Thompson.*

This wasn't the time or place to be distracted. Even if the storm subsided, the one he was weathering for his parents lent enough reason for him to stay focused all on its own.

This interview could be the difference between his dad recovering and—

Another honk cut off a thought he couldn't bring himself to finish. Two headlights tunneled straight for him. Reflexes kicked in. He thrust the car into reverse, twisted backward, and sped in the opposite direction. Rain gushed down the back window. He couldn't see, couldn't tell what was behind him. With no other choice, he slammed on the brakes and crossed his arms to brace for impact. Oncoming headlights speared across the windshield, but in that split second, all Chase could see was the glare of regret.

A single turn wouldn't have skyrocketed Livy's pulse if this were any other neighborhood. But even after ending her call with the adoption agency hours ago, her nerves were still shot.

Each prompt from her GPS burrowed the implications left from her conversation with Tanner's caseworker into her a little deeper. Choices. Consequences. Things set in motion she couldn't change. Even if she could, would it really be best?

Honestly, she'd never allowed herself to doubt that her son was growing up in a solid home. Had never let herself worry if the Bradleys had turned out to be the kind of adoptive parents they'd seemed like they would be during the selection process. But after spending time with Sophie, she couldn't help it now.

From the passenger seat, Bandit stretched a paw onto her thigh, somehow knowing she needed him. Livy glanced at the address she had from their profile and circled the wheel onto the corresponding street.

Bandit's nails snagged the seat when the car came to a stop. Parked on the opposite corner, she looked from her sticky note to the number on the house's brick siding. Though numbers weren't her thing, they usually didn't lie. This was it. The home someone else was providing for Tanner in ways Livy never would've been able to. Shoot, even daydreams didn't amount to a house this nice.

Taking in every manicured angle, she rubbed Bandit behind the ears. Money wasn't everything. She'd learned that firsthand in London. Bricks and mortar could easily hide a crumbling home inside.

Bandit lifted a curious ear as Livy unbuckled her seat belt.

"I know. I'm not sure it's a good idea either." She scratched his head and drew in a deep breath. "But good or not, I need to do this." Even if it didn't make sense. Even if it changed nothing. She had to know.

Bandit nudged his nose to her arm when she stopped with the door halfway open.

"You sure this isn't crazy?"

Round, brown eyes looked up at her, and she almost laughed. If this wasn't crazy, she certainly was, sitting here talking to a dog. Then again, it had to be better than playing Snow White in the woods.

The memory of Chase's laughter grazed the softest of smiles across her face until the scene he'd pulled at the group home ransacked the moment completely. He wasn't the only one who had a right to be angry. He shouldn't have pried. Shouldn't have followed her or...

"*Real love doesn't abandon, Liv.*"

His words sank to her core. Even when she pushed him away, he still didn't abandon her.

Tears blurred the house in front of her with a film of her many mistakes. For the hundredth time over the last three days, she wished Chase were with her. Truth was, he would've been if she'd let him. If things were different—

Across the street, the front door opened, and a woman nearly as pristine as her yard stepped out with a four-year-old boy holding her hand.

Livy's fingers clenched the door handle. So big. He'd gotten so big already. She absorbed every detail. His blond hair brushing above curious blue eyes, the Spider-Man backpack hanging on tiny shoulders capable of carrying more than Livy would ever be strong enough to carry herself. Perfect, happy, and proof that after nine months of the fiercest battle she'd ever fought, love had found a way to overcome loss.

Mrs. Bradley helped Tanner into his car seat and handed him an action figure. His face lit up, and something inside Livy came undone. He might have Livy's eyes, but his smile belonged to the mom who held his heart. He trusted her, loved her. Whether a block away or right beside them, anyone could see it.

And rightly so. Though clearly well-off and wholly put together, Mrs. Bradley held a softness about her. The kind that went hand-in-hand with a mother's natural instincts. Livy wasn't blind to the truth in some of Sophie's concerns about the system. But while sitting there now, she couldn't deny this was one case that had worked out for the best.

Relief should have been sweeping through her. Gratefulness—joy even. And honestly? It was, but a hollow emptiness never failed to trail just behind.

Hot, stagnant air poured in through the open door. Livy didn't release the handle. Didn't move from the seat, not even when Bandit nudged her to get out before the SUV pulled away. She watched, waited, maybe even hoped Tanner would somehow recognize her.

Why she'd expect him to see anything but a stranger, she didn't know. The SUV passed without a single glance falling in their direction, and Bandit's brown eyes moped at her.

"Don't look at me like that. I came to make sure he was taken care of. That's it." She pulled her door in, got her seat belt caught in it, and wrangled it free. "No one said anything about meeting him or interfering in any way." No one said seeing him, even from a distance, would hurt this much either.

On instinct, she reached for her cell and scrolled to Chase's number. It took four rings to register that she didn't know what to say. It didn't matter. She just needed to hear his voice. Needed to hear—

His voice mail clicked on, and in a matter of seconds, a muddled blend of relief and disappointment stormed into the other jumbled feelings Livy wasn't prepared to sort through right now.

She opened her email instead, looked up at Tanner's house once more, and found herself asking his caseworker the question she feared most.

A call came in right as she hit send. Livy answered, a little surprised to see Quinn's name on the screen. "Please tell me you have a batch of fresh cupcakes made." She could sure use one of those lifesavers. Or maybe a dozen.

"Rough day?" Quinn laughed. "I'll tell ya what. If you come over right now, I'll make you a box to take home. Not that I'm bribing you for anything. Okay, maybe I am. I could actually use your help with something. You mind swinging by?"

Livy tried to fasten her seat belt with her left hand. "Of course not. But I'm not in town right now, so it'll take me a good hour to get there. Hey, by the way, do you know where Chase is? My call went to voice mail."

"I'm sure he'll call you back when he gets a break."

"A break?" Her hand froze with her belt stretched halfway out.

"He caught a job in Chicago. Left early this morning. He didn't tell you?"

"Oh, um, he probably just didn't get to it. We've sort of been..." Fighting? It sounded so weird to think, much less say out loud.

Cooper hollered something from another room.

"Are you sure that's in the same place as...?" Quinn's pause stretched into the sound of the Weather Channel increasing in the background.

Livy's earlier tension clawed into her muscles again. "Same place as what? What's wrong?"

"The storm in Chicago that brought Chase there. It looks bad."

"How bad?" And why did this blasted seat belt hate her so much right now? She gave the uncooperative thing another yank.

Quinn's voice thickened. "The airport lost contact with one of the planes. There are accidents all over."

The belt finally jammed into place with a clank that sent a shudder up Livy's spine. "But you've heard from Chase already, right? He got there okay, didn't he?"

Quinn's silence couldn't have been louder.

Heat pressed in from every side. "Tell me he's okay, Quinn." She tilted the vent toward her face and closed her eyes. "Quinn? Tell me."

CHAPTER SEVENTEEN

Currents

Livy paced across Quinn and Cooper's living room with her phone to her ear. *C'mon, Chase. Pick up.*

"Hey, you've reached Chase Thompson's voice mail. You know what to do."

She'd never hated the sound of a beep more in her life. Frustrated, Livy left another quick message and ended the call at the same time Quinn ended hers.

"The airlines are worthless when it comes to giving out information." Quinn set her phone on the narrow table in the entryway and backed against it. "Why can't my brother have a normal job like everyone else? I mean, seriously. Following hail storms across the country? It's crazy. Surely, the body shops around here do enough work year-round to pay him a decent wage."

Cooper entered from the kitchen, carrying a cupcake in one hand and a sleeping Brayden in the other. "Working a few months out of the year for the same salary as a 9-5? Sounds like a no brainer to me."

Quinn made a face at him. "Do all men think alike?"

A lopsided grin followed Cooper's shrug. "Only when they're surrounded by girls who think alike." He laughed at Livy's matching crossed arms aggravatingly proving his point. "Will you two relax already? I'm sure Chase is fine. He probably just doesn't have reception right now."

"You're really maddening when you're being logical, you know that?" Pulling her lips to the side only drew Cooper's to them.

"And you're really adorable when you're being illogical." He kissed her again, set the cupcake on the table, and headed down the hall. "Why don't you two talk about the coffee shop instead? It'll get your mind off things."

Livy shook her head as Cooper trailed into Brayden's bedroom. "They really do think alike, don't they?"

"Welcome to my life." Quinn exaggerated a huff but couldn't shake the honeymoon glaze lingering in her eyes.

Livy couldn't blame her. Cooper was one of the best guys out there. She always knew things would turn out well for him once he finally stopped running. Smiling herself, she picked up a framed wedding photo of them on their dock, fireworks going off above the lake. "I still can't believe you guys got married on the Fourth of July."

"I'm sorry, how long have you known my husband?" She raised a sassy brow.

"Point taken."

"Hey." Cooper gently eased Brayden's door shut, came back, and wrapped his arms around Quinn from behind. "Only an *epic* wedding day for my bride." Picking up his cupcake, he winked at her as if sharing an inside joke. "Speaking of epic…" He bit into the cupcake top and showcased a dreamy grin. "The two of you running a coffee shop together could be magic."

Quinn air-kicked him toward his study. "Just be glad I don't have a wand right now."

Unfazed, Cooper tossed their cat, Trooper, onto his shoulder and disappeared into his office.

"I thought he didn't like that cat."

"He puts up a good front." Quinn stuffed her cell in her back pocket. "But those two are inseparable. If he's not carrying Brayden around, he's got Trooper on his shoulders."

The image gave her a chuckle. But as she returned the picture to the table, a pang of an all-to-familiar emptiness pushed back. Her closest friends had all found the love and families they deserved. Drew and Ti, Cooper and Quinn. She didn't have a single doubt Chase would find the same too.

Quinn handed her a mug. "Coop's probably right, you know. About Chase not having reception."

"Yeah." Livy took a sip of the Italian roast. "I'd still feel better if I could talk to him." Not being able to get in touch with him gnawed at her, more from fear that his silence was by choice. What if she had pushed too far this time?

"He'll call." Whether borrowing assurance from Cooper or drawing from her own, Quinn smiled warmly and nodded for Livy to join her on the couch. "So, listen, that thing I needed your help with? It has to do with the Finch's old café. Chase told me about the pizza chain planning to open up there if we don't do something to stop it."

"Stop it?"

"Yeah. He said there's some city law that if enough of us lobby against it, Mrs. Finch will have to find another buyer."

"A loophole." Livy shook her head, somehow not surprised Chase had found one and had once again gone out of his way to clear the road for her to act on his faith in her.

"Guess you could call it that." Quinn exchanged her mug for a notepad and pulled a pencil from her hair. "I'm thinking of featuring an article about it in our magazine. Maybe get something to the local paper too. Would you be up for helping me get a few quotes from other local business owners? Ava's out this week with some family stuff. I could really use an extra hand."

Livy mindlessly traced her fingertip up and down her mug as she looked around Cooper and Quinn's high-ceilinged living room. Like the expensive brick house her son was growing up in, the family inside was what made it a home. A family might not be in the cards for her. She couldn't undo her past. But if there was any chance of both Tanner and Chase being proud of her, she needed to do whatever it took.

"Actually, I think I can do something even better." Livy set her mug on the end table and pushed up from the couch. "Just give me a minute to make a couple of calls first."

Quinn nodded, and Livy strode out to the back deck overlooking a gorgeous view of Lake Gaston. Leaning against the railing, she found Tessa's number, hovered over it, but then scrolled to Chase's number one more time instead. *Please pick up.*

"Hey, you've reached Chase Thompson's voice mail. You know what to do."

Her lashes fell at the beep chiming through the line. "Chase, hey, it's Liv… again. If you can't tell, we're a little worried about you back here. You don't want to know how many cupcakes Quinn and I've eaten today. All I can say is I'm gonna need all new jeans after the chocolate binge you're putting me through right now, buddy."

Her laughter tapered as she ran her nail along a groove in the wood. "Seriously, though, I'm calling to make sure you're okay, but also because there's something I want to talk to you about. A lot of things actually." Would he give her the chance to apologize? To explain about the group home, Tanner?

She swallowed her uncertainty. "So, that's it, I guess. Just needing to hear your voice." Needing to tell him he was right about everything and that she wouldn't disappoint him this time.

An unrelenting lump marched up her throat. "I'm sorry I waited until today to call. Please… call me back when you can." She hesitated before hanging up, then folded her arms on the rail and exhaled into the wind. Where was he?

An osprey squawked above the sky's glassy reflection shimmering over the lake. Music played from the neighbors' pier. But as Livy wrestled to quiet her heart, all other noise faded into the sound of Chase's voice promising her she'd never lose him.

What if that was one promise he couldn't keep?

The oncoming car swerved to the right just in time to miss Chase's front end. It stopped with the driver's window lined up to his.

After his pulse finally evened out, Chase cracked his window far enough to catch a glimpse into the other car. "Earl?"

"I thought you might need some help out here," he called over the clamor of raindrops slamming into the pavement.

"By trying to drive me off the road?"

"Sorry 'bout that. Was trying to dodge that pothole back there." He patted his dashboard. "I just got her an alignment last week."

Drops of rain ricocheted off the window onto his face. "Do you always launch a search and rescue mission in the middle of a storm?"

"Only when my recruits are crazy enough to go driving in one." His hearty laugh countered another round of thunder. "C'mon, kid. Follow my taillights. The shop's just off that next turn."

Crazy or not, after reaching the shop safely, it'd taken less than three minutes into the tour for Chase to remember why he liked Earl so much. The old man didn't just work on classic cars, he loved and respected them as much as Chase did.

Earl grazed a finger along a 1966 Pontiac GTO showcased near the front of the garage. "She's a beaut', isn't she?"

"Like something out of a movie."

"Just wait." Earl flipped the lights. A section at a time, the industrial lighting showcased row after row of refinished models. The buzz of electricity surged with the kind of palpable energy you'd find in the middle of a live auction.

Chase laced his fingers behind his head while taking a sweeping look around. He'd labeled himself a daydreamer, but this was far beyond what he'd pictured. "It's incredible."

"Not too shabby for a place to call work, eh?" Earl squeezed Chase's shoulders from behind. "Seeing it in person is a real game changer. Didn't I tell ya?"

With a swift pat to the back, he led Chase over to an office, where two gentlemen he introduced as his partners each shook Chase's hand.

The one with an overgrown gray beard reclined against the edge of a metal desk. "It's good to finally meet you, lad. You ready for a test run?"

Chase cast a glance across the semicircle of faces waiting for his response, peered behind him into the garage, and scratched his chin. "You want me to work on one of these cars *now?*"

"We got a '55 Chrysler 300 in yesterday, just waiting for you to get your hands on her." Grizzly Beard pulled a clipboard off the desk and rested the bottom edge against his thigh. "Not to put any pressure on you, lad, but Earl here hasn't stopped tooting your horn since he got back from the Carolinas. Seems you have a reputation to live up to."

Yep, no pressure at all. Chase rubbed a hand up and down the back of his hair. "I don't know about that, but I'll do the best I can."

"That's good to hear." The old man met him across the room and landed a solid grasp to Chase's upper arm. "'Cause the best is all we accept."

If he read the intense look in his eyes right, "the best" didn't come with much leeway.

"You sure you're not trying to heap on the pressure?"

A raspy laugh similar to Earl's shook Grizzly Beard's stout shoulders. "Maybe a little." He nodded to the door. "C'mon. We'll get you set up in Bay One."

Chase's uncertain glance at Earl met an undaunted nod of confidence. This must've been what Livy felt like every time he brought up the coffee shop. It figured he'd get a heaping dose of his own medicine. Smiling to himself, he brushed off any hesitation and focused on why he was here to begin with.

Once he dove in, his admiration of classics mixed with his training and pushed all pressure further into the storm with each minute that passed. It wasn't work. It was fun.

Earl tossed him a rag as Chase rose from the stool he'd been wheeling around the car on.

Chase wiped the Bondo off his hands and checked the clock. "Did your partners already leave?"

"Got cranky wives to get home to." Earl winked. "Teasing. Their eyesight ain't what it used to be. Don't you worry, though. They'll inspect your work first thing tomorrow in the daylight."

"You too?"

"Aw, I've seen enough already." He traced a hand over the classy twin tower taillights. "You'll pass with flying colors, kid. I'm not worried about that in the least."

That made one of them. Chase looked from the coupe's smooth rear-quarter panel to the creased wrinkles jutting out from the corners of Earl's eyes. "Something else have you worried?"

"By the time you reach my age, you learn worry's nothing but wasted energy." He hung the key to the Chrysler in a key box on the wall. "But I'm not gonna sugarcoat it for you, son. You have some competition—qualified candidates eager and ready to accept our offer."

Chase slung the rag over his shoulder. "I wouldn't expect any less."

"That's what I like about you. And you know I'll go to bat on your behalf." Sliding him a fatherly glance, he nestled a newsboy cap on his head. "As long as it's what you truly want."

It would help if Chase knew the answer to that himself. He used his Swiss Army knife to pick off a dried spot of Bondo left on his nail. "I appreciate all you've offered me so far. And I don't mean to string you along at all, but…"

"But you have choices to make." Earl fastened the top button on his raincoat. "I understand. No one wants you to make them lightly." His gaze glided past him to the counter where a blue light blinked on Chase's cell.

Reception. Finally. He'd been too caught up in the work to check or notice until now. He hustled over to his phone.

"Just remember, kid, all choices have ripples." He unhooked what must have been his own keyring. "It's up to us to decide which way we want the current to run."

He made it sound so easy, so certain.

Earl crossed the floor toward the doorway but stopped beside him first. "We need an answer in two weeks, or we'll have to go with one of the other candidates."

"Fair enough."

He patted Chase's shoulder again. "I'm gonna lock everything up. Walk you out in a few?"

"Sure, that'd be great." Eyes on his phone, he swiped the screen. "I just need to—"

"Weigh those choices." Earl waved behind him on his way out. "Holler when you're ready."

Chase pulled up his messages the second he was alone. Mom, Quinn, and even Cooper had called, but hearing Livy's voice was what he'd been waiting for most.

"... Please... call me back when you can."

Chase scrolled to her number without wasting time figuring out what to say.

Answering on the first ring, she didn't give him the chance anyway. "Chase Thompson." A wave of relief merged into her frantic answer. "Tell me you're alive. Because if you're not, I'm gonna kill you."

He laughed. "Um, you know that doesn't even make—"

"Shut up and talk to me. Where are you? I mean, I know you're in Illinois, but are you okay? None of us could get through to you, and I swear Coop's about ready to bust out some tranquilizers for Quinn and me. Don't get me started on how much coffee we've had today. Or cupcakes. For real, don't ask."

She took a breath. "Oh, and speaking of that... your loophole? Very clever. Quinn's all over it, but I wanted you to know I'm making my own. Well, sort of. I decided to apply for a business loan. Evelyn's not the only investor out there, right? Just 'cause she turned me down doesn't mean every bank in the area will." She paused, probably chewing her pinky the way she did when she was thinking. "You don't think this is crazy, do you? Ugh, it is, isn't it? I don't know. I felt so sure before, but now... Chase?"

"Yeah, I'm here." And ever amused at her adorable, spastic ramblings. Man, he missed that. Missed her, even after just a few days.

Leaning an arm into the door trim, he stared across the dim garage. Earl and his partners deserved an answer soon. Dad deserved access to the meds he needed. And Livy deserved a life she still wrestled to believe she was worthy of. Chase rubbed his eyes. Did he really have a say over which way the current ran?

He scanned the garage full of dream cars and the dream job that went with them—all within grasp, ready to help him overcome the financial barrier preventing him from taking care of his parents. The choice should be easy. There was just one problem. Broken or not, he couldn't shut off the part inside him that would go dark without Livy in his life.

"Chase? Please say something. What are you thinking about?"

What he always thought about—the one who held his heart most.

"You."

CHAPTER EIGHTEEN

Key

Livy jogged to her front door. With Chase being gone all week, the doorbell hadn't gotten much use lately. "Just a minute." She balanced her mug so it didn't spill and swung open the door but might as well have walked right into it. She did a double-take. "Ti?"

She posed like a model, a series of bangles clinking down her arms. "In the flesh."

Livy peeked over Ti's shoulder to her empty smart car parked on the street. "What are you doing here?"

"Um, hello, you *do* remember the 'burns his britches' comment, right?" Flashing her contagious smile, she pulled Livy into a hug. "What do you think I'm doing here, chica? I came to rescue you from yourself. Now, c'mon." She dragged Livy inside by the hand. "We have work to do."

"Work?" Whatever that meant, Livy was positive she didn't want any part of it. "Ti, I—"

"Eh." She made a zip-it motion with her hand, which Livy automatically obeyed. Jeez, she was getting good at her new mom role. Ti tugged Livy onto the middle of the living room floor with her, set Livy's coffee mug aside, and rested their joined hands on her crisscrossed knees.

The clock ticked between wordless blinks. If Ti stared any deeper, she'd drive Bandit right out of his therapist job.

Livy scrunched her lips to the side. "You didn't bring your oil diffuser, did you? Because this is about to get weird."

"Girl, from what your eyes are telling me, you need a lot more than a little aromatherapy."

"Um... thanks?"

Ti's two-tiered earrings jangled as she sat back. "You're hopelessly in love with Chase. Admit it."

Blunt as usual.

Livy swiped her mug off the floor. "I'm not *hopelessly* in love with him." She looked from the picture of her and Chase on her end table back to Eagle Eye picking apart her soul. "I'm..." She traced the top of her mug with her nail until her shoulders finally fell. "Daft. Utterly, *hopelessly* daft." Tears confirming it, Livy set her coffee down again and faced her sweet friend. "How could I let myself fall completely in love with a man I can't be with?"

"We *are* talking about the same guy you're totally going to end up marrying, right?"

Livy made a face at her. "That's the issue." She scooted across the floor and flopped back against the closest husband pillow, missing Chase being in the one beside her. "He's the kind of guy you dream of marrying. Since he was a kid, he's been praying for the family he's always wanted. For the girl he's been waiting for all this time." She balled a throw pillow under her arms. "He's saved himself for his wife, Ti, and I..."

She closed her eyes at memories that would never release her. "I'm…"

"The girl he wants."

"But I can't—"

"Yes, you can." Ti scooted across the floor and leaned a shoulder into hers. "Remember what you told me the summer I met Drew?"

Livy rolled the corner of the pillow down. "That's different."

"Sure it is. 'Cause this doesn't look at all like you're sabotaging the things you think you don't deserve." A pointed brow daring her to deny it kept Livy from arguing. "You told me who I am isn't what holds me back. It's who I think I'm not." Ti laced her fingers through Livy's and rested her head on her shoulder. "Don't give in to that same lie."

Teary again, and probably in more need of that silly oil diffuser than she wanted to admit, Livy drew her knees to her chest and whispered, "I can't hurt him, Ti."

"Then give him the honesty he deserves." She swatted Livy's leg with the back of her hand. "And put a little faith in love. It covers more than you think, girl. Trust me."

Drew and Ti's story had proven that true. Livy had even reminded Cooper of the very same thing last summer. But what she'd told Ti back in Ocracoke was true too. Somehow, love was always easier to give than to accept.

She breathed in, out. Leaning on Ti's faith, she sat up. "Okay."

Ti followed. "Okay?"

"Okay, I promise I'll tell him when he gets back from Chicago. You're right. He deserves to know, and I..." Her brows rumpled. "Will *try* to trust things will work out."

A flicker of sunlight caught Ti's smile. "And I'll *try* to resist leaving the bottle of lavender oil I have for you in the car." She hopped to her feet. "But seriously, I'm ordering you a diffuser when I get home."

"Of course you are." Livy started after her when she crossed the room to the door. "Wait, you're leaving already?"

"Maddy's helping Drew make spaghetti and meatballs tonight. No way I'm missing that love fest." Ti spun around in her sparkly flip-flops, pulled her keys from her pocket, and aimed them at Livy. "But if I don't get a wedding invitation in the next month, I'm coming back."

Ignoring the bait, Livy shook her head at her crazy friend. "I can't believe you drove all this way just to stay for ten minutes."

"It's not that far of a drive. Even if it were, you know I'd still come in a heartbeat if you needed me."

What was with Livy's emotions lately? She tugged Ti into a hug before she cried. "Thank you," she said, her thick voice adding everything she couldn't get out.

"You can thank me by going and living happily ever after with your cowboy." Ti untangled herself from an embrace Livy wasn't quite ready to let go of, opened her car door, and stopped halfway in. "Are you guys going to ride off on a horse after your wedding? You are, aren't you?"

"Bye, Ti." Eyes rolling, Livy waved her on. "Give my love to everyone." Some days, she missed her old life in Ocracoke.

But after living in Littleton this past year, she couldn't imagine being anywhere else, and she knew exactly why.

Back inside, she made a beeline for her abandoned coffee cup. Before she reached it, Bandit scrambled out of wherever he'd been sleeping and almost slid face-first into the front door. He pawed at it, whining.

Livy strolled over to peek out the window. "Aw, did you want to meet...? Oh." She squinted toward the Toyota parked in Mrs. Finch's driveway. "Now, how'd you know your mama was home already?"

With his tail wagging fast enough to sand the veneer off the floor, Bandit barked until she opened the door. Once outside, he sprinted across the yards, landed his front paws on the passenger door, and licked every inch of the window.

Livy jogged over as Mrs. Finch was getting out. "Someone's sure glad you're back."

"That makes two of us." She ruffled the dog's ears as he doused her in welcome-home slobber. "You haven't been getting in trouble without me, have you, you big goober?"

If she only knew.

"No getting into any trouble, Mama." Tessa closed the trunk and wheeled a walker toward her mom. "Doc Jenkins said to take it easy for a while."

Mrs. Finch glared at the walker. "How can I possibly get in to anything while handcuffed to that silly old thing?"

"Somehow, I'm sure you'll find a way," Tessa called on her way to the front door.

Mrs. Finch winked at Bandit, and Livy hid a smile. Still as spunky as ever. And apparently as determined as Chase had guessed she would be.

Livy scratched her calf with her sandal. "You know, Chase wagered you'd be back home by the end of the week."

"Well, of course he did, hun. That boy's got a good head on his shoulders." Leaning on her walker, she slanted an intuitive look Livy's way. "That kind of instinct's worth trusting."

Fantastic. Now, she had a second pair of soul-searching eyes reading into her today. Livy lifted a hand to her neck and looked out to the street.

Thankfully, Mrs. Finch didn't let the pause linger.

"How's that bid for the café coming, sweet pea? I'm afraid I can't keep up with the taxes much longer, and I'd sure love to see you in there instead of a pizza chain."

Livy glanced from Mrs. Finch to Tessa unlocking the front door. This wasn't incredibly awkward or anything. "Oh, um." She swiped at a hair tickling her arm, hating the thought of letting her down. "I sort of made a real mess of my first interview, but I'm gonna do everything I can to land a loan this time. If there's any chance I can meet my son, I have to make this work before then." She was running out of time. Any day now, she'd be hearing back from Tanner's caseworker on whether the Bradleys had agreed to let her visit him.

"I see." Mrs. Finch's eyes dimmed, and something about them made Livy's do the same.

She looked away, wiped her arm again. Why couldn't she find that sorry strand of hair?

Tessa came back down the walkway. "You ready for some coffee?"

"You know I am." Mrs. Finch patted Bandit's head. "Livy, hun, would you mind watching him a little longer for me?" She steadied herself with the walker again. "Some things you just can't rush."

There was that intuitive gaze again.

Livy knelt in front of Bandit, who went right to her. "I'd be happy to."

"Thata girl." She waved Livy up for a hug. "Now you'll have an excuse to come visit an old widow every once in a while."

Livy squeezed her tight. "No excuses needed."

Mrs. Finch leaned back and dished out the sassy smile Livy had missed. "You bring that good-looking Thompson boy with you next time, and I'll be sure to have some sweet tea ready."

Livy laughed. "The key to his heart."

"Now, sweet pea." She patted Livy's hand. "We both know I'm not the one who holds that." Before Livy could deflect yet again, Mrs. Finch motioned for Tessa to help her to the house and winked at Bandit one last time. "You be sure to save some mischief for me, you hear?"

Livy would've laughed if all of Mrs. Finch's insinuations weren't reminding her of the promise she'd just made to Ti. Even the messes Bandit got himself into couldn't top the one Livy might make by telling Chase everything.

It'd be okay, though, wouldn't it?

Searching for the faith everyone but her seemed to have, Livy faced a sky on the hinge of dusk and sighed. One more night 'til Chase was home. One more day 'til she found out if the truth would cost her the key Mrs. Finch was so sure she held.

CHAPTER NINETEEN

More

Chase parked in front of Livy's house and breathed at the sight of her sitting on the porch like she had when he'd first met her at her parents' place. Just as gorgeous now, she curled an arm around her long legs and a bashful smile around his heart.

He'd been away from her for a week before, but something about this time got to him. He swallowed while climbing out of his truck's cab. Only halfway up the driveway did he notice she was on her cell. He slowed a few feet away as she ended the call.

"That was Jed." Livy set her phone on the step. "I haven't talked to the guy since that day he was here. Then he calls out of the blue last night to tell me he's going to make a trip home on his day off. Now he can't fit it in."

The lack of surprise in her voice tugged at Chase's insides. *Wait.* He rewound what she'd just said. "You haven't talked to him since before we went camping?"

"No, why?"

Way to jump to conclusions, Thompson. Chase shook his head. "No reason." He leaned against the railing and helped her to her feet. "I'm just surprised he hasn't figured it out yet."

"Figured what out?"

Holding her gaze, Chase slid her hair free from behind her ear. "That you're a girl worth always coming home to."

The vein in her neck thrummed under his touch as he edged in to kiss her cheek.

When he leaned back, she stayed in place with her line of sight glued to the grass. An awkward silence replaced the familiar camaraderie they'd left somewhere back on their camp site over a week ago. He'd really messed things up, hadn't he?

Chin down, Livy ran the bracelets on her wrist up and down her arm. "I know I don't have a right to say anything, but why didn't you tell me you were going to Chicago before you left?"

Chase faced the cloudless sky and inhaled. He'd been so frustrated with her for not trusting him enough to be honest, but in all reality, he'd kept things from her too. "I was going to stop by on my way to the airport, but..."

She took a hesitant step forward. "But?"

He lowered his head, smiled sadly. "I ran out of time." He'd thought he had anyway. Thought he'd lost his chance with her. "I should've told you. I'm sorry."

"No, I'm so sorry." The words flew out like they'd been suspended against a springboard for months. "I never should've kept secrets from you. I was scared. Afraid of what would change. Of what I could lose." The fear in her voice reached for her eyes. "Then with that storm and not knowing whether... If anything were to happen to you..."

"Hey, I made you a promise, remember?" Breathing in the familiar fragrance of coffee and fresh laundry, he closed her in both arms and held on to a dream he wasn't ready to let go of yet. If he still had a shot, he wouldn't jeopardize it this time.

Livy hooked her arms around his neck and pressed in tight. The awkwardness subsided. And this time, the silence felt like home.

She lowered to her heels, slipped her hands in her back pockets, and pulled in her bottom lip just like he'd pictured her doing a dozen times while he was away. Dodging his eyes, she crossed and uncrossed her arms twice before stowing her hands in her pockets again. "There's something I need to tell you."

The gravity in her voice launched a seed of unease sprouting through his tendons. He'd been so determined to know what she'd been keeping from him, the possibility that he might not be ready to hear it had never registered. Until right then.

"There's actually something I need to tell you too." He willed his usual playfulness to sound more natural than it felt. "But right now, we have coaching sessions to catch up on."

"We don't have to keep doing that."

"Of course we do. We lost a whole week." And he didn't want to waste a second more.

When she didn't look convinced, he dipped his head under hers. "If you're going to be meeting a lender about a loan, now's the time to get that confidence level where it belongs, right? Think of it as more of a dual-purpose practice date this round." With her hand in his, he led her toward his truck.

"Wait, now? Where are we going?"

He smiled over his shoulder. "You'll see."

A coffee shop definitely wasn't what Livy had expected. But now that they were here, enveloped in an aroma of roasted beans and flavored liqueurs, she had to admit it was exactly what she needed. Even the eclectic artwork lining the walls sang her love language.

At the counter, Chase leaned an arm beside the register and hitched the kind of smile capable of speaking a thousand words to her—the fact that he was up to something being top of the list.

She mirrored his pose. "A coffee date, huh? You do know *I'd* be the coach on this one, right? I mean, coffee *is* sorta my jam."

His freckles quirked. "Good thing. 'Cause your *jam* is about to be put to the test. That is, if you're up for a little friendly competition."

Against that merciless grin? Probably not the wisest idea. "What are you talking about?"

He lifted off the counter. "It's time to show off those skills under pressure."

Um, he did know her, right? She and pressure didn't exactly mesh together so well. Hello, she couldn't even pee in the presence of random forest animals.

One of the café's employees set two aprons in front of them, to which Chase offered a quick chin flick of thanks.

He slid the strap of one over her head and picked up the second. "All you have to do is beat me in a game of roast off."

Livy cracked a laugh. "Did you just say roast—?"

"Roll with it." He took his cowboy hat off to put on the apron. "Four drinks. Ten minutes. Two taste testers."

"You want to race me in making coffee?" He had to be joking. "Do you even know how to use an espresso machine?"

Grin to the side, Chase tucked his hat back on. "Patience and persistence."

Livy looped the straps around to the front of her apron, tied them in a knot, and eyed her opponent. "This is one time you're gonna eat those words, Chase Thompson."

Visibly holding in a laugh, he scuffed the back of his hand under his chin. "We'll see." He flagged down the guy behind the counter. "Phil, you ready for us?"

"You're all set up in the back, bro."

"Thanks, man." Chase swung an arm in front of Livy toward a door off to the side.

She went through first, surveying the utility room and the little coffee bar area they must've set up for Chase's mastermind showdown. The guy really was something else.

A list of four drinks ran down a sheet of paper in between the two stations. Cinnamon Dolce Latte, Caramel Macchiato, Iced Skinny Mocha, and a simple Flat White. She could taste the delectable flavors just thinking about them. "After I toast you, we get to drink at least one of these, right?" The mocha was seriously calling her name right now.

"*If* you toast me."

Please.

Chase set a countdown on his phone and placed it between them. "On your mark."

Livy grabbed an espresso tamper. "Are you sure you want to do this?"

"Get set."

She countered his maddening grin. "Don't say I didn't warn you."

"Go."

Keeping the timer in sight, Livy had the first two drinks done before Chase had even figured out how to use the steam wand. She fought a laugh, but when a dollop of foamy milk sprayed up his nose, she lost it.

"Here." She took his hands and showed him how to use the frothing pitcher correctly. "See? You want to..." She looked up to find Chase's eyes on her instead of the pitcher. *Breathe.* One look. That's all it ever took to show her how much he cared about her.

Regaining her composure, she motioned to the milk still on his nose. "You saving that for later?"

The corner of his mouth curled. "Saving it for *you*."

She backed up. "Don't even think about it."

Right. Unstoppable mischievousness teemed in every step toward her.

"Chase!"

Too late. He caught her hands, nuzzled his head to the side of her neck, and wiped the now-cold, frothy milk onto her skin. "Five minutes left. You're not getting distracted, are you?"

From having his lips nearly graze her ear? Distracted was one word for it.

Fighting for restraint, Livy maneuvered under his arm back to her station. "Too bad for you, *I* can multitask." She grabbed the chocolate drizzle bottle, squirted it in Chase's direction while spraying whipped cream over her next drink, and then circled the drizzle on top. Perfect.

The timer went off as Livy turned to a chocolate-striped face closing in on her. "You lose," she gloated.

"I don't know. I think I might have to disqualify you for interference." He wiped a finger across a streak running down his chin. "Or at least level the playing field."

He stole the squeeze bottle before she ever moved and squirted it across her face like an artist lost in creating an abstract masterpiece. His hat fell off when she chased him, hands blocking the gooey spray.

Phil and a woman with a tag that read *Trish Allen, Manager* walked through the door. "You ready for us?"

Livy and Chase both froze. Ready to crawl under the table to hide, maybe. Despite what they must've looked like, they attempted to pull off a halfway dignified response.

"Yep." Chase picked his hat up and strode over to the one drink he'd made. "Just adding the last touches."

"I see that." Trish looked between them on her way to the table. At least she was smiling.

Chase rubbed his hands together. "Livy might've made more than me, but we still have the taste test."

"No, we don't." Face scrunched, Trish set Chase's mug down. "Definitely a 'no' to whatever *that's* supposed to be."

His laugh bounced around the stainless-steel equipment. He motioned to the four mugs lined up in front of Livy. "Hers are safer. Trust me."

Phil and Trish each tested out her finished drinks. Trish held on to one. "Girl, all I can say is you can have a job here any day."

Livy slid Chase an impressed glance. "Really?"

Phil clapped Chase on the back. "You, on the other hand, bro, better stick to cars."

Another laugh. "Point taken."

Trish followed Phil out but stopped at the door and took another sip of the macchiato. "If you ever need someone to vouch for you, give me a holler."

Once the door swung behind them, Livy joined Chase at the three-part industrial sink. "You planned this, didn't you?"

Beside her, he took the pitcher and dried it with a rag. "Planned what?"

"Getting me a referral from a local café manager."

"That was all you."

"Uh-huh." She rinsed out his mug. "Just like your loophole was all Quinn."

"Hey, you're the one who set up a meeting with the bank all on your own." He wiped a spot of chocolate she must've missed on her cheek. "And look what you just did here. Tackled an assignment, showed up your competition, and let that confidence shine." He winked. "Whether a date or an investor, they're gonna walk away impressed with Livy Hensley."

She would've waved him off if his thoughtfulness weren't pulling at her heartstrings. Once again, he'd gotten her to see the potential he saw in her. Had gotten her to feel confident, hopeful, even talented. She toyed with her apron belt. "Maybe."

"Definitely." His grin pulled to the side as his thumb glided over her cheek. "I mean, who couldn't take this chocolate-drizzled face seriously?"

Fighting the urge to pop him with the rag, Livy brought her hand to his wrist instead. Wrong move. It took all her willpower not to draw his palm to her lips. Her eyes gravitated to his instead. Swallowing, she ran her fingers away from his hand up his defined arm. Her lashes feathered together, no amount of deep breaths helping. Attraction, she'd known. This was more, deeper. It had been from the very beginning.

Chase tipped his head at her. "Are you all right?"

Only if turning hotter than the steamer passed for all right. She had so much to explain, so much to tell him. But standing here now, the only words coming to mind were the only ones that mattered. She loved him. And it was time he knew how much.

She turned toward the table and filled a to-go cup with the rest of the mocha mix that had been calling her name. If anything would help, it had to be coffee. She chugged a good half of the cup, breathed some more, and curved her braid over her shoulder. "Chase, when you were gone, and we couldn't get ahold of you, I realized something."

The same apprehension from earlier when she'd mentioned she had something to tell him shaded his eyes again.

"Hold that thought," he whipped off as quickly as she normally talked.

Okay, something was definitely wrong here. Before she could ask, Chase had her hand in his and her feet trying to keep up with him.

"Date's not over yet."

As nervous as she was to tell him how she felt, she was even more afraid to ask what he had planned next.

CHAPTER TWENTY

Ripples

Chase hooked his thumbs in his belt loops as they strolled along the road circling the lake. Between the glimmers of moonlight reflecting off the water and the faintest sound of music from a nearby pier, he couldn't have cued the setting any better. Even the humidity seemed to take a bow for the evening. Instead, a cool breeze fanned Livy's fresh cotton scent around his already-uncooperative lungs.

With her hands around her coffee cup, she took in the lake as though it held answers she was searching for.

Chase released a slow exhale. It would've been easier to coach her to have confidence if he could've found some of his own. He hadn't meant to cut her off back there, but something about the gravity in whatever she'd wanted to say triggered a reflex to stall. He needed more time. Needed to be sure he'd shown her why they should be together before she made her choice.

He had the rest of the night still. He could do this.

Keeping things light, he nudged her with his shoulder. "If this were a real date, I might put an arm around you right now."

A slanted look tipped his way. "If this were a real date, I might let you."

"We should probably test this out. You know, for practice."

"Uh-huh." She leaned into his side. "How's this?"

He savored the feel of her nestled under his shoulder the way he'd always known was right. "Perfect," he whispered. Considering she didn't pull away, maybe *more* than perfect. "Thanks for letting me take you out tonight."

"Have you met my hard-nosed coach? He doesn't let me give up on something I've started."

"Sounds like the guy knows what he's doing."

"He seems to think so."

More like he *hoped* so. Would it be enough?

Chase ran his hand down her arm. "Well, it helps when your student's already a natural at dating."

Livy snorted. "A natural at falling for guys I can't keep interested long enough to stick around. Yep, that's definitely one for the resumé."

He stopped at her jaded tone. "You mean Jed?"

"Among others," she mumbled. She stared across the lake again and dragged her nail along the cardboard sleeve around her coffee cup. "Honestly, I can't blame him. I haven't exactly been Miss Consistent around him."

Chase took his hat off and fiddled with the brim. "Maybe that's 'cause you're not in love with him."

Her chest rose and fell to the rhythm of the cicadas in the background when he turned to face her. "What if risking love changes everything?"

Was that what she was worried about?

Chase tugged his hat back on and kept his head down a moment before looking up with every certainty inside him. "We'll never find what we want most if we're not willing to take risks."

The sheen building in her eyes nearly matched the glassy lake top. She blinked toward the fuchsia crape myrtles bordering the bank. Another breeze swept up the seconds passing by unanswered. A strip of bark dropped into the still water. The farther out the ripples fanned, the farther a gradual smile drove away whatever Livy was still guarding inside.

"If you're dying to say what I want includes a wedding in a barn, the rest of this mocha might end up on your shirt."

Chase's shoulders relaxed at her playful tone. He rubbed his knuckles down his jaw. "You gotta admit, marrying a hunky cowboy wouldn't be so bad."

"Mm." She turned, started down the road again, and glanced behind her. "Let me know where I can find one."

"Ohh!" He jabbed a fist to his heart. "Merciless."

Her laughter trailed into the sound of geese honking up ahead.

"If it makes you feel any better," she said over her shoulder. "Jimmy Sterling didn't have nearly as cool of a supervillain name as Boots."

Off near a bush, a goose zeroed in on Livy, extended his long neck to the ground, and hissed. Oh, this could be bad.

"Um, Liv?"

"As much as Wesley drives me crazy, I gotta hand it to him for nailing that one."

The goose stretched his wings out.

"No, Liv, you might want to—"

"Milk it for all it's worth?" Laughing, she whirled around. "You better believe I'm—" She took one look at the goose and morphed into a statue.

Chase looked between them, his arms extended like a referee. "Don't move."

Too late. The silent standoff ended the second Livy backed up. The goose charged, and she sprinted in the opposite direction. "Chase!"

"Stay calm. I'm sure he's not gonna hurt..."

The goose cleared the ground and flapped straight for her.

"... you."

Livy ran in her heels with her coffee cup flailing above her like some kind of peace offering. Unimpressed, the bird knocked her smack upside the head with his feet. The coffee cup dropped to the ground, Livy right behind it. She covered her head, swearing at the goose like he could understand her.

Chase rushed beside her. "You all right?"

"Is he gone?"

The goose circled around and soared back to what looked like a nest under the bush. That would explain things.

"All clear."

She rolled onto her back. "Tell me that didn't just happen."

He tried not to laugh at a scene only Livy could pull off. Epic fail. "Oh, no, an all-out chase with a goose definitely just happened."

She sat up and flicked an acorn at him. "So much for my *hunky cowboy* rescuing me."

"Hey, Papa Goose was protecting his family. There's no getting in the middle of that. Trust me."

Something shifted in Livy's eyes as she peered up at him from the grass. She studied him. The street quieted. And in a matter of seconds, the hilarity of the random messes she got herself into faded with the fog rising around the lake.

A pang of self-consciousness passed through him at the look on her face. "What?"

With a smile too fragile to last, she grazed her fingers through the hair around his ear. "You may have a lame super-villain name, Chase Thompson, but you're gonna make an amazing father one day. I know I get a lot of things wrong, but that I'm positive of."

The unexpected compliment spoke straight to the doubts she couldn't have known about and drove him back against his heels. "You don't know how much I want you to be right." Or how hard he'd tried to prove it.

"What are you talking about?" She looked at him with every ounce of faith he wished were his own.

He dragged a finger through the loose rocks between the grass and road, not wanting to dig up his past, his doubts. "Nothing. Everything going on with my dad right now is getting to me. That's all." The need to tell her about Earl's offer throbbed in his chest. "That's actually part of why I went to

Illinois last week. While there, I sort of... had... an interview."

"An interview?" The hundreds of questions written on her face nearly drowned him in the ones he still hadn't answered himself.

"For a job with Gateway Classic Cars."

"*The* Gateway Classic Cars?"

He laughed. "That's what I said. I still can't believe they made me an offer. It all feels kinda surreal."

Blue eyes searched his, making this even harder than he anticipated. "Did you take it?" she asked slowly.

"Not yet. I have until Tuesday to decide." The weight of the decision drove his shoulders toward the ground. "It's a great opportunity. One that could open the doors for me to get my dad the treatment he needs." He rubbed his wrist. "Honestly, there's a lot there I've always wanted, but... it'd mean leaving Littleton." And her.

A painfully quiet minute lapsed with nothing but crickets filling in the conversation he wasn't sure how to continue.

Livy set a hand on his arm, and when he raised his head, only compassion looked back at him. "It's your dream job, Chase. No one would blame you for moving on. Believe me, it's easy to find a hundred reasons to leave."

He held on to her gaze, wanting so much for her to understand. "But I just need one reason to stay."

Seconds stalled in the wind.

She turned toward the lake again, and her voice barely crested the distant flutter in the trees. "Someday, you'll find that reason."

"Someday, I can wait for." He brushed a feather off her bangs. "You'll be an amazing parent too, you know. An amazing wife. Whether you get married in a barn or not," he said with a wink. "There's so much future for you, Liv. As sure as you are about mine, I am about yours."

Panic stormed the hope losing the battle for her eyes. Her pulse raced under his thumb. "I should get home," she rattled off faster than the flag whipping back and forth at the end of the nearest dock. She jumped to her feet, leaving Chase in a whirlwind of confusion and frustration on the grass.

He took his hat off, raked his fingers through his hair, and tugged it back on. Would he ever get this right? Ever find the right time, the right words? She felt something for him. Even if she wasn't ready to admit it to herself yet, it was there. He could feel it.

A frustrated exhale worked its way up his chest as he rose. But when the creases around Livy's eyes mirrored the internal war he wanted to rescue her from, he backed off. He shouldn't be pushing her all over again.

She picked up the coffee cup she'd dropped. "Being a zombie in the morning isn't gonna help my chances at the bank. And knowing my luck, Bandit's probably turned my place into a scene from *Marley and Me* by now."

Hidden tremors betrayed her fast ramblings. "Did I tell you Mrs. Finch is home already? She still can't get around very well, so I agreed to watch Bandit a little longer. I'm probably crazy for keeping him inside, but he flaunts those blasted puppy dog eyes at me, and—"

"Livy." He lifted her chin and tried again when she still didn't look up from the ground. "Liv…"

A long blink and an even longer inhale slowly brought eyes torn between emotions toward his. "You shouldn't have to wait for someday, Chase."

He drew her close, rested his chin over her head, and whispered a truth he wouldn't stop fighting for her to believe on her own. "Neither should you."

Unlike when they were trying to pull the hatchet out of that log at the camp site, this time when she leaned into him, he knew she wasn't playing dating games. She was scared. Of what, he still wasn't sure. The only thing he knew was he'd hold her forever if she'd let him.

He didn't press the conversation on the drive home. Didn't try to fill the silence with music or idle talk. Instead, he let the promise in his words settle into the hidden crevices where only hope could reach.

Back at Livy's place, he took her hand as she unbuckled her seat belt. "Before you go, I need to apologize."

"No, you don't." The words sounded as fragile as the vulnerability keeping her head down.

"Yeah, I do." He took off his hat and waited for her to look up from the floorboard. "I told you love doesn't abandon, and I meant that, but loving you doesn't give me the right to cross boundaries. I'm sorry for not respecting your choice to keep parts of your life private. I had no right to ask for your trust when I wasn't willing to give you the same. You deserve better than that."

Tears filled a look deep enough to house the silence filling his truck. One moment stretched into another before Livy finally turned for the door, hesitated, and then stretched across the seats. She pressed a kiss to his cheek and an even softer whisper to his heart. "I love you, Chase."

He caught her hand once more. Neither of them moved. Their shoulders rose and fell in breaths saying everything they weren't.

She had to have felt his feelings for her pulsing through his heartbeat, but he didn't care. "One more date, Liv. A real one. Tomorrow." He rubbed the backs of her fingers. "Please."

Livy hung her head, still without facing him, and closed her eyes. "Tomorrow."

She'd made it out of his Chevy and into her house before he released the edge of his hat and the words he wasn't ready to let go of yet. Staring up at her front window, Chase breathed in. Somewhere beyond the doubts and insecurities, she had to see that the someday she longed for was right in front of her.

And he had one week left to prove it.

His nerves twitched. Knowing what he had to do, he traded his hat for his phone and scrolled to a number he'd probably regret calling.

Cooper answered on the third ring. "'Sup, hoss?"

"Hey, man, I have a favor to ask. I need your help with something, and I need it fast. But..." He peered through the windshield to the lamplit porch he was still hoping to kiss Livy on one day. "If you so much as tell *anyone* about this, I'll kill you."

Cooper placed the hand Chase had already pulled away twice back to his waist and tugged him close. "Now, dip me."

"Come again?"

"Dip me."

Chase's gaze zigzagged around all four corners of the living room's ceiling while he tried to avoid bumping faces with him. "There are limits, man."

Getting this up close and personal with his sister's husband was most certainly one of them.

"If you want to show Livy you can dance, you need to be smooth, skilled." His dimples danced all on their own. "Debonair."

If Chase managed to be anything other than nauseated right now, he'd really be accomplishing something.

"You've gotta be willing to take the lead." Cooper pulled Chase's torso tight to his.

"Oooh-kay, this isn't happening." Chase pushed away and pinched the bridge of his nose. "You know what? I'm just gonna wing it."

"Bad idea, hoss. You know how many times you've stepped on my feet in the last hour?"

About as many times as Chase regretted thinking that coming to Mr. Ladies' Man for dancing lessons was a wise move.

Of all the things Livy could love, why did she have to pick the one thing that sent Chase's nerves into a tailspin?

Cooper grabbed his hand again. "C'mon, you gotta at least nail the dip."

The dip in his sanity was already one too many.

Footsteps shuffled in through the front door. Chase and Cooper broke apart but not soon enough. Even Brayden laughed at the pair of them. Quinn let go of her son's hand and raised an overly amused brow their way. "Um, what are you two doing?"

"Nothing," they said in unison.

Nothing other than incriminating themselves. At least Cooper had held up his side of the deal in keeping the lessons a secret.

Cooper turned off the music from his iPhone dock while Chase dug out his Swiss Army knife, which suddenly became the world's most interesting gadget known to man.

The second he risked tearing his focus from it to his sister, she slid him a dangerously perfect replica of Cooper's dimple-bookended grin. That was definitely his cue.

"You know, I was just leaving." Apart from dodging her amusement, he was out of time anyway. He brushed a quick kiss to Quinn's cheek on his way by.

"Where are you running off to so fast?"

"He's got a date." Cooper swept Brayden off the ground into a whirling hug.

Brayden giggled his infamous request. "Again! Again!"

Quinn smiled from them to Chase. "A date, huh? Care to fill me in?"

Not particularly. "Later," he called as the door closed behind him.

A lot of good escaping his sister's scrutiny did for his nerves. His muscles had relaxed once he'd gotten in his Silverado. But by the time he pulled up to Livy's house, the tick of the clock running out pounded in his chest. He took one last swig of his sweet tea, fit his hat on, and stared himself down in the rearview mirror. "You can do this."

Bandit all but tackled him halfway up the lawn.

"You better watch out," Livy said from the porch. "That dog turns into Houdini when we're not looking." She pulled herself up by the rail. "I used to think Mrs. Finch kept leaving the back door open, but now, I swear he opens it by himself somehow."

Chase led Bandit up the steps and inside the house by the collar. "Nothing like a little mystery to keep life interesting." He moseyed back down and kissed her cheek. "Speaking of which, ready for our last date?"

Her eyes narrowed. "If you weren't so cryptic about it on the phone, I might've at least known how to dress."

A glimpse over her sundress, jean jacket, and cowgirl boots gave Cooper's dimples a run for their money. "You couldn't be more perfect."

In the wind, her hair fell loose from her braid, and his heart fell a little more.

She twisted a button on her jacket enough times to unlock the familiar awkwardness becoming too frequent between them lately.

Claws clinked against the window beside the door. They both turned toward Bandit's wet nose smeared across the glass below big brown eyes it took a heart of steel to deny.

Three seconds of staring at his slobber running down the pane turned into a spastic game of him licking every trickle before it reached the sill.

Chase and Livy glanced at each other, and that was it. Genuine laughter broke the silence hovering between them.

He fiddled with his knife in his pocket. "Thanks for letting me take you out one more time." He wasn't sure she would after she'd flung her walls up again during their walk by the lake. Given how hesitant she looked right now, he'd guess she wasn't so sure herself.

"One of the girls at Long Shots owed me for covering her shift." Looking off to the side, she ran her fingers up and down her arm. "I asked Wesley to keep an eye out for Bandit, but I probably shouldn't stay out too long. He got in a scrap with one of Mr. Hood's beagles last night." The smallest smile crinkled her eyes. "I think they're fighting over a new lady friend on the other side of the woods. Silly dog's been whining at the back door all day."

Chase knew the feeling. He squeezed his shoulder blade. "I don't blame him. When we find a lady worth fighting for, it's hard for us not to go all in."

Rather than evading eye contact this time, Livy looked him over, and a hint of the sass he was starting to miss played with her lips. "If 'going all in' includes trading your T-shirts for a button-down, those ladies better watch out." A full smile hung on her words. "You clean up nicely, Chase Thompson."

"Thanks." He rolled up the sleeves on the shirt Cooper had lent him. "I'm trying to impress my date." He leaned a hand beside her on the rail. "Is it working?"

Not missing a beat, Livy adjusted his messy sleeve-roll job and patted him on the chest. "Who needs sharp clothes when all you have to do is turn up that southern charm?"

This close to her feisty grin, he'd be lucky to pull off coherent, let alone charming. Sunlight zeroed in on the back of his neck, heat spreading limb by limb.

Livy stepped away and circled her bracelets around her arm in one of her adorable nervous tics, and Chase adjusted his hat.

Before another wave of awkwardness could pull the tide out from under his plans, he fanned an arm toward his truck. "Guess we'll find out who's right." With a little luck, and way too much debt owed to Cooper, hopefully she'd finally see how all the dates leading to tonight proved they should be together.

She hopped into the cab of his truck and leaned through the open window when he closed the door for her. "What are you up to?"

"Who said I'm up to anything?"

"That crooked grin you can't shake, for starters." She studied him. "I swear, even your hat is smiling."

He tipped the front of it. "Can't blame a southern boy for looking forward to a summer country drive with a pretty girl." Around the hood of his truck, Chase climbed into the driver's seat in time to meet a deadpan stare.

"A summer drive."

"Hey, never underestimate the magic of a back-road sunset."

"Wow, country magic, huh?" Livy slipped her sunglasses on as if they could shield her laughter. "You're really pulling out all the stops on this one, aren't you?"

To win his best friend's heart? A little magic might be his only hope.

CHAPTER TWENTY-ONE

Limits

Fields of wildflowers surrounding an endless dirt road swayed close enough to the truck's windows that Livy could almost run her fingers through them. Could almost believe the things she wanted most weren't out of reach. But even here—in a place where country magic didn't seem so far-fetched—daydreams had their limits.

Livy twisted her lip back and forth, her promise to Ti gnawing at her. Last night, she'd wanted to tell Chase the truth. Had *needed* to tell him. And she would have if he hadn't dropped that bombshell about the job offer on her. This opportunity for him changed everything.

She let go of her lip and chewed her nail instead. Less than one week left. Tuesday, he'd decide whether he was leaving Littleton. How could she tell him she wanted to be with him now? As much as she didn't want him to leave, she wouldn't complicate his decision. His life, his choices—they should be easy for him. He deserved that, and so did his dad. If Chicago held the answers to helping him, then that's where Chase needed to be, no matter what it meant for her.

Livy grasped on to the country road's tranquility, breathed in, out, and buried her feelings deep below her diaphragm. She had to make it through their last date with her heart intact if she was going to find enough courage to say goodbye.

The engine's idle purr drew her gaze away from the fields to a curious look that seemed to wonder if she'd noticed that they'd parked.

"A thousand pennies for your thoughts?"

Livy clamped them farther down until she trusted her voice enough to pull off the lightheartedness she needed to make it through this. "Just anxious for this back-road magic you promised." She hopped out and winked.

"Then you better get ready." Chase joined her around the opposite end of the truck and lifted her onto the open tailgate. "Your terrace, ma'am."

She feigned a seated curtsey, but when he brought over two mugs and a thermos, she scrunched her nose at him. "Um, you know I love you, but please tell me you didn't try making coffee on your own."

His gentle laugh warmed over her. "Don't worry. I stole it from Quinn and Cooper's."

"What were you doing over there?"

He squeezed the back of his suntanned neck. "Don't ask."

"You kidding?" Livy twisted toward him. "Now, I *have* to know."

He chuckled. "Let's just say, you're not the only one who needs a coach from time to time." Chase lowered his mug. "Mm. Speaking of—" His cell rumbled against the truck bed.

Cringing at the interruption, he went to silence it but then stared at the screen.

From the glimpse Livy caught, it looked like the same Chicago number he'd said he didn't recognize back at her place the night Mrs. Finch had fallen.

"You need to take that?"

He looked up, brows knit together. "Nope. Whoever it is can wait." He slid the phone into his pocket. "Sorry. I was about to ask how things went at the bank this morning?"

"Oh." She fiddled with the hair tie at the end of her braid. "Really well, actually."

"Really well, as in you got the loan?"

Eyes brimming with hope and expectancy waited for the answer he'd always believed in, and all Livy could do was nod.

Chase didn't give her more than two seconds to put her mug down before he had her up and twirling in the air. "I knew you could do it." His enthusiasm swept through her until she felt like she was soaring.

When he finally lowered her boots to the grass, she kept her arms around his neck a moment longer. Too long. Her pulse sped, her smile fading.

He must've noticed. Yet, though his hands let go of her waist, his eyes didn't come anywhere near releasing her. "I'm so proud of you, Liv."

The simple words plucked dormant strings in her heart that had turned brittle with doubt long ago. Her heart compressed as her eyes roamed over him. This whole time, little by little, he'd been awakening a song inside her that years of shame had stolen. How could she do anything but offer him that same selfless friendship?

He swept her bangs to the side. "What is it?"

Don't you dare cry. "Nothing." She pulled away and brushed her fingertips through the tall grass. "It's just that the acceptance is only provisional right now, so I'm trying not to get too excited yet, but you know me. I'm already decorating the café in my head." She plucked a purple wildflower from the ground and coiled the stem around her finger. "I know I shouldn't get ahead of myself. Anything can happen, and if it doesn't work out, I—"

"Liv." Chase turned her around. "It never hurts to dream."

She swallowed at the dream his eyes made her want to live every day. "It's more complicated than that." And way too costly.

"It doesn't have to be."

Knowing he truly believed that dragged the broken flower out of her hand. She escaped back to the tailgate and the coffee she was going to need five more cups of if she had any chance of keeping her composure.

She laced her fingers through the mug handle. "Either way, I want to thank you for encouraging me to try again for the loan."

"You always had the confidence you needed." He sat beside her and nudged a shoulder into hers. "It just took a little faith to uncover it."

Borrowed faith, maybe.

"Still, I'm hereby officially eating my words. Your confidence coaching actually paid off."

"In dating too?" The slow, quiet words drifted across the open field.

Livy set her mug down and slipped her hands under her legs. "I never heard back from Jed, so I guess that's your answer. It's not your fault, though. Damaged goods don't tend to sell very well."

Chase turned to her then, and the way he looked at her singlehandedly ruined any chance of her heart staying intact. "Is that what you think you are?"

The cool metal dug into her fingers. "It's easier to think that way." Safer.

"I don't understand."

A part of her hoped he would never have to.

Searching for how to start, Livy avoided his eyes and expelled a long breath. "When I modeled in London, I thought I finally had it all. Money, a future, love." She stumbled over the last word and the truth it'd left her with: Everything she'd sought to fill her was as expendable as she was. "Turns out I lost a lot more than I gained."

White dandelion seeds floated through the air like scattered wispy snowflakes. And for a minute, Livy pictured her mistakes and emptiness blowing away with them.

She'd wanted Ti to be right about love covering more than she thought, but what if it wasn't enough?

"Do you believe in grace?" She let go of the truck bed. "I mean, the kind that's big enough to make things right. Even the worst things you can't change on your own."

Looking into the field, Chase adjusted his hat. "I want to." An ache of doubt splintered through his usual assurance. He didn't talk much about how his dad's illness affected him, but every now and then, the pain wore through.

Livy watched a Carolina wren soar above the purple and yellow flowers painted in the sunset. "This is how I picture it. A borderless field of sunlight. No shadows or dead ends." She lifted her face toward the sky. "Just warmth, peace. Can you imagine standing in the middle of a place like that? Completely vulnerable with nowhere to hide. And the crazy thing is, you don't even feel like you have to, because in the center of something that freeing, it's almost like you've finally found your way home, you know?"

When no response came, waves of self-consciousness rushed clear past her hairline. There she went again, letting her artsy thoughts and runaway mouth take off before she could rein them in to some level of normalcy.

"Sorry, I didn't mean to—"

"Dance with me."

And he thought *she* was the random one? Livy turned, expecting to see humor and wit ready to tease her. Instead, Chase had his eyes on her as if she captured him more than the stunning imagery surrounding them.

Smiling softly, he dropped his focus to the hands that had comforted her so many times. "You said you used to daydream of dancing on your dates, right?"

"Um, yeah, but…"

He looked up then, and Livy would've been lucky if she could stand on her feet, let alone dance. "Rule number one of dating—every girl should get her dream."

Chase helped her to the middle of the truck bed, and with one little smile, the freckles accentuating his eyes ushered in his exasperatingly attractive charm. "I know it's not a barn loft, but the view's not half bad."

Livy pulled her lips to the side. "And what about Jimmy Sterling?"

There were those tiny dimples again. "I can unbutton my shirt and show off my summer tan, if that would help."

She swatted his arm, and he drew her close. The intensity from earlier returned to his eyes. "Dance with me," he said again.

"Right here?"

He took her hand in his and rested his cheek to her temple. "Right here," he whispered.

If the truck weren't made of steel, she might've melted through it. She'd never known this kind of tenderness from a man. Had never known a love more devastatingly gentle.

"I haven't had the chance to write that country song I owe you," he teased. "So, you'll have to imagine it for now."

No, she didn't. The cicadas, the wind, the rhythm of Chase's heartbeat—it was already a song she'd never forget.

Her fingers tightened around his shirt and around the one dream she couldn't stop herself from pretending would never end.

It felt like he was concentrating, maybe even... counting? Wait a second, Chase Thompson wasn't comfortable dancing? Charm without moves. Oh, the fun she could have with that one. In any other context, she would've. But right here—

right now—his adorable imperfection was nothing but perfect.

His heart's tempo gradually slowed under her ear as the sun dipped a little farther behind the trees. Livy closed her eyes and held on. Between the simple, understated sway and the safety of Chase's embrace, this had to be the closest she'd ever come to dancing with grace.

Minutes drifted in and out until he finally took his hat off and nestled it onto her head. "A real cowboy should always give his girl his hat."

His girl. Something about those words coming from him killed her in all the right ways.

Keeping it playful, she tipped the front of the hat the way he often did. "Now the *real* country magic can happen."

"I think it already has." Inching closer, he brought his thumb to the side of her chin.

Composure, space—it all vanished when he looked at her like that. Livy gripped his sleeve, breathed.

A raindrop splashed onto his forehead. Another. Livy followed his stunned look toward the dark clouds caught up in pockets of the day's remaining sunlight.

Chase blinked through the rain. "Sun shower? C'mon."

Once off the tailgate, she stopped him. "Wait." Livy stretched her neck back and her arms out. "When was the last time you danced in the rain?"

A surprised expression took her in, a slow grin building. She knew that look but had nowhere to run. And frankly, this was one time she didn't want to. He scooped her up and spun her around in fits of laughter and sunshine and a shower that couldn't have been more freeing.

She didn't know what had gotten into her. Just that she couldn't leave. Not when everything she wanted was right here. Maybe it was because she knew dancing led to...

"Liv." His chest rose and fell with urgent breaths.

Though they'd stopped in the middle of the field, her heart kept spinning.

This. Dancing led to this—unequivocal, uncontrollable desire to be with him.

His eyes held hers, and before she had time to think, she lifted a hand to his unshaven cheek. Raindrops ran into her fingers, longing into fear. Her palm drifted to his chest. And right then—whether from Ti's nudging or Chase's back-road summer magic—Livy couldn't stop the words from coming.

"You told me I should kiss Jed to find out how I feel, but what if the man I really want to kiss me is standing right here?"

Rain beat onto the brim of his hat, his pulse under her hand. Slower than the adrenaline in her body could handle it, Chase moved even closer, took his hat off her head, and threaded his fingers in her hair. "Then I'd kiss you the way I've wanted to since the day we first met."

Ever since their camping trip, she'd almost lost herself in starting to believe she was the girl he'd been waiting for. But to see it on his face, to hear he had feelings for her too...

Love pounded in her heart with hope, dreams—things that never lasted.

Raindrops merged with tears incapable of washing away the memories tied to them: Nights of counterfeit love she'd wanted to be real. Mornings alone, proving they weren't. A hundred empty kisses and even hollower lies. Loss, consequences, scars she couldn't pass on.

"Chase, I..."

His thumb grazed the corner of her mouth, his touch soft, sincere—the opposite of everything she'd ever known. But when she found his eyes again, she only heard one thing.

"It's a great opportunity. One that could open the doors for me to get my dad the treatment he needs... But I just need one reason to stay."

One reason. Her lashes crashed together, the snow globe of dreams shattering. "I shouldn't be... I'm sorry. I can't." This was a mistake. All of it. She shouldn't have come today. Shouldn't have made things worse. She backed up, turned.

"Sorry? Liv, hold on a minute." Chase caught up. "Talk to me. What just happened?" He caught her hand when she pulled away again, but she didn't turn back around. Couldn't. "Is this about Chicago? Because, honestly? I don't know what I'm supposed to do yet. I have no idea how to help my dad, or if I even can." He turned her around. "But I know I can't lose you."

Her chest caved. This whole time, he'd been torn over what to do because of her. Worse, part of her almost wanted him to be. Her selfishness tightened her grip around his sleeve, and she knew right then. She had to tell him what he needed to hear, not what she wished could be different.

A slow breath lifted a smile that knew as many fractures as her heart. "You can't stay for me, Chase."

"Then come with me."

She searched his eyes, and for longer than she should've let it, hope nearly dismantled her resolve. "I can't leave." She'd spent so long thinking she'd never see Tanner again. That she didn't deserve to. She still wasn't sure she did, but if there was even the slightest chance grace was real enough to give her a second chance, she had to stay and try.

Shadows swallowed the last glimpse of light as she fixed the unruly section of hair forever matted from his cowboy hat. "I meant what I said last night. Your someday is going to be more amazing than you can imagine." She lifted on her toes to kiss his cheek and held on a minute longer.

"Liv..."

"We should go. Please."

The sound of rain watering a field where magic bloomed now filled the silence washing it away. Once in his Silverado, it followed them down the sloshy dirt road, back to the firm grip of pavement and the even firmer grip of reality.

Livy clenched her seat belt, praying it would hold her together a little longer.

A few more turns brought them to a car with its hazard lights flashing parked on the side of the road. Chase pulled up behind the Lexus, slipped his hat on, and paused with the door halfway open. "I'll be back in a minute. Just want to make sure they don't need any help."

When it came to Chase, she wouldn't expect any less.

He jogged up to the car and knocked on the window. A brunette with a jacket draped over her head stepped out and stood in front of him for less than ten seconds before tackling him in a hug. The kind that said they knew each other. Well.

The streaks of rain coursing down the windshield blurred a clear enough view for Livy to make out what they were saying. Probably better that way. Still, when the two jogged over to the truck together and opened the door, something in Chase's expression turned Livy's stomach inside out.

"Liv, this is Kaley. We..." He knocked his hat up to scratch his forehead.

Clearly familiar with his nervous tics, she extended a hand to Livy when he stalled. "We've known each other a long time."

Kaley turned toward him, cozied under the umbrella. "Hey, is Mikey's shop still open? I couldn't remember their number for the life of me. Then when you didn't answer my call, I tried looking under the hood myself, and you know how well that went." She laughed. "I guess driving all the way from Chicago wasn't my greatest idea, huh?"

Chicago? The calls he'd been ignoring in front of Livy... They'd been from Kaley? Chase's comment about Mystery Girl from the day he pitched his coaching gig sank into her gut. *"Actually, it's someone I've known for a long time."* The pieces came together and drove Livy's shoulders into the back of the seat. His trip last week... *"There's a lot there I've always wanted."*

Including a girl worth waiting for?

CHAPTER TWENTY-TWO

Echoes

After making sure Kaley got a tow and a ride to her sister's, Chase drove Livy home. The last of the raindrops smeared across the windshield, disappearing with any chance he had of salvaging the night.

His Silverado rolled to a stop beside the curb. Livy had hardly spoken since Kaley started recounting their past as if she hadn't walked out on it well over a decade ago. He couldn't blame her. One minute he was telling Livy he wanted to kiss her. The next, he was introducing her to his ex-girlfriend. She probably thought he was as big of a player as Jed.

Chase shook his head. One last date—one last chance to break through the walls holding her back—and somehow, he'd messed it up. He turned the air off, but the feeling of being so close to breaking through to her pressed in with his damp clothes.

He couldn't give up yet.

Lost in thoughts he'd give far more than a thousand pennies to hear, Livy twisted and untwisted the hair at the end of her braid.

"I'm sorry about Kaley." He pulled the keys from the ignition. "We dated in high school and—"

"You have nothing to explain. I'm the one who lost my head out there." Blue eyes sadder than he'd ever seen them turned away from the window. "Guess you were right about not underestimating those back roads." She glanced at her house, the strain of deflection wearing through. "Speaking of magic, I should go make sure Bandit didn't pull any Houdini acts while I was gone."

"Liv, please." It was all he could get past the knot in his throat.

She bunched the scalloped hem of her dress between her fingers while holding back tears it gutted him to know he'd caused. Three breaths passed before she looked up again. With a smile that could've wept, she tipped his hat. "Rule number two—every hunky cowboy deserves a happy ending." She kissed his cheek. "Thank you," she whispered before drawing away. "For everything."

Something about her touch—the ache in it, the conflict—tore down his middle. It kept him in place and his emotions churning until the collision wrecking his insides launched him out of the truck.

"Hang on." He hustled up the walkway. "How can you think anything about watching you walk away is a happy ending?"

She stood in front of the steps, gripping the rail. When she finally turned, the tears she'd fought in the truck glistened under the porch light. "Because I'm not a part of that someday you're looking for, Chase."

He stopped short at her words. "Why? Because of whatever happened in London?" Everyone had baggage. His reaction to Kaley showing up had just proven that.

Livy whipped her head up. "Because you don't know me, okay?"

The jolt almost brought him to his knees, but he wouldn't let her push him away this time. Reaching her, he brushed his thumb across her damp cheek. "Then stop shutting me out and give me the chance."

Her lashes closed at his touch. "Please don't make this harder. Your future's in Chicago." She pulled away, and something inside him broke.

"And where's yours? Running back to a guy like Jed?" The humid air left from the rain nearly suffocated him. "I'm sorry, Liv, but that creep doesn't care about you. The only reason he made time to see you and cleaned your house is because he's trying to sweet-talk his way into your bed." He didn't mean it to come out that harshly, or to come out period. But even if she didn't want to be with Chase, he couldn't watch her lose herself to some jerk.

She didn't so much as blink away the resignation in her response. She looked down and twisted the ring on her pointer finger. "I know."

"Then why would you...? Don't you see...?" The tree branches swaying in the wind seemed to beg him to stop, to listen.

Livy released a slow breath as if she'd been holding it since the day she moved to Littleton. "That group home you followed me to? One of the girls there was dating this classic player. He had all the right words, all the right moves to make her believe she was something special to him." Tears ran into the raindrops she hadn't wiped away. "To an insecure girl desperate to feel valuable, that attention is almost like a drug. You crave it, feed off it. Even when it leaves you emptier the next time you're alone, you keep going back."

Her arms came undone, Chase's heart even more.

"And you think you're like her?"

"I *am* like her." She pushed off the rail and stopped a few paces away with her back to him. "I'm *that* girl, Chase. I'm the cliché who turned to all the wrong places for the love she never got at home." With a shake of her head, she stared across the dark yard. "Those consequences don't just go away."

Her hair blew in the wind as she turned. "I'll always love you for wanting to see the best in me. But as much as you want to, you can't undo my past any more than I can."

Was that what she thought he was trying to do?

Aching to prove her wrong, he moved closer. "Just because you made some mist—"

"I have a son, Chase." She wrestled to make herself look him in the eyes. "I have a son, and I don't even know who the father is."

Her shoulders quivered to keep from falling, and right then, nothing mattered but holding her close. "Liv."

Her arms a fortress, she hedged a wall paved in fear between them. Tears brimmed as she faced him again. "I lost him. I lost my career. Lost myself, my future."

She wiped her cheeks and straightened away from him. "And no amount of volunteering at group homes or confidence coaching or daydreaming is going to change a scarred girl who had to give up her child and can't get close to a guy anymore without panicking, because *that's* who I am. That's the girl you think you know." Shadows in the yard flickered over the ones trapped in her eyes. "Someone like Kaley's worth waiting for, Chase." Her voice waned to a whisper. "Not me."

Her words might as well have thrust a gear wrench through his rib cage. All this time, that was the secret she'd been keeping, so afraid of what he would think of her. He could see it on her face. The fear of disappointment, the guilt. Shame. She stood there, waiting, expecting him to discard her the way others had.

Without releasing her gaze for a single moment, he brushed her bangs back as he always did. And with all the compassion inside him, he brought her into his arms and into the kind of acceptance she still didn't understand. "If you honestly believe that, then I'm not the guy you think I am either." He rested his cheek to her head. "Your scars aren't who you are." This was. The girl he had always and would always love.

She pressed in, and he held on tighter. He couldn't heal brokenness. He knew that. And heaven knew he had his own battle with faith. But if his arms could be extensions of grace, he'd hold every piece of her that came undone until she trusted it enough to make her whole again.

Wesley sailed around the corner of the house out of nowhere and leaned against his knees. "You're back."

Livy flinched out of Chase's arms at the interruption, but not before Wesley sized him up. Focusing back on Livy, he broadened his scrawny shoulders. "Going for the jealousy play. I feel ya." He strutted toward them. "At least Boots is smarter than that H.R. Wells joker you had over here the other week. Wait. He's not like the *evil* Wells, is he? 'Cause I don't want to have to lightning bolt his sorry butt into the Speed Force if he's playing my girl, but I'll do it."

Between calling Livy his girl and tossing around *The Flash* references like they were reality, the kid didn't exactly make it easy to keep a straight face in even the tensest of moments.

Chase gave him a good-faith tip of his hat. "Don't worry. I promise to protect Livy." He glanced at her, praying she'd trust him enough to know that included her heart.

"Good." Wesley grabbed the sides of his plaid button-down in a not-so-subtle display of the red-masked hero on his T-shirt. "But don't think that changes things between us."

Chase tried not to smile. Livy, on the other hand, didn't seem amused. "Did you check on Bandit?"

"You mean Boombox?" The kid paced back and forth with enough friction to burn a path in the grass. "That dog's got some serious bass on him. I mean, hey, I respect doing what you gotta do to go after your girl, but all that barking ain't necessary. I was like, seriously, dawg, take it down a notch."

He slid Chase a keep-it-real expression. "Am I right? Especially with Mr. Hood already rolling out there with his shotgun. You ever hear those old beagles howl? If my aim was dope, I'd get up in one of 'em trees out there and—"

"Wes." Chase clamped both hands on his shoulders to cut off his tangent. "I need you to focus, buddy. Are you saying Bandit got out again?"

"In the woods. I swear it's like he can vibe himself over to see that poodle mix whenever he wants." His shoulders sank like a fallen hero's. "I tried to find him but..."

Livy didn't wait for him to finish. She took off around the back of the house. "Bandit!"

Great. Chase motioned Wesley to his house. "Head home, all right?" Not leaving time for argument, he sprinted to the backyard. "Liv, wait up." He caught her at the edge of the woods. "Did you miss the part about Mr. Hood and his shotgun? You're not going out there in the dark. It's dangerous."

"Exactly." A flare of determination fired up her cheeks. "I can't leave Bandit out there. Mr. Hood hates him. If he has the chance, he'll..." She breathed in.

"That's not gonna happen." He dipped his head under hers. "Hey, look at me. Mr. Hood might be a crotchety old man, but his heart's not that cold."

A dull ache poured from her eyes. "Not everyone's as redeemable as you think they are."

He grabbed her hand when she turned, wanting to shake words of truth all the way to her bones. "And not everyone's as quick to disappoint you as you think they are." What did he have to do to make her see that?

Her chest heaved as fast as his. Face to face again, neither moved, neither spoke. She had always carried a fear he couldn't fully uncover. Now, with her secrets in the open, it pulsed in the way she looked at him. Raw, vulnerable. The yearning to make her feel safe rooted inside him with such magnitude, he risked a step closer.

"Livy?" someone called from the corner of the house.

They both turned.

She squinted through the dark. "Jed?"

You've got to be kidding me.

She looked from him to Chase and back. "What are you doing here?"

"I caught a break in our schedule. It's just for the night, but I thought we could…" His words trailed when he got close enough to lock eyes with Chase.

He thought they could what exactly? Chase's veins heated, but Livy stood between them, looking lost. After everything she'd just told him, she couldn't seriously still be interested in—

Two gunshots popped off in the distance. Livy's shoulders flinched. Another shot echoed between the trees. A howl.

"Bandit!" Fear and adrenaline throbbed in the split-second look she flashed Chase before bolting into the woods.

He darted after her. Fog rose off the ground, still wet from the earlier rain. Underbrush whipped across his ankles, but he didn't slow. He dodged a hanging branch, cleared a fallen log, and pushed off trunks on his left and right.

Shadows encroached on the splinters of moonlight filtering through the leaves. And when another howl trailed on the wind, the woods turned even darker.

Livy gasped ahead. She stared across a gully toward a glimpse of an animal Bandit's color lying behind a large pine.

Chase shifted a glance from Mr. Hood lowering his shotgun a good twenty feet away to his target and back to Livy. Slow, cautious steps brought him up behind her. "Li—"

"Livy?" Jed yelled several turns behind them.

The beagles sent a round of barks shaking through the branches.

Livy cast a glassy-eyed look at Chase and buried herself in his arms.

"It's okay." He cupped the back of her head and held her close. "I've got you."

Jed crossed the last few feet to catch up. "Someone want to tell me what we're running …?" He slid a once-over down her and Chase. "Never mind."

With the gall to look offended, he ran his tongue under his top lip and pulled out his cell. Busy shooting off a text, he switched the toothpick he'd been chewing to the opposite side of his mouth. "Do me a favor. Next time you're already booked for the night, give me a heads-up before I make the drive out here."

He chucked the toothpick on the dirt as he turned, and it took every ounce of Chase's restraint not to drop him to the ground next to it. If Livy hadn't grabbed his arm to stop him, he would have.

The beagles howled across the gully again. An echo of pain jolted her forward. She stopped after three steps as though torn, and then jogged after him. "Jed, wait." She turned him around. "It's... We're..."

"You're what?"

She looked back to where Chase stood waiting for her answer as much as Jed. He didn't move, only prayed the certainty in his eyes would take away the doubt in hers. Instead, it deepened even further.

A blend of tears closed behind her lashes, sealing off the last of his hope before she ever said the words. "We're just friends."

CHAPTER TWENTY-THREE

Wrecked

Livy lined up four magazine tear-outs on her kitchen table and stepped back to study them. Ten seconds later, she swapped one with a fifth from the pile in the corner. "What do you think, Soph? Do these wall decals go okay with these light fixtures?"

Sophie strolled in from the kitchen with a glass of iced coffee. She sifted through the ones Livy had left to the side and pulled out two. "What about these?"

Livy gave a little sigh at the perfect match. This was why she had asked Sophie to come help her work on design themes. "See, I told you I needed another girl's input. If you weren't here, I'd have to ask…" No one.

The pang of missing Chase burrowed into the gouge she'd left in her heart five nights ago. Not giving Sophie a chance to probe, she quickly added, "You have a killer knack for decorating."

"Learned from the best." Leaving the returned compliment behind her, she flitted into the living room with her drink. "I still can't believe you're really doing it. Your own café. Seriously, how legit is that?"

Legit? Smiling to herself, Livy pulled out the chair in front of her and almost sat on a layer of dog hair. She wiped it off. Sheesh. The little furball hadn't even stayed with her that long, and she would've sworn his hair was coming out of the vents.

She sank onto the chair, and before she could stop it, her smile yielded to an ache that had been festering all day. All week, really. Alone, the house had felt as empty as she did.

Even though the wounded animal they'd caught a glimpse of in the woods the other night turned out to be a coyote, Bandit was still missing. Letting Mrs. Finch down gnawed at her almost as much as Jed showing up Thursday night had.

He was the last person she'd wanted to see, and she'd told him as much once Chase had gone. Truthfully though, if he hadn't come, her resolve to let Chase go would've crumbled.

It had gutted her to say they were only friends, but she knew him. Knew he'd give up things she couldn't live with letting him sacrifice for her. As much as it hurt, she wanted what was best for him, for his family. One day, he'd understand. And one day, she prayed her heart would breathe again.

But right now, the love in his eyes still haunted her. The compassion, forgiveness—things he shouldn't have felt after finally seeing who she was. He was supposed to walk away.

Confusion suffocated tears stirring deep in places forever wrecked by grace. Even now, she couldn't make sense of arms that had embraced every exposed, destructive piece of her heart.

"Holy hotness," Sophie said out of nowhere. She spun around in the living room with a framed picture of Livy and Chase at one of his parents' cookouts. "I figured Jed had to be gorgeous, but wow. You were holding out on me."

Livy stretched her hair tie around the end of her braid to the max and looped it one last time. "Um, actually, that's not Jed. It's Chase."

Twisting away from the living room didn't delay the question she knew was coming. Sophie walked it straight toward her. "Hold on a minute. You have a picture on your end table of a guy you're not even dating?"

"He's my best friend." *Was* her best friend. She swirled the ice cubes in her glass of sweet tea, the sound thrumming with memories.

Sophie set the frame on the table. "Yeah, sorry. There's no way you can be just friends with someone this hot. You're into him, aren't you?"

Livy straightened the already-straightened stack of magazines, wishing she could come up with an answer half as sturdy.

"Oh my gosh, you are. You're totally crushing on him." She dragged the chair beside Livy out and plopped down like she'd just scooted up to a press conference. "How long has this been going on? What about Jed?"

"Soph, relax. This isn't *Highschool Musical.* I'm not *crushing* on Chase, and Jed is..." She might as well be honest. "Kind of a jerk, actually." She swiveled in the chair to face her. "It took me a while to admit he was just like Luke, but you were right." About a lot of things.

Seconds passed in thoughts and regrets.

Staring at the table, Sophie circled the bottom of her cup on its edge. "Why do we always have to go for the jerks?"

Livy picked up the frame, sighed. "Honestly? I think when you grow up without someone teaching you what real love is, you end up turning to the counterfeit kind instead."

Sophie stopped fidgeting with her cup and nodded to the picture in Livy's hands. "Is Chase the real or counterfeit kind?"

Swallowing the pain of an answer she'd always live with, Livy ran her thumb over the glass safeguarding a dream where it couldn't shatter. "More real than I deserve."

She batted away pointless tears, set the frame face down on the table, and scanned over the magazine pages in front of her. Regardless of where they stood, she knew he'd want her to finish this project.

Livy tucked one leg under the other and studied a photo of a café located somewhere in Portland. She took in the angles, the themes. But the longer she tried to focus on the visual artistry, the more she knew even the most creative decorating wouldn't change the fact that the center of it all was missing.

Her thoughts wandered to the flyer she'd already designed to advertise the first open mic night she had planned for her shop's grand opening. Of all the ways she could break her heart by getting ahead of herself, that, by far, topped the list. Still, she couldn't let it go.

"Um, Liv?" Sophie's grin zeroed in on Livy's unintentional origami project. "This café gig isn't turning you into a tweaker, is it?"

"What? No, of course not." She smoothed out the page she'd mindlessly folded in no less than ten different directions. "I just have a lot on my mind." She rose. "And what do you know about tweakers anyway?"

An are-you-kidding-me expression blew her way. "You know how many messed-up homes I've lived in?"

Livy's heart winced. The girl probably had more street experience than anyone her age should have.

As usual, Sophie didn't only notice the concern Livy tried to hide. She balked against it. "Don't look at me like that. Just because I've been around druggies doesn't mean I'm destined to be one. I make my own decisions."

"I know." Livy gave her arm a soft squeeze. "Which is exactly why I asked you over today. Those decision skills of yours are going to save me from drowning in indecisiveness."

As Sophie stirred her straw around the ice cubes left in the bottom of her cup, the hard lines of indifference she strove so hard to maintain gradually surrendered to a smile. "You know, given all those skills, you should probably start paying me by the hour."

"Don't press your luck, girl." Livy tossed her a notepad and a wink. "But… if things go as I hope, there might just be an hourly job waiting for those *legit* skills of yours pretty soon."

Sophie's face lit up. "For real?"

Livy's heart constricted at how easily it surprised Sophie when someone showed the slightest belief in her. "For real. But for now, sorry, your only payment is free coffee."

She picked up her near-empty coffee cup and shrugged. "I can live with that."

Good. Because it was all she had to offer.

Livy motioned to the pad with a list of supplier websites written on it. "I'll go make another pot if you finish pricing out some equipment for me. I started on that first site last night, so check out the costs on the other two for comparisons. There should be a spreadsheet already open on the laptop in my bedroom."

Sophie saluted before hopping up. Halfway down the hall, she stopped and turned with her lip caught between her teeth and the list clutched in her hand. She lifted on the balls of her feet. "Livy?"

"Yeah, love?"

"Thanks." She twisted the paper. "You know, for having me over to help out and stuff. It's pretty cool of you. Especially after last—"

"Hey. Already forgotten." Livy was the last person with any right to cast judgment, particularly when she made nearly identical mistakes. "Just don't tell anyone how messy my bedroom is. Deal?"

Sophie donned a no-promises look as she spun back around.

Livy smiled. Yep, she definitely needed Soph's company to get her through today. Well, that and coffee. This sweet tea wasn't coming anywhere close to cutting it.

In the kitchen, she set up her French press, got the water boiling on the stove, and opened a fresh bag of coffee beans. Smooth Guatemalan aromas swirled into the air like a godsend. Would she get to do this for a living soon? It still seemed unreal. A little nerve-wracking, sure. But something indefinable pulsed in the possibilities this could open up for her. Something almost like—

"You have a kid?" Sophie's indignant tone exploded across the kitchen.

Livy knocked over the bag of coffee. "What?"

She shoved Livy's laptop onto the counter. "You left your email open, so don't bother denying it."

A reply from Tanner's caseworker regarding meeting him glared off the screen like a shiny two-edged blade.

"Soph—"

"You didn't want him?"

Livy's chest sank. "It wasn't like that. It was—"

"Complicated? Spare me the sob story. I've heard them all." She stopped in the doorway. Her shoulders slumped, her voice falling. "You were supposed to be different. The one person I could..." She shoved down tears churning with betrayal. "I can't believe you've been lying to me this whole time."

The hoarse words emanated such hurt, Livy could hardly move. "I'm sorry."

Indifference flaring again, she crossed her arms. "What's another kid abandoned by parents who don't care about him? We're just a number in a system, right? Someone else's problem to deal with."

"You know that's not what I think."

A moment after looking away, she lost her grip on her elbows. "Wait. Is that why you've been spending time with me? To make yourself feel better about ditching your own son?" Her eyes darkened. "It is, isn't it? I can see it on your face."

"No." Livy shook her head, desperate to shield her from the truth. She reached for her. "Let me explain."

"Save it." She jerked away. "Next time you want to use someone as your charity case for some kind of penance, do everyone a favor and keep your messed-up junk to yourself. We have enough people letting us down."

Her words a knife, the serrated edge sawed through every flimsy attempt Livy had made to atone for her mistakes. And though silence fell across her apartment, the voice of accusation had never screamed louder.

Tears bound her in place until the teakettle's whistle finally broke her free. She snapped the burner off and breathed her way into the dining room where the clock continued to tick in place of words unable to make things right.

Sophie kept her head down and her hands around the top of the chair. "I can't believe I thought you might've actually wanted..." She tugged her purse off the chair. "Forget it. I should've known better."

She strode for the front porch.

"Soph, wait. Where are you going?"

"To catch a ride. And don't worry about what to tell Jackson." Already opening the door, she hurled a glare across the room. "You're not the only one good at lying."

The slam of the door shuddered across Livy's shoulders, followed by another flinch from her cell ringing on the table. She grabbed it on her way out, only half looking at the screen. "Hello?"

"Miss Hensley, it's Bethany from BB&T. Do you have a minute?"

Outside, Livy shoved her bangs off her forehead and squinted down the street. Sophie had already made it to the corner. "Um, it's actually not the best time."

"I'm afraid time is of the essence."

The sobered pitch in her voice stopped Livy at the bottom of the steps. She looked from Sophie back to the house where an email giving her the opportunity to meet her son hung in the balance. "Is something wrong?"

Bethany's five-second delayed response might as well have been thirty minutes. "It's about your application for the loan."

CHAPTER TWENTY-FOUR

Enough

Chase sat back in one of the wicker chairs Mom insisted he own, cradled his guitar in his lap, and watched the fireflies hail the end of a long day. He changed chords and picked with his fingertips until a song he and Dad used to play together filled his quiet backyard.

His focus strayed to his Nova in the corner, his thoughts to the past few weeks. Goals, choices, decisions. He was never really in control of any of them, was he?

"Uh-oh," a familiar voice said from the side of the house. Kaley strolled across the yard with her hands in her jean shorts' front pockets. "It's worse than I thought."

Chase propped his guitar against the chair. "What is?"

"You, sitting out here, playing music instead of working on your old Chevy." She stopped at the edge of the slab. "Whatever's on your mind, it has to be pretty bad."

She shouldn't still know him so well. "Nope." He rose and weaved through the patio furniture toward his toolbox. "I was just taking a quick break."

She followed. "Mm-hmm."

Chase grabbed the sander he'd left on the ground and squatted next to the right rear quarter panel. He rubbed a hand over the steel, looking for imperfections and any chance to avoid a conversation he wasn't up for.

Clearly missing the hint, Kaley leaned against the taillight. "Sorry for just showing up. I tried calling." She dragged her heeled sandal along her calf when he didn't say anything. "I thought... maybe we could..." She lifted a shoulder. "Talk."

When had that ever gotten them anywhere?

Chase glanced up at green eyes he'd spent years forgetting. Though they'd lost their hold over him, they still held memories. Some good, some bad. But enough for him to know he couldn't dismiss her as easily as part of him wanted to.

He nodded to the front of the house. "You got your car fixed?"

She looked behind her. "Yeah. Thanks for your help with that by the way. If you hadn't come along, I would've had to call Bethany, and you know how much help she would've been."

"Is her husband afraid to get his hands dirty, or something?" The summer heat drilled into the back of his neck. If Mom were there, she would've popped him a good one. Mumbled or not, he should've kept that retort to himself. He wiped his brow with his sleeve. "Sorry, I shouldn't have said that."

"It's nothing that isn't true. If Chris can't cross-examine his way out of something, it's not worth his time." She fiddled with her keyring. "Guess that included his marriage. They got divorced several years back."

So, the golden lawyer turned out to be a schmuck. Big surprise.

Another glance in Kaley's direction caught a telling grin. "You're picturing the look on my dad's face when that went down, aren't you?"

"No." Chase braced both hands on his thighs. "Okay, maybe, but I shouldn't be." He peered up at her. "I'm really sorry your sister had to go through that."

"If she didn't let my dad control her every decision, she probably wouldn't have."

The irony in her remark weighed down the space between them like a lead sinker.

"I know what you're thinking, and you're right about all of it." She slid her keys into her pocket and twisted toward him. "But more than anything, I should've apologized a long time ago for the way my dad treated you."

Chase placed the sander in his toolbox and fished for a rag to wipe his face with. "There's nothing to apologize for. You can't fault a guy for protecting his daughter from a floundering kid headed nowhere."

Already kneeling beside him, Kaley set a hand on his. "That's not what you were."

He looked from her tender touch to the matching sincerity in her eyes.

The neighbor's dog barked, and Chase slipped his hand and gaze free. He dug his Bondo putty out and went back to work on the panel. Just because her father's words stung didn't mean they were wrong.

"I might not've thought so then, but I owe him for getting me on track." Instead of working his way to landing a job on a hail team, he probably still would've been making minimum wage as a helper in the local mechanic shop. "I wouldn't have much to offer anyone if he hadn't driven me to make something of myself."

"And you do now?"

The failure of getting nowhere with Dad's insurance company bled into his inadequacies of not being able to break through to Livy. He stared at his reflection in the dull steel, knowing full well not all imperfections were as easy to remove. "I'm working on it," he whispered more to himself than to her.

"Is that why you're thinking of taking the job in Illinois?" Kaley shrugged when he raised a brow. "Small town."

Of course she'd heard. There wasn't room for secrets in a place like Littleton. At least he didn't used to think so. Flashes of Livy confessing she had a son collided with unanswered questions he thought he'd let go of ages ago.

"I used to love that about this place," she said. "The smallness. Summers at the lake that made it feel like the whole world existed right here." Nostalgia clung to her words like the Spanish moss hanging on the cypress tree branches above them. "You don't know how much I miss that."

Chase met her eyes then, the repressed question needing an answer. "Then why was it so easy for you to walk away?" From her roots, their plans, him?

"I didn't walk away."

"No, you're right. You ran. To other guys, to parties." Chase chucked the dirty rag into his toolbox and rose. "Jeez, Kaley, you ran all the way to another state."

"It wasn't like that." She blinked toward the grass. "I was scared."

"Of getting stuck in a small town with a dead-end mechanic?"

"Of watching you start to believe that's all you had to offer." Kaley pushed off the Nova and walked right up to him. "I'm not the only one who used to think Littleton was enough. You were content with our life back then. Content with who you were before my dad crushed that in you. If we'd stayed together, we would've ended up like Bethany and Chris."

"I wouldn't have let that happen."

Her eyes softened. "It already was." She set her palm on his chest. "I watched him break your spirit, Chase. Outside our house that night, I heard what he said to you."

Chase turned, head down. "That was a long time ago."

"And yet you're still living with it." She reached for his shoulder. "Don't you see it? This 'track' you think he set you on—this drive to make enough money to take care of your family—it's ruled by the fear of not being enough. I've watched people do this my whole life. You're shutting out everyone else's help so you can prove you can handle things on your own."

His jaw tensed. "That's not what I'm doing."

"No?" Kaley turned him around. "Then why are you running off to Chicago?"

"Because..." His chest heaved, but the answer he didn't want to admit drained the fight in him before he found the words.

"I'm sorry." Kaley stepped back. "I honestly didn't come over here to fight or dredge up the past or..." When her gaze intersected his, she broke the connection as though re-centering herself. "I actually came because of something I overheard Bethany telling Livy earlier about the loan she applied for. I know I shouldn't be telling you this, but I thought you'd want to know."

If he read the look on her face right, she didn't need to finish. "The bank retracted their offer?"

"Something about London. A flag that must've come up in a credit report. I didn't catch all the details, but it didn't sound good."

His heart tanked. After the things Livy had already been through, she didn't need hope to disappoint her one more time.

Chase peered to the patio table where he'd left his cell. The urge to be there for her pushed against the strains of pride that had kept him from calling all week.

With a look that seemed to know what he was thinking, Kaley picked at the fringe on the edge of her shorts. "I had a feeling." Another pained smile met the question in his eyes. "I'm happy you found her, Chase, but a word of advice? Don't let another girl push you away like I did."

He scratched the base of his neck, wishing it were that easy. "You must've missed the part where she chose another guy."

"You mean the wrong guy?" A rueful chuckle brought out the single dimple in her right cheek. "Yeah, I've been down that road, remember? He's not who she wants to be with."

An awkward pause bounced between them. If he was supposed to respond to that, he honestly didn't know what to say.

Thankfully, she spared him. "Look, just trust me when I say what she wants for herself isn't the issue. What she wants for you is what's holding her back."

Chase rewound her girl riddle through his head—slowly. "So…?"

She laughed softly. "So, you can stop trying to prove you're worth loving. She already knows that. What she needs is to believe *she* is."

"That's exactly what I've been trying…" A backlash of how he'd been pushing Livy to become more craned his neck to the sky. Like a gavel over an edict that she wasn't already enough, his desire to drive her to a place where they could be together had inadvertently driven them apart. Worse, he'd masked his own need to prove himself underneath it all.

He raked his fingers through his hair and shook a smile at Kaley. "You've always been smarter than me, you know that?"

"Not always." She dipped her chin. "But regret has a way of helping you see what you missed." She smoothed her thumb beside the corner of his eye. "So do these." Her fingertips drifted into his hair, her gaze into his. "I didn't come back to Littleton just to visit my sister, Chase. When I heard you might be moving to Chicago, I couldn't help thinking maybe…"

He lowered her hand to her side. "Kaley."

"I know. With the way I left things, I lost my place in your heart a long time ago." Eyes caught in a storm he couldn't rescue her from, she brushed the top of his hair to the side. "But that doesn't mean you won't always hold mine."

When he didn't respond, she batted away the beginning of tears and squeezed his hand. "I should go."

She'd made it around the side of the house before the moment freed Chase to catch up.

"Kaley, hang on." In the middle of the driveway, he drew her into a hug he wished could be enough. "I'm sorry I didn't fight for you when you needed me to." All this time, he'd blamed her for running away, but really, he had too. Maybe now they could both fully move on.

She breathed against his chest. "Just don't make the same mistake again." She lifted on her toes and pressed a kiss to his lips. "Take care of yourself, Chase."

A car door closed behind them. He looked over Kaley's shoulder to a shattered expression staring at Kaley in his arms. His heart dropped.

"Livy?"

CHAPTER TWENTY-FIVE

Faith

The minute Livy convinced her legs to move, she jetted back to her Fiat.

"Wait. Don't leave." Chase jogged over and cut her off from opening her door.

She fumbled her keys. "I shouldn't have come. Something happened, and I thought…" That was half her problem. She obviously hadn't thought at all. She'd just… needed him.

Off to the side, Kaley tiptoed down the driveway like a teenager trying to sneak out of Chase's room at night.

The keys dug into Livy's palm. She'd told him he belonged in Chicago with someone like Kaley, and she'd meant it. Just like she'd meant to be strong enough to believe it. "I'm sorry. I shouldn't be here."

"Liv—"

She closed her car door and started the engine before Chase could convince her to stay.

Tears she had no right to cry blurred her drive all the way to the parking lot that he'd rescued her in weeks ago. Their relationship had been so much less complicated before then.

Things couldn't have stayed that way. As much as part of her might have wanted them to, her heart wouldn't have let them. She knew that now.

She parked in the back corner, away from the streetlamp casting light over how long she'd lied to herself. Somewhere under the weight of so many regrets, truth had lost its voice. Even now, the whisper beneath it all felt so faint, so distant. But for the first time in her life, she knew what real love looked like. And it didn't matter if her heart ached, or if she got her happy ending, because all she wanted was for Chase to have his.

She drew in a breath, and with it, the assurance of what she needed to do. With slightly shaky hands, she tapped out a text she should've sent when Mrs. Finch first passed on her daughter's number.

Tessa, hey, it's Livy. Can we talk? It's about your mom's café.

A knock on her window flinched across her shoulders. She turned.

And quickly regretted it.

Cleavage Livy didn't need to be eye level with right now—or ever—jostled in front of her. Leaning over, her coworker fingered a necklace disappearing into her shirt. "You all right, toots?"

Did it look like she was all right? Livy left her tears in her car as she climbed out. "Fine."

Jen let go of the chain around her neck, dug through her purse, and held out a tube of concealer. "Here. Lance is already in one of his moods. I wouldn't push it."

"I'm good. Really."

Jen jutted the makeup at her. "Have you looked in the mirror? If you want to earn your wage in tips tonight, you better take it."

Livy almost told her where she could stick the concealer but took it instead. Begrudging the truth never changed it. "Thanks."

With a bob of her head, among other things, Jen walked toward the bus station in heels no waitress should be wearing. How her feet tolerated them her whole shift, Livy had no clue. Or maybe she did. She looked from the concealer to the back door of the bar and sighed. The longer you endure pain, the easier it gets to cover it up.

After hiding her own aches under a layer of makeup, Livy threw herself into the distraction the after-work crowd always brought. The nonstop orders, the clamor of pool balls and empty chatter, the inevitable stains on her shirt. Any other night, it would've been enough to keep her hustling. But as she spritzed and scrubbed down the table she'd just cleared, the conversation she'd had with Tessa while on her break collided into the one she'd had with Cooper last year.

Maybe Grandma Jo's right about things working themselves out, but I can't help wondering how much we mess things up by getting in our own way.

At the time, it had seemed so easy to say. So easy to believe in the good things waiting for him if he'd stop running away from them. But for her...

"Good ole Thompson didn't go and break your heart, did he?" Jeremy strutted over from a corner table where he'd been eyeing her for most of the night.

Shivers crawled over her skin like they had when he'd tried to corner her in the parking lot. Not giving him the satisfaction of catching on, Livy wrung out her rag. "You're lucky I didn't press charges against you the other night."

"For what?" He lounged against the edge of the booth. "Last time I checked, there were no laws against talking to a pretty girl."

What about the back of her tray talking to the bridge of his nose? So tempting. She held it to her side instead and nodded behind him to his friends with their arms around three girls they'd picked up tonight. "Looks like you've got enough pretty girls to talk to."

"There's always room for one more." He pulled out a twenty-dollar bill from his wallet, creased it along the middle, and moved close enough for his ashtray breath to assault her nostrils. He ran the corner of the bill down her cheekbone. "In a place like this, I'm sure you could use an extra tip."

Blood heated in her veins at his insinuation. She shoved him away. "If you even think—"

"Jeremy, my man." Her boss jogged over, his smooth-talking skills following each stride. "Good to have you back tonight." He clasped Jeremy's hand and shot Livy a glare. "I trust my girl's treatin' you as one of our valued customers."

The snark in Jeremy's twisted smile burned into her skin. "You might wanna give your waitresses a few hospitality lessons." He stuffed the twenty into his jeans' pocket. "I'd hate to have to take my business elsewhere. Especially when the dessert here is so..." A hungry gaze roamed over her. "Enticing."

Livy strangled the rag in her hands and the words in her throat.

Lance cut off any chance for her response to escape and steered Jeremy back to his table. "I'll tell you what. That last round of drinks is on the house."

Once Lance had weaseled in enough flattery to appease the jerk, he marched back over to her. "Where's your head, Hensley?"

"*My* head?"

"You've been acting off for the last three weeks. One minute, you're shuffling around here like a dazed zombie. The next, you're giving customers lip like you don't want to be here."

Truthfully, she didn't. She heaved the bucket of dirty dishes onto her hip and stared past him. Like a mural painted over the grimy wall, the scene from her and Chase's date at the café practically begged her to take up the manager on her offer. The job wouldn't be the same as owning her own shop, but at least she'd have her dignity there—a chance to be creative and invest in what she loved.

Lance took the bucket out of her hands. "And what are you doing bussing tables? Doing Billy's job for him doesn't mean you get to take his cut of the tips. Jeez, Livy. I expect better from you."

"Says the boss who's too busy sucking up to drunk locals like they're dropping hundreds in his lap to give a rip about the employees they're harassing."

Uncrossing her arms did nothing for the crossed look Lance drilled into her.

With a calculated glance around the room, he wormed his fingers through his sweaty hair and lowered his voice. "Flirting comes with your job, sweetheart. You knew that signing on, so don't try pulling this high-and-mighty crap now. What's really going on? Are you using? Is that why you've been so off lately?"

You've got to be kidding me. "You're unbelievable, you know that?"

"Hey." Lance grabbed her wrist as she turned. "You best mind who you're talking to if you want to keep your job."

A flare of indignation that had been building for months burned through her layers of reservation. She pulled her arm free, shoved her tray into his stomach, and added her balled-up apron to it. "Then I guess it's a good thing I don't want this job anymore." She strode for the exit without looking back.

Outside, the night's cool breeze rushed across her overheated skin. And right there in a parking lot that had chained her to a past she wanted to forget, she breathed a breath of release.

Chase was right. She should've done this a long time ago. A wave of freedom rushed through her. On instinct, she pulled out her phone to scroll to Chase's number but stopped on an email notification first.

She stared at the name on the screen. Tanner's caseworker. With slight reluctance, Livy tapped open the message.

Good news. The Bradleys just notified me of an unexpected opening in their schedule. They can move up your meeting with Tanner to tonight at 6:30, if you're available. I realize this is last-minute, so let me know as soon as you can.

Excited for you,

Lara Crawford

Tonight? Livy backed into the dim streetlight and checked the time—5:45. In less than an hour, she could meet her son. In. Less. Than. An. Hour.

Her nerves swerved into a tailspin. She pulled the hair tie out of her braid and scanned over her freshly-stained work clothes—*old* work clothes, considering she'd just quit her job.

Dread twisted in her stomach. Pacing, she combed her fingers through a section of hair matted together in who-knew-what. Brilliant. She had forty-five minutes to come up with a way to spin why she was a jobless waitress who looked frazzled enough for her ex-boss to accuse her of using drugs. Yeah, no chance of that affecting first impressions or anything.

She slumped against the light pole again. What was she doing? Even if she got herself cleaned up in time, could she really hide the mess inside her right now?

"You can't tell me it didn't take guts and faith to work those shoots... That girl's still in you. We just gotta bring her out again."

From somewhere above the relentless questions, the whisper of Chase's belief in her stilled the voice of doubt.

This whole time, she'd been so set on shielding him from who she'd let herself become in London that she'd lost sight of the hope and confidence she'd once had. They were more than a little broken now. And maybe they always would be. But if the kind of grace Chase had shown her was real, she'd hold on to it with all she had.

Livy pushed off the pole and tapped out a reply to Lara.

I'll be there.

She inhaled, let it go, and took the first step toward a new beginning.

"Livy?" Jackson's Subaru careened up to the curb. Swinging the door behind him, he left the engine running and skirted around the front bumper.

He didn't have to explain something was wrong. His expression cut to Livy's core before he said a word.

CHAPTER TWENTY-SIX

Unspoken

Livy glanced at her cell as the hospital's elevator doors dinged open—6:08 p.m. If she skipped a shower, she could still make her meet-up with Tanner. But right now, Sophie needed her.

Jackson led the way to the room number the receptionist had provided them. With light after light passing overhead in a blur, all Livy could think about was her last conversation with Sophie. The fighting, the damage she'd caused to Sophie's already-fragile trust in others. If anything happened to her before Livy had the chance to make things right...

A nurse rounded the doorway to the room as they approached.

Jackson motioned inside. "May we?"

After a quick scan over the chart in her hands, she brought it to her side. "Mr. Holgate?"

"Jackson." He extended a hand. "I run the group home where Sophie lives. This is Livy Hensley, one of our volunteers."

Livy winced at a replay of Sophie's accusation about her reason for volunteering.

If the nurse noticed her reaction, she was kind enough to pretend she didn't. Instead, she nodded her understanding. "You're welcome to go in and see her." Her patient smile warmed over them when Jackson hesitated to open the door. "I don't know why Miss Pendleton ended up in a drug house tonight, but I'm willing to bet she could use a familiar face right now."

Drug house? The room started to slant.

They'd never talked about her mom's drug abuse. In fact, Livy sometimes wondered if Sophie even knew the real reason she ended up in foster care. Either way, she'd always stayed clear of that life. Why now?

Jackson shook his head. "There must be some kind of mix-up. Sophie's made her share of poor choices, but drugs?" He stumbled over the word. "That's not her. She wouldn't use." Jackson brought his fist to his mouth. "Did you do a drug test?"

"We did. It came back clean. But given her concussion and the laceration above her eye, we'd still like to keep her overnight for observation."

"Concussion?" Jackson's fist tightened. "Who would...?"

Livy didn't blame him for not getting the question out. The thought of anyone hurting Sophie burned to her bones.

"We're guessing a dealer. If she turned him down, it might explain the roughhousing."

Livy gripped her stomach in search of the breath this whole conversation had knocked out of her.

Eyes softening, the nurse touched Livy's arm. "The number of patients we see from that part of town never gets easier. But when I see a case like Miss Pendelton's, it reminds me to be grateful for second chances."

Someone from farther down the hall called to her, and she waved the chart in return before offering Jackson and Livy a final warm smile. "Excuse me."

Left to go inside, Jackson scrubbed a hand down his five-o'clock shadow and turned away from the door instead.

Livy knew he was thinking the same thing she was. "This isn't your fault."

"You sure about that?" Jackson faced the ceiling and pinched his forehead. "I know I'm not her parent, and I probably get the discipline part of this role wrong half the time. But I'm telling you, when you're responsible for a kid her age, you'd do anything to—"

"You're doing the best you can." Livy rested a calming hand on his shoulder despite feeling anything but calm herself. "She knows that."

Underneath her protective shell, Sophie craved the love she so vehemently closed herself off from receiving. Livy had to believe she'd find the courage to open herself up to that love, even if it could disappoint her. They were too much alike for Livy to give up on that hope.

He squeezed Livy's hand in a silent thank-you, inhaled, and led them into the small room.

Sophie sat propped up in her bed with a blanket pulled up to her lap and stitches above her eye. The room's dim light flickered over finger-shaped bruises discoloring her arm like a tattoo branding her with abuse.

Fierce waves of anger nearly knocked Livy over. Jackson brought a hand to her back, and she motioned she was okay. They'd deal with that part later.

The *click* of the door opening drew Sophie's gaze in Livy's direction. She flicked it back to the TV before the door settled into its frame. "Haven't you used up your quota of pity on me this year?"

Jackson stepped forward. "Sophie."

Livy held up a hand to stop him. Sophie had a right to be angry with her as much as Livy had a right to explain.

"You're right. I messed up. I should've told you about Tanner from the beginning. I was wrong to keep that from you, and I'm sorry." She eased forward, swallowed. "I don't blame you for being upset—"

"I'm not upset." When she caught Livy's concerned look at the bruises around her wrist, she slid her arm under the blanket and strained to keep an indifferent gaze glued to the TV. "This has nothing to do with you. I already told you. I make my own choices."

"And tonight, you chose, what? To go tweaking? I thought you said—"

"It doesn't matter."

"It matters to me." Livy strode forward, her arms and heart unraveling. "Don't you see that?"

A wounded stare overrode the tears Sophie struggled to blink away. "If you didn't think using drugs was worse than using people, maybe I could." Her blood pressure cuff compressed around her arm, her words around Livy's chest.

"I wasn't using you—"

"Please, just leave." With her gaze fastened on the TV again, Sophie bundled the top of the blanket under her arm.

Livy started for her. "Soph, let me—"

"I said, go." The stark beeping from the monitors beside her bed added a hundred exclamation points.

Livy gripped her elbows across her torso to keep from blanching at the darkness crowding out the vulnerable girl she knew was underneath it all.

She looked at Jackson in the corner, visibly fighting the urge to intervene. It wouldn't have mattered if he'd tried. With one more glance back at the girl she'd hurt too deeply to receive forgiveness from, Livy turned for the door and the realization that some people's second chances eventually ran out.

Outside the room, she backed against the cold wall, covered her mouth, and inhaled a shaky breath.

A little girl holding her mom's hand stared at her on their way to the next room down. Livy quickly ran a knuckle under her eyes. Regardless of who they were about to visit, the girl didn't need to go into the room thinking people came out of them crying.

Yet instead of fear or apprehension, the strength Livy had wanted to show the girl beamed back at her as if she somehow knew Livy needed it right then more than she did.

Livy tilted her head, hanging on to the silent connection until the echo of her cell ringing bounced against the hallway's white walls. She hustled to answer. "Hello?"

"Livy, it's Lara Crawford. Mrs. Bradley just called. She said you didn't show up."

Shoot. She lifted the phone from her ear—6:52 p.m. *No, no, no.* She couldn't miss this appointment. Not when her son was expecting her to keep her word. "I'm so sorry. An emergency came up, and I..." It didn't matter right now. "Please tell her I'm on my way." She pushed off the wall.

"I'm sorry, but I'm afraid it's not going to work."

"No, I can make it work." Her shoes squeaked to a stop in front of the elevator. She jammed the button six times. *Come on.* "It'll take me no more than thirty minutes to get there. Not that I'll be speeding," she backpedaled. "I'm a great driver. I promise. Safety first, always. I know a few shortcuts, and I can stay later if they don't mind. This is really important to me. I know these aren't the perfect circumstances, but I've been hoping—"

"Tanner's not ready, Livy."

The elevator doors chimed open, but she didn't move. "I'm sorry. I don't understand. Not ready for what?"

Lara breathed through the line with the weight of words unspoken. "Your son's not ready to meet you."

Seated on the edge of Quinn and Cooper's dock, Chase pulled one leg up and leaned an arm over his knee. The sunset blended into the lake like watercolors waving together without beginning or end. Alone, he soaked in the lake's solitude.

It wouldn't last much longer. He'd been around enough storms to know one was building on the horizon. But as close or severe as it might be, it didn't compare to the storm he couldn't still inside him.

For the tenth time, he glanced at his cell lying on the pier. Time was up. Earl needed the answer Chase still hadn't found.

A slow breath slid his arms to his sides and his palms to the warm cedar boards. A foot away, a Carolina wren hopped toward him and cocked its head. Neither moved until chirping brought who he guessed to be a mate soaring to the dock. In one fluid song, the two birds careened across the water already starting to churn in the wind.

Grace amid the storm. Would it be enough this time?

Footsteps sounded behind him. "Sorry," Quinn said on her way down the dock. "I thought I'd be back sooner. Mama's all in a tizzy 'cause Dad won't come in from the barn, and she's insisting we're about to have a real gully washer." Half laughing at their mom's country sayings, Quinn joined him on the edge of the pier. "Who knows, maybe Dad sensed it too. You should've seen him gathering up his woodwork projects like a tornado was about to tear through there or something. It was so weird."

When Chase didn't reply, she leaned an arm into his. "Hey, you all right?"

"Yeah." He lowered his leg and stretched his back. "Fine. Just needed the lake for a bit, I guess."

"I don't blame you. It's a special place." She peered around the dock, no doubt lost in memories she shared here with Cooper.

Chase hid a grin. The two of them might've nauseated him at times, but truthfully, he couldn't be happier his sister had found the family she'd always wanted and more than deserved.

"Where's Brayden?"

"Inside with Cooper." She leaned back on her hands. "Probably getting slipped some coffee while I'm not looking."

"Better coffee than free dance lessons." Chase's chuckle wavered against the memories he still wrestled to make sense of.

Rather than jump on the opportunity to rib him about the dancing fiasco, Quinn drew her knees up to her chest and gazed across the water with him. "You want to talk about it?"

It figured she'd sense something was on his mind.

Chase twisted his phone in half circles on the planks. "Actually, there's something I need to tell you." Question was, where to start. He pocketed his cell and straightened out his jeans at the knees as dark clouds rolled in from the far end of the lake.

"If you tell me this is about Kaley, I'm seriously going to shove you in the water right now."

He laughed. "You do remember how that's turned out for you every other time you've tried, right?" He'd lost count of the number of times he'd tossed her off piers while growing up.

"Everyone's winning streak is bound to end at some point. Now, spill it already."

Amusement tapering, he clasped the ridged end of the boards on either side of his thighs. "It's about Dad. About his insurance, actually." He flicked the top of his hat, regretting keeping things from her for this long. "Their plan changed this year, and—"

"I know."

His gaze shot up from his lap. "You do?"

"Jeez, Chase. Give me a little credit, will ya? Just 'cause I'm still living in my honeymoon stage doesn't mean I'm completely oblivious." She wrapped her arms around her legs and set her chin over her knees. "And this is Mama we're talking about here. The woman can't keep a secret to save her life."

"Why didn't you say anything?"

"I figured you'd tell me when you were ready." She peered across the water again. "I know what it's like to need some space to sort through things on your own."

"I'm not sure how much good that's done." Answers still felt as out of reach as the bottom of the lake.

"Last year, you told me I had nothing to prove to Dad." Her hands slid down to her ankles. "Maybe that's the only answer you need right now."

Was it? Chase rustled his fingers through his hair and slipped his hat back on. "You know, he hardly recognized me the last time I was home."

"Is that why you haven't been back?"

He caught a pointed glance. The kind that saw through any attempt at denying it, even if it hadn't been a conscious decision.

Under a canopy of branches, Chase watched the beginning of the rain play the faintest percussion over the lake. "Remember when Mom used to make him come get us out back when supper was ready?"

"And you'd beg, 'ten more minutes, ten more minutes,'" she mocked him.

"Okay, A, I didn't sound like that. And B, we got to stay out longer, didn't we?" He smiled at images of Dad standing on the back porch. "Make it five, and—"

"Don't tell your mom," she joined him in finishing Dad's infamous response.

Laughing, Quinn crossed her ankles above the water. "Shoot, half the time he stayed out in the fields with us, getting just as dirty."

"It didn't stop him from trying to play it off." His ridiculous excuses were almost as comical as the look Mom gave him each time he tried to pull one over on her. Man, he missed those summers. Missed the way things used to be. It wasn't supposed to turn out like this.

He hung his head and blew out a breath. "I'd give anything to have those five minutes back again."

"Me too." Her torn words drifted into a surge of wind picking up above the trees.

Chase tucked her under his arm, and she leaned her head on his shoulder. "He's still with us, you know," she whispered.

For how much longer?

"The medicine's not helping anymore. Even if I take this job in Chicago, it won't accomplish any more than staying here will." He chucked an acorn into the water. Ripples spiraled like the consequences he didn't have control over. "I don't know how Mom does it. Watching him fade every day, knowing there's nothing any of us can do."

Quinn peeked over her shoulder up toward the house. "Sometimes I wonder more how *Dad* must feel, having to rely on Mama to take care of him now. He's always been the one to fill that role, you know? But then I have these moments with Cooper when I can't shake something Dad said to me last year."

She faced Chase then. "He told me pain's what's kept their vows to love each other through anything as real now as they were the day they'd promised them."

Chase had always admired their parents' marriage. Had grown up dreaming of creating that same kind of legacy. Now, he couldn't stop wondering if he'd spent his own life chasing something he couldn't hold on to.

"What if it's not enough, Quinn? Faith, family, our home... they used to be what got us through anything." He closed his eyes against the wind. "I honestly don't know what to do if we lose that."

Head down, she fanned a string of Spanish moss that had blown onto the pier into the water. "Actually, I think something like this is exactly why Dad built our home on that foundation. So that no matter what else falls apart, it will still hold." She looked up from the wood. "Even when we can't see how."

Mom's words from the morning Chase had flown out to Chicago rushed in on the tail of Quinn's.

"I'd rather die believing without seeing, than to go through a day of this life without faith."

She'd known even then that the medicine had stopped working, hadn't she? Had known they'd eventually lose him. But instead of turning to herself for a way to fix it as Chase had, she turned to faith and her vow to stand beside her husband for better or worse in what time was left.

Quinn bumped her shoulder into him. "Besides, I seem to remember this *really* obnoxious brother of mine reminding me last year how family sticks by each other no matter what." Sobering, she moved back to meet his eyes. "You know that's true for you too, right?"

"I know," he said softly. It had taken him longer than it should have to remember it, but he knew.

"You sure? 'Cause I feel like you need to know it's okay to lean on someone else sometimes." Her eyes slanted. "Someone *other* than Kaley Phillips."

He laughed. "Actually, she—"

"Isn't the one who got Tessa to agree to reopen Mrs. Finch's café."

He stared at her. "What?"

Quinn scrolled to something on her phone and held it out to him. He took it and looked over a graphic of a flyer advertising the first reinstituted open mic night at the café's grand opening. His eyes stopped over the text stating all proceeds would go to dementia research.

Chase clutched the phone. "Livy did this?"

"She's in love with you, Sherlock."

"But how did she—?"

A squeal lit off beside him. Quinn covered her head with her arms to block the beads of rain smashing through the oak leaves above them.

So much for calming the storm. The earlier soft raindrops now blew sideways in thick sheets. Chase and Quinn made a run for it up the dock.

"Wait." She stopped him at the bottom of the stairs leading to the deck. "We can't leave Dad out in the barn."

"As long as he's under shelter, he'll be fine."

A crack of thunder challenged his response.

"No, you don't understand. He was lining up his woodwork outside like some kind of inventory check or something." Quinn grabbed his arm. "You didn't see him, Chase. He's not gonna leave that stuff outside, no matter how bad it gets."

Knowing Dad's tie to his woodwork, he didn't doubt it.

The flag at the end of the pier whipped back and forth as hard pellets drummed onto the dock like gunfire.

Quinn scanned the yard. "Is that hail?"

A *crack* sounded above them. Chase barely got Quinn out of the way before a branch crashed into the rocks along the bank and splintered in all directions. He knew the signs of a storm to be afraid of. Knew what kind of damage they could leave.

Adrenaline picking up, he grabbed Quinn's hand. "We need to get to Dad. Now."

CHAPTER TWENTY-SEVEN

Fallen

A yelp from his parents' backyard echoed the claps of thunder coming closer and closer together. Without waiting for Quinn to catch up, Chase sprinted around the corner of the house, cleared the fence in one leap, and ran through the rain and hail pummeling the barn's wooden frame.

In the middle of it, Dad frantically turned toward the wood pieces not yet in the wheel barrel beside him.

"George, please." Mom reached for him again.

A dark look flashed in a streak of lightning as Dad broke her hands free from his wrists.

She fell to the ground, narrowly missing the border of bricks encasing flowers the hail had beaten into the soil.

Chase wrenched off his rain jacket while dropping to his knees and flung it around her. "Are you all right?"

"Don't worry about me, honey." Streaks of water ran from the hair matted to her forehead across wrinkles that seemed to have deepened over the last month. She wiped her hands and nodded behind him. "You just get that stubborn daddy of yours out of this mess before he gets himself hurt."

"Mama?" Quinn's knees splashed into a muddy puddle beside them. Hood up, she blinked through the sideways rain blowing into her face and helped Mom get her arms through Chase's jacket sleeves.

"Oh now, stop your fussing. I'm not on my deathbed, sugar." The minute Mom shifted to stand, a wince sent her reaching for her hip.

Quinn's eyes begged Chase to tell her what to do.

He peered back at Dad, still straining to haul heavy wood pieces into the barrel. Hail blew across the open field behind the house. The nearest red maple's branches whipped from side to side, cracks sounding down one of the limbs. Chase didn't have time to hesitate. He scooped a shoulder under Mom's and heaved her to her feet.

"I've got her." Quinn looped an arm around her waist as Chase steadied her.

Mom shooed him off. "Go on, now. Your daddy needs you."

While the girls made their way across the sodden yard, Chase rushed to the wheel barrel. "Pops, it's time to go. We gotta get inside."

"Not without my work."

Another *crack* above them swept the tree branch into the side of the barn. Chase reached for Dad's hand. "There's no time."

He pulled away. "I'm not leaving." A welt from the hail swelled along his brow, distorting eyes Chase almost no longer recognized. Yet even distant, they held a familiar pang of determination. The kind that throbbed with the need to be fearless. Whether against the storm or his disease, Chase wasn't sure. But standing there with a fallen hero who needed to know he still had fight left in him nearly brought Chase back to his knees.

Dad nodded an earnest plea for him to understand.

One of Mom's plastic chairs flipped over and blew into the table. Chase whipped toward the house. He needed to get them to shelter before things escalated.

Reading his thoughts, Dad turned caved shoulders to the drenched wood pieces and struggled to pick up the old owl figurine he'd carved back when Chase was in Boy Scouts.

Chase caught the bottom edge and lifted the weight off Dad's shaky arms. A flash of recognition met Chase's eyes then. He stopped, stared. Maybe they weren't soldiers. Maybe it wasn't a battlefield. But something about the moment beckoned a bond his dad seemed to know wasn't broken.

The maple's branch beat into the barn again. Soaked leaves and twigs trampled over them. And while the storm continued to rage, all outside interference dwindled to un-spoken words shared between a father and his son.

Without letting go of the owl, Dad tipped his head, and a smile from the past overrode the present. "Ten more minutes."

Rain tunneled into a slow grin streaked with tears Chase had kept harbored for too long.

His dad's gray and watery gaze held on to his as though desperate for it to keep him there in a memory he didn't want to lose. He stretched out a hand. "Chase, son—"

Wind howled into the thunder. The plastic chair whirled across the grass, and with another piercing smack against the barn, the branch finally cracked above them.

Time stalled. Chase blinked, breathed. Before he could move, the branch knocked Dad to the ground. Shards of wood and hail sprawled across the yard like shattered glass.

A scream rang from the house, and adrenaline tore through him. At Dad's side in a second, Chase hefted the broken branch off his chest. "Pops, talk to me." He leaned an ear over his nose. Though short, shallow breaths whispered through the thunder, his body lay still. Unmoving.

"Chase!" Quinn yelled from the back door, Mom leaning over her shoulder from behind.

"Stay inside." Chase turned back to Dad and tapped his face. "C'mon, Pops. I need you to wake up." He hunched over him to block the rain. "Mom and Quinn need you. You hear me?" Tears burned in his throat. "*I* need you." Hail beat into his back, the cost of what he could lose cutting deeper.

Time rarely played fair. Too short, too fast. Life barreled forward, leaving memories relegated to a past easily forgotten in the chase for the future. He couldn't go backward. Couldn't keep things from changing. But while breathing in, he faced the dark heavens and prayed for five more minutes with the man who'd taught him to make every minute count.

A weak grip curled around his forearm, followed by an even weaker rasp. "Chase."

He blinked through the water running from his hair to Dad's fingers balled around his sleeve. He clasped a hand over his. "Pops?"

"You planning to keep an old man out in this weather, or you gonna get me inside already?"

Head hanging in relief, Chase let out a tension-releasing laugh. Of all moments—in the middle of a storm that had nearly broken his body—Dad found the sarcasm he'd lost over the last few months. Chase ran a hand down his wet face. "If that *old man* would stop fighting me, maybe we'd already be inside."

"Now, how would you become the man I taught you to be without a little fight in you?"

For a minute longer, Chase sat in the rain, staring at a rare glimpse of the dad he missed more than anything.

"Dad!" Quinn skidded into Chase's back, swung around him, and grabbed Dad's free hand.

"I thought I told you stay inside."

A peaked eyebrow challenged Chase's tone. "Guess you're not the only stubborn one in this family."

No doubt about that.

"I think your daddy's got you both beat." Mom towered above them, hands perched on her hips. "Stubborn as a pack of mules. The whole lot of you."

All three of them shared a look the way they used to when they went in with their pitiful excuses for being late to supper. Laughter tumbled out until Dad reached for his head, and a blood covered hand silenced them all in a heartbeat.

CHAPTER TWENTY-EIGHT

Choices

Livy pushed through the crowded hospital entryway and bumped into Chase hurrying in the opposite direction.

"Whoa." He steadied her by the arm as they whirled under the canopy outside. "Liv? What are you doing here? Are you all right?"

All right? She wanted to be—*needed* to be—but everything was falling apart. She stepped back and kept her eyes down. "I'm fine."

"You're not fine." He dipped his head under hers. "Livy."

Though tears rarely ever listened to reason, the mix of fear and comfort found in how well he knew her didn't leave Livy a fighting chance. Everything pounding inside her welled up with the intensity of the storm robbing the day of sunlight.

"Hey." He pulled her close. "Whatever it is, it's going to be okay." Cupping a hand to her hair, he kissed the top of her head. "I've got you."

Even when he had every reason to let go.

Livy clung to his back, to him. "He doesn't want to see me." She breathed against his shirt. "My son. I was late to our visit, and he changed his mind. And now I don't know if I'll ever…"

"You will." His whiskers brushed over her hair with assurance, and everything in her wanted to believe him.

A woman who looked like Chase's mom scrambled up the walkway with a rain jacket pitched above her head. Livy tugged Chase out of her path just before she almost ran into them. "Mrs. Thompson?"

She gasped. "Oh, for heaven's sake." She lowered her hand from her chest and clutched Livy's forearm instead. "Sorry, sugar. I should be minding where I'm going." She shook out the wet jacket and draped it over her arm. "I was in such a tizzy when we first got here, I forgot my pocketbook in the van. And that impossible receptionist won't do a blasted thing 'til I fetch her our insurance card." She rustled through her oversized purse, mumbling things that would've had Livy laughing in another time and place.

She looked at Chase to fill in the gaps of whatever she was obviously missing.

He tipped up the front of his hat and ran the back of his wrist across his forehead. "There was an accident at the barn. My dad, he's…"

Livy's heart thudded in her ears. She gripped Chase's arm. "Tell me he's okay."

When Chase didn't answer, Mrs. Thompson patted Livy's shoulder. "He'll be fine, dear. If there's one thing my husband has, it's a hard head." She slanted a pointed look at Chase.

"Something he and our son seem to have in common." Leaving a shadow of pink across Chase's cheeks, she took extra care to smile at the hand Livy still had wrapped around Chase's arm before heading inside.

Livy brought her fingers to her neck and waited for the entryway's doors to close behind Mrs. Thompson. She breathed out, wanting to kick herself. His dad needed him, and here she was, blubbering on his shoulder about her own problems. "I'm sorry. I didn't realize..."

"There's nothing to be sorry for. Like I said, everything's gonna be okay."

Livy stared at the unfailing confidence she'd wrestled for so long to make her own. Willing back more ridiculous tears, she cleared her throat. "Still. You should go be with your family. Please."

"I will." He stepped closer. "But right now, I need to be with you." He took his hat off and dropped his gaze to the scuff mark he was making with his boot. "Quinn showed me the flyer. How'd you change Tessa's mind?"

Livy twisted the tips of her braid. "I might've told her a story of this *charming* young man who sang for his high school sweetheart there, and how they're going on thirty-seven years of marriage now." She let go of her hair. "What girl wouldn't want to keep a good ole country love story going?"

Instead of dishing out a joke about Livy's own country daydreams, Chase seemed to marvel at her as though she were part of the storm. "You say I'm the one always taking care of people, but you're pretty good at it yourself."

A trail of leaves blew past them, her breath caught up in the wind. Lightning flashed across the dark clouds in the distance. But for one moment, even the rain couldn't dampen how good it felt to be near Chase again. For things to feel the way she wished they could stay.

He fit his hat on again, the look on his face backing her against the column. "Thank you. I can't tell you how much everything you've done means to me." Eyes conflicted, he stepped closer. "But if Tessa reopens, you'll lose your chance to buy the property. I can't let you give up your dream."

"You're not. You're helping me preserve a different one." She reached for his hand. "This is the right thing to do. I think I've known it all along. It just took hitting my face against a few closed doors to understand why."

She forced down a swallow. "Chase, I meant what I said the other night. About Chicago, Kaley, all of it. I want you and your family to be happy." *Needed* them to be. Her heart couldn't take anything less.

His Adam's apple bobbed. "I appreciate that." He curled his fingertips under hers, not letting her draw away. "But Kaley's not the girl I'm in love with."

Warning herself to stay strong might've worked if the emotion in his eyes weren't unraveling her.

"I meant what I said too. Your regrets aren't who you are, Liv." He flung his hand up the minute she tried to interject. "I'm not saying choices don't have consequences. But running around, trying to make up for ways we think we fall short? It doesn't work. Believe me."

The space between them diminished another inch. "Regardless of whether you open a coffee shop or continue volunteering at the group home, or even if you never find Bandit again, you're already enough. I never should've made you feel otherwise with all this coaching stuff. You have nothing to prove. Especially to your son."

She drew in a shaky breath at the faith in his eyes.

"I know that's what you're worried about most, but he's gonna love you."

The knot tormenting her chest seized her throat. "How can he? I left him, Chase. You said it yourself. Real love doesn't abandon."

"Is that what you think?" Crestfallen, he lifted heartbroken eyes to hers. "Sacrificing to give him the best home you could wasn't abandoning him. You put him first, same way you're doing with me. With my dad." Chase stepped closer. "Your love's always been real, Liv. Give your son the chance, and he'll see that too."

Her chin trembled. "You can't know that."

He freed her hair from behind her ear as he often did and left his fingers along her neck. "Take it from a boy whose heart you held the moment he met you. You're impossible not to love."

Another inch, another breath, and she could hardly speak through the hammering in her chest. It pressed her back deeper against the column closest to them and her gaze deeper into his.

"I told you a relationship should be easy. That choices should be easy." Chase glanced toward the hospital entrance and exhaled. "But when it comes down to it, they're not. None of this is. Love, sacrifice—it's hard, even scary." He rested his forehead to hers. "But maybe that's how we know it's right."

Livy held on to him, not wanting to let go of the only right thing in her life.

"I understand why you think I should go. I understand why you want me to say I'll be happy in Chicago with someone else. And you know I'd do anything for you, Liv." His lips grazed her ear. "But don't ask me to tell you something I can't."

With eyes more vulnerable than she'd ever seen them, he pressed a kiss to her cheek. "I might be able to lie to myself," he whispered. "But not to you." His arms slid to his sides, their absence defying a night still caught in a storm that wouldn't let her go.

The hospital doors opened and closed. The wind continued to howl into the rain. All around her, noise after noise collided with the hundreds of responses churning inside her. But in the middle of it all, her heart grabbed hold of the only one that mattered.

His cell rang as she reached for him. Five more people passed in both directions before Chase finally drew his phone from his pocket. A glance at the screen weighed across his shoulders, and somehow, she knew.

He scrubbed a hand down his mouth and turned. "Yeah, hey, Earl. I take it you got my message. I'm sorry for dragging this down to the wire.… Uh-huh. I understand… There's no need. I've made up my mind."

Seeing him rub the grooves on his fingertips left from his guitar strings made Livy want to curl into a ball right there on the walkway. Her muscles tensed, torn between answers. Though that choice wasn't hers to make, the one that was had never been clearer.

Chase looked from the hospital entrance to her, his heart as heavy as the clouds. And in a matter of seconds, the choice that could alter everything rose above the storm. "Yes," he breathed into the phone. "I'm sure."

CHAPTER TWENTY-NINE

Home

L ivy held her cell between her ear and shoulder while wringing out the family-size tea bags over the pitcher in Mrs. Finch's sink. "Thank you so much for this opportunity, Trish. I'm really looking forward to working with you. And thanks again for letting Chase set up that little coffee war in the back the other week. I'm glad he connected us."

"Me too." The manager of the café across the lake laughed. "You just keep Chase Thompson away from my coffee presses, and we'll call it even. Actually, *any* coffee presses."

The pain of knowing Chase wouldn't be around to give her a hard time about it stole the heart in her laugh. His phone call with Earl last night had made it pretty clear he was taking the job in Chicago. Given the urgency on Quinn's face when she'd said they needed him inside for something to do with Mr. Thompson's insurance, Livy couldn't blame him. The only question left was how soon she had to say goodbye.

"See you Monday," Livy added before ending the call.

Mrs. Finch set a cutting board beside a fruit bowl. "If you wrap those strings around those bags one more time, we're gonna end up eating our iced tea instead of drinking it." She nodded to the tea bags about to burst in half.

"Sorry." Livy slid her phone to the counter and set the thoroughly squeezed bags in the sink. "Lost in thought."

"I gathered." The aged woman lined up two lemons on the cutting board and stretched a shaky hand to the knife block.

"Here. Let me." Livy cut one slice and waited for Mrs. Finch's approval before continuing. "I admit I'm better with coffee, but if you don't mind sharing your secrets, I'll try to make the tea as close to yours as I can."

"The only secret to sweet tea is the sugar." She leaned in. "Same ingredient for love." With an impish wink, Mrs. Finch dumped the tea bags in the trash can, dragged a navy-blue Tupperware canister across the counter, and peeled open the lid. "I reckon you've shared a sugar or two with the Thompson boy, no?"

A hunk of sliced lemon propelled off the cutting board.

Mrs. Finch's raspy laugh followed the rogue fruit slice across the kitchen floor. "Well, that answers that. The only thing funnier than the look on your face, hun, would be the look on Bandit's after eating that lemon off the floor."

Her eyes dimmed, and Livy's heart sank with regret all over again. "Oh, Mrs. Finch, I'm so sorry. I never should've—"

"Don't worry yourself one more second. That silly mutt will come back when he's good and ready."

Livy stared out the window to the woods, thoughts taking her back to the morning Bandit had taken off after that fox in the mountains. Like Mrs. Finch now, Chase had been so sure

Bandit would find his way back. *"You're like home to him. That'll always be enough to lead him back to you."*

She set a wrinkly hand over Livy's. "I haven't added the sugar yet, sweet pea."

"Sorry." Livy stopped her mindless stirring. "I was just…"

"Thinking. Mm-hmm." She poured in a scoop of sugar from the canister.

Livy dragged the wooden spoon around the bottom of the pitcher, questions still churning. "How did you do it, Mrs. Finch? Find the courage to let go of your family's business, I mean?"

She dumped another scoop of sugar into the tea, followed by the lemon slices. "I knew it'd work out."

"But how?" she said more to herself.

"Courage doesn't come without faith, dear." Mrs. Finch gave her a pointed look. "And I reckon you have more of both than you think, or you wouldn't be doing the same thing with your own dreams."

Gaping at her only brought out the intuition in her aged eyes even more. Yet instead of saying more, she held out a spoon to Livy. "Would you like a taste before I put it in the fridge to cool?"

Wait, was she seriously changing the subject? "No, thank you," she rambled off. "I'm sorry, what did you mean a second ago about the 'same thing'?"

Mrs. Finch balanced the pitcher of tea in both hands, turned, and shuffled across the tiles without her walker. "You mind my asking why you gave up on opening your own coffee shop?"

Apparently, changing the subject was what she did best. Livy plugged the sink and turned on the faucet. "I haven't given up on it."

"Then why are you taking a job somewhere else?"

Gazing out to the woods again, Livy turned off the water and left her hand on the handle. The more she thought about it, the more Chase's words from the first day in front of the vacant café swelled inside her with the very thing it had taken her this long to trust. "Because sometimes, you just know when the timing's right. And I want to wait for that, you know?" She swirled a soapy rag through the water. "That dream's a part of me. It's something I really believe I'm meant to do, but I don't want to be driven by the fear of my son being ashamed of me if I'm not successful. It's not about that." It never should've been.

The refrigerator door opened, snapping Livy out of another daze. "There's no room for shame in love, dear."

Livy smiled in the face of grace. "I know that now." She'd been wrong about experiencing real love for the first time when she met Chase. She had the moment she'd found out she was pregnant. Through each ultrasound, every kick. And especially the day she had to let Tanner go.

"When I gave Tanner up for adoption, I had to trust things would be okay. It was the only way I'd get through it." She set the cutting board in the drain rack and grabbed the dishtowel. "Heaven knows I lost that faith along the way. I kept trying so hard to make things happen on my own and couldn't understand why nothing ever worked out." She looked at Mrs. Finch. "But—I don't know—maybe I needed to find my way back to that place of trust first. For Tanner, the coffee shop." Maybe even for Chase.

"Like I said, hun, I reckon you have more faith than you think, or you wouldn't be trusting your dreams to work out the same way I have with my family's café." Another wink swept toward her from the fridge. "Which is why you're finally ready to inherit it."

She dropped the dishtowel. "Wait, what?"

"Now, I know your hearing isn't as bad as mine, sweet pea."

"Sorry. It's just... I don't understand. Tessa already agreed to reopen the café."

Mrs. Finch made it to the kitchen table and eased onto the nearest chair as though needing a breather from the walk across the floor. "There've been a few times she's offered to carry on the family business as a favor to me, but I never let her. My girl's always been the happiest teaching music."

"But she's already moving back here and everything?" How could Livy take it out from under her now?

"She's coming home to take care of her old mama." She pointed at Livy. "But don't you dare go telling her I admitted I need taking care of."

If her teeth weren't busy worrying her bottom lip, Livy might've laughed.

"Trust me, sweetie. She was relieved as I don't know what when I told her I wanted you to have it instead." Mrs. Finch tilted a patient smile at her. "I've always known you were the right person to inherit the shop. I've just been waiting for you to realize it too."

When Livy still couldn't get more than a couple of blinks out, Mrs. Finch chuckled. "Well, don't just stand there looking like the porch light's on but no one's home. You have a shop to design." She aimed a finger at her. "And I don't want you feeling like you have to keep things the same either. You make it your own, sweet pea. I don't want it any other way."

Emotion clogged her voice. "I don't know what to say."

Mrs. Finch swayed her head. "You could start by asking the previous owner to star in your first open mic night. I've been known to pack in a full house a time or two in my day."

Of that, Livy had little doubt.

A motherly smile landed on her. "Just remember, having faith doesn't always mean sitting on your hands. And we're not just talking about business here, are we, hun?" Rather than say more, she slanted a glance to Livy's cell on the counter.

The woman was about as subtle as Ti. Smiling to herself, Livy picked up her phone and hovered a thumb over Chase's name. Wanting to talk to him was even less of a question than wanting to be with him. She just wanted to be sure she wasn't interfering with... A glimpse of someone in her yard caught her eye through the window. Someone who looked like... "Sophie?"

Livy had made it halfway out the back door before grabbing onto the trim to stop herself. With the screen open, she turned to Mrs. Finch, who waved her on with a *Country Living* magazine. "I'll be here when you get back." Flaunting a wink rivaling Chase's, she flipped open the first page. "But no promises the tea will be."

Livy jogged over and wrapped her arms around her neck. "Thank you for believing in me."

"Aw, now. You make that part easy." Mrs. Finch squeezed her hand. "Go on, now."

As anxious as she was to find out what Sophie was doing here, another part of her was scared to know. She stopped at the screen again to iron out her shirt and any fears holding her back before crossing the lawn.

Sophie stood beside the firepit, her lip caught in her teeth and her hand still covering the bruises on her arm.

Livy stopped behind a lawn chair and ran her fingers over the top of the cushion. "Hey."

"Hey." Uncrossing her feet did nothing for the tense silence weaving between them until it was thicker than the after-storm humidity. She pointed behind her. "Jackson's out front, in case you were wondering. I asked if we could stop by on the way home."

Home. Livy exhaled on the inside. But when Sophie kept her chin down and twisted the bracelet Livy had given her without saying more, she held her breath again.

Another minute lapsed before Sophie looked up. "Is it true you came to see me last night instead of meeting your son?"

Livy sent a quick glance to the house, picturing Jackson in his car, hoping he'd done the right thing by telling her. She slipped her hands in her back pockets and lifted her shoulders. "I was worried about you. Still am." She angled her chin to catch Sophie's gaze. "Is everything—?"

"I went to look for my mom last night." Sophie darted her focus to the patio as fast as she'd shot off that bombshell.

"Your mom?"

"I know she didn't run off to New York to be a singer." She scuffed her Toms against the edge of the firepit, her voice ragged. "It just hurt less to picture her as a brave artist instead of some deadbeat meth head who probably doesn't even remember the daughter she had by mistake."

All the painstaking effort she put into hardening her shell broke against the pavement along with Livy's heart. The veneer melted, and instead of a vexed teenager, a vulnerable little girl longing for the love every child deserved stood in front of her.

She picked at her chipped nail polish. "When I found out you gave up your kid, too, I guess I kind of lost it." She shrugged. "I know it's stupid, but after how much time we spent together, I thought maybe you'd want to..." Chin quivering, she toyed with the corner of her shirt. "You know, adopt me. Then when I thought it was all fake, it felt like..." She looked up from her shoes long enough for the sorrow in her eyes to gut Livy.

"Like your mom was abandoning you all over again?"

Still without facing her, Sophie wiped at her tears. "I know it was dumb to try to find her. But I kept thinking, if she could just see me one time. If she knew I was looking for her, she might come back for me."

"Oh, Soph." It all made sense. Her defensiveness about drugs, her sense of betrayal, abandonment, the lashing out to keep from hurting. Livy crossed the intricate layers of pain between them and held her close.

"Why wasn't I enough, Liv?" Broken, she gripped Livy's shirt. "Why wasn't I enough to make her stay?"

She squeezed Sophie tighter, wishing she could take away every scar. "Love, your mom didn't give you up by choice."

"But she could've gotten clean. Could've come back for me."

For a period of time, that was true, but Sophie didn't need to hear about state laws right now. She needed to know it wasn't her fault.

"I'm willing to bet she wishes she could go back and change that now." Before Livy could stop them, Chase's words from last night rose with the tears climbing her throat. "Take it from someone whose heart you held the moment she met you. You've always been enough, Soph." Livy stroked her hair. "If you didn't already have such a great family ready to adopt you, I would've been lucky to have you as a daughter."

Sophie leaned back. "Really?"

Livy nodded, a full-on mess of tears now. "Yeah."

Jackson sneezed from the corner of the house. When the girls broke apart, he stood there, looking like an uncomfortable dad scouring for a dozen excuses to remove himself from all things emotional.

Laughing through tears, Sophie motioned him to them. "Don't worry, Jackson. We're not gonna cry all over you or anything."

He crossed the yard and drew her into a side hug. "It'd be okay if you did, you know."

She leaned her head against him, and Livy couldn't have been more grateful Mr. Hood's beagles chose right then to bark loud enough to camouflage the tiniest sob sneaking through.

Apparently, not well enough, because Sophie looked at her then. "What's gonna happen with you and your son?"

So much for no more tears.

Livy twisted the tips of her hair until all the questions and emotions and fears that'd been balled up inside her slowly untangled. "Honestly? I don't know how it's all going to work out, but I know he's gonna keep growing up with amazing parents who love him. And until he reaches a place where he wants me in his life, I'll keep waiting."

After a minute, Sophie's gaze flitted from Livy to Jackson and down to the patio again. "Do you think the Millers still want to be my parents?"

Jackson squeezed her arm. "As a matter of fact, they called me this morning."

"They did?" Once again, the surprise of someone being genuinely interested in her flickered in her eyes, but something deeper in them had changed.

Livy smiled at Jackson. Though neither of them could promise her what the Millers' home would be like, they could both promise she'd always be loved.

Jackson kept his arm around Sophie's back as they headed around the house. Something about watching them walk side by side painted a vision of Chase with his daughter, raising the family he'd always wanted here in Littleton. And right then, Livy knew she couldn't wait any longer.

She grabbed her cell from her pocket without thinking it through and hustled up to her back door. "Come on. Pick up."

"Hey, you've reached Chase Thompson's voice mail. You know what to do."

She hung up, twisted the doorknob, and almost smacked her nose dead into the pane when it didn't budge. She shook the knob again. "Don't tell me." With her hands cupped to the window, she glared at her keys mocking her from the end table. "You've got to be kidding me." She banged a palm on the door. "You've got to be freaking kidding me," she yelled this time.

Only she could lock herself out. She backed against the door and scrolled to Quinn's number. "Hey," she started in the second Quinn answered. "Tell me Chase hasn't left yet."

"He's at the airport, but—"

But nothing else mattered. Livy hung up, jetted around the house to her car, and kicked the tire when it reregistered that she didn't have her blasted keys.

Pacing the walkway, she wrenched her bangs back. Uber. She'd get an Uber. She dropped to the porch step and pulled up the app.

More barks sounded nearby, alternating with her pulse. Livy closed her eyes under the sunlight. *Please don't let me be too late.*

Something wet touched her knee. She flung her eyes open to Bandit's slobbery tongue panting right in front of her face. One whole second. The crazy dog didn't wait more than one whole second to paw his way into her lap.

Laughing, she pulled him down by the collar and kept his furry cheeks in her hands. "Do you have any idea how much trouble you're in, mister?"

"More than me, I hope." Chase rounded the corner of the driveway in worn jeans, a black T-shirt, and his cowboy hat.

Livy dropped her cell beside her feet.

A solid minute had to have passed—this time, without a single blink. Chase ran his knuckles down his rough jawline when Livy just sat there, staring like a girl with a schoolyard crush. But with the sun clinging to every inch of the hardworking country boy she'd fallen in love with, she could barely hold on to Bandit, let alone her heart. After all they'd been through, she'd stopped trying.

Another lick broke Livy's paralysis.

Laughing softly, Chase tapped his thigh, and the dog zoomed to his side. He squatted to give him a good rubbing. "I saw him in that field across from the Gilberts' while I was driving. I backed up, whistled for him, and he jumped right over my tailgate like he knew exactly where I'd take him."

Livy wiped Bandit's slobber from her cheek. "I can't believe he came back."

Stopped on the walkway with his hat shadowing his face, Chase rubbed the callouses on his left hand. "I told you he'd always find his way back to you."

Seeing Chase here, knowing she never wanted him to leave, Livy gripped the edge of the step. Everything she needed to tell him beat through her pulse against the concrete.

He breathed in. "Liv, I—"

"Don't go." She bolted to her feet. "Don't move to Chicago. I know I told you you should, but I was wrong. Your parents don't need your money, Chase. They need *you*." She glanced at Mrs. Finch's house, so relieved her daughter had decided to move nearby.

Chase stepped closer. "Livy—"

"Believe me, I know roots can get messy and complicated and even scary when things start changing. And I can't tell you how much longer you'll have with your dad, but I know you have right now. So, please."

He swallowed again, and she had to beg her heart to slow.

"Stay. With your family." She raised both shoulders. "With me. Because that someday you've been chasing... it's right here. In the town where your dad first sang to your mom. That legacy's yours, too, Chase. One I want to keep building with you."

He took his hat off and brought it to his side. While his hair rustled in the wind, the look in his eyes never wavered.

Bandit let out a soft bark as though unable to take Chase's pause any longer than Livy could.

She reached for his fingertips. "I can't promise you any dates with fancy oyster dinners if you stay," she said through a grin. "You can forget sharing a bowl of popcorn. And all things camping are *definitely* out."

Locked on his brown eyes, Livy reveled in his smile. "But I can promise there'll be two ridiculously worn husband pillows, an *endearing* number of self-incriminating comments, and an embarrassingly quirky best friend who wants to spend every day with you, living like all we have is right now. Because I'm in love with you, Chase Thompson. I always have been."

His chest expanded as though breathing for the first time.

Still without looking away, the country boy she'd fallen for the first day they met on her parents' front steps backed her up to the ones behind them. "I'm sorry, can you repeat that last part?"

As if his darn freckles weren't already showing how much he was enjoying this, the sideways grin flirting with his lips had to go and hitch his charm to a whole new level.

Shaking her head, she shoved him. "I think you heard me, Boots."

He kept his hand over hers on his chest. "I think I need to hear it again."

"Is that right?"

"Mm." He took his hat off, and she could barely restrain herself from showing him exactly what she meant.

Playing the coach this time instead, Livy ran her fingers from the tousled hair above his ear to the whiskers along his jaw. "Well, in that case, I said..." Slow and brimming with meaning he couldn't miss, she feathered the softest "I love you" against his lips.

A dimple-worthy smile curved into hers. "I'm definitely going to need to hear that a few more times."

If he kept up that look in his eyes, he'd be lucky if she could remember how to speak at all.

Bandit barked beside them. Laughing, Chase waved him on to Mrs. Finch's house. "Not this time, boy." He found Livy's gaze again. With one hand along the nape of her neck, he pressed his cowboy hat to her back. Slow and tender and perfect, he kissed her with every ounce of his promise that she'd find a guy who treated her the way she deserved.

Too soon, he broke away, kissed her once more, and leaned his forehead to hers. "I'm not going anywhere, Liv." Raspy breaths full of passion and commitment met hers. "I never was."

She set a hand on his wrist. "But you were at the airport."

"I went to make arrangements for Earl to pick up my Nova."

"You're selling it?" She leaned back. "I don't understand. That car's everything to you."

"Not everything." He uncaged a strand of hair tucked around her ear. "You told me taking care of things doesn't mean I can't let others help me, and you're right. So, Quinn and I are both pitching in to keep Nurse Murphy on board as long as we can."

He wiped specks of dirt off the brim of his hat. "I know money can't save my dad. Maybe none of my choices can." Exhaling, he looked up with such conviction, Livy's fingers tightened around his sleeve. "But whether I can see how it'll help or not, I choose to stay. This is my home. My life. And I don't want to miss a moment of it."

Livy took in every brave, sacrificial, honoring inch of the amazing man in front of her, overwhelmed with the truth in Mrs. Finch's words. *"Courage doesn't come without faith."*

"Besides." With his familiar cadence returning, Chase fit his hat back on. "Before I got sidetracked with a crazy dating scheme to win over this *really* cute girl, I promised her I'd fix her dishwasher, so..." He laced his fingers behind the small of her back. "I should probably find a way to make it up to her."

"Oh really?"

"Mm-hmm." His freckles edged closer. "Think I could swoon her with a country song?"

She slid her palms up his chest to the back of his neck, the memory of their dance warming through her. Sunlight crested the trees. Every shadow disappeared. And without any reservations, Livy settled into the gift of grace she'd never had to earn. "You already did."

"Does that mean I can take you on one more date?" He leaned back far enough to flaunt a loaded grin. "'Cause I hear Quinn and Cooper have an *epic* end-of-summer party coming up."

Heaven only knew what that meant.

CHAPTER THIRTY

Someday

Chase's mom sidled up beside Quinn in the living room with a tray of peach cobbler in hand. "Now, sugar, when you asked if you could move your party to our house for your daddy's sake, you could've warned me how many handsome fellas you'd be bringing with you." She fretted with her hair. "I would've at least worn my Spanx."

Chase nearly spit out his sweet tea. Quinn turned red as usual, but Ti obviously couldn't help egging her on.

"Right?" She twisted the fringe strips on the end of her dress. "Seriously, this many gorgeous eyes all in one room has me dying for my camera right now."

Drew cleared his throat behind her. Laughing, Ti turned and roped her arms around his waist. "Don't worry, babe. You have the sexiest dimples by far."

"I don't know, girl." Beside them, her friend Cassidy shifted her one-year-old daughter to her opposite hip and leaned into her husband. "You do recall the firemen calendar comment you made when you first met Ethan, right?"

Ti cracked up when Ethan's cheeks beat Quinn's in the party's first—and surely not the last—round of pure awkwardness.

Quinn sent a whimsical grin across the room with enough inside meaning to lure Cooper toward her. "Sorry, ladies. When it comes to dimples, my man wins hands down."

The guys all looked at each other, shook their heads, and kissed their wives—something Chase could barely keep waiting to do himself. Everyone else faded in the background as he watched Livy help Dad keep Wiggle Worm Brayden on his lap. He wasn't about to wager on who had the best dimples. But when it came to who was the most blessed guy in the room, his heart didn't hold a single doubt that he won that contest every single day.

Ti squealed from the window. "Bree and Josh just got here."

Cassidy handed their daughter to Ethan right as Mom held out a plate of cobbler to him. "You look like you could wet your whistle, darlin'. What can I get for you?"

Ethan pulled their daughter's finger away from the cobbler's whipped topping. "Um..."

Oblivious to Ethan's confusion, Mom already started for the kitchen. "Do they drink sweet tea in New York? You know, my husband and I almost went to see the Statue of Liberty when we first got married, but ooh-wee, we sure enough didn't make it past that Motel 6 outside town, did we, George?" She poked her head around the corner toward Quinn. "Sugar, I know the honeymoon is over, but if you still need some tips, your daddy and I can—"

"Eh, eh, no." Cringing, Quinn flung her hand up. "Mama, seriously, that conversation is never happening. Like, never ever."

Redirecting to Chase wasn't happening either. The second Ti opened the door for their friends, he grabbed Livy's hand and whisked her out the back.

She laughed. "Afraid your mom might embarrass you next?"

"Were you not in there for the last thirty minutes?" he deadpanned. But when Livy sank into his side, the moments before them were all that mattered.

He slid his fingers through hers and soaked in the afternoon. The sunshine, the cicadas, the summer breeze. It held everything he loved about growing up here and—he kissed Livy's cheek—every reason he wanted to stay.

She circled in front of him with her hands around his back and set her chin on his chest. "The barn looks great, by the way."

Chase peered toward the repairs he and Dad had made together after the storm. "Thanks." He fanned her curvy hair off each shoulder. "Wait 'til you see the inside."

Her mouth pulled to the side. "You're not gonna try to make out with me on a bale of hay, are you?"

"Maybe." If his arms knew he was teasing, they might've let her go. Not that it mattered. Barely inside, Chase brought his lips to hers, unable to wait.

Livy backed against the door with her fingers entwined in his hair. She grazed her palm along his jawline and kept her eyes closed a moment longer when he broke himself away. "If you plan on following that up with something more amazing, you've got your work cut out for you."

"I've always loved a challenge." Chase flipped the lights, led her up the ladder to the loft, and savored the feel of her fingers tightening around his when she saw the table he'd set up.

"Lilies." She stepped forward, stopped, and pinched her lips together. "And Cheerios?"

"*With* a banana and candlelight." Chase joined her. "You did say if a guy had all three, you'd never look back."

Her sweet laugh flitted around the twinkle lights strung through the rafters. "You really do know how to win a girl's heart, you know."

"Not as easily as you won mine." He set his cell on one of the rustic old benches, turned up the volume to the country song he'd finally written and recorded for her, and drew her into a dancing hold. He tipped his hat. "Your dream date in a barn loft, ma'am."

With eyes full of love he could get lost in, Livy stood on her toes to kiss him again. "It's perfect." Her grin pressed against his. "And for the record, you make a *way* sexier cowboy than Jimmy Sterling."

"You sure?" Chase pulled at the hem of his T-shirt. "'Cause we can settle this tan-off once and for all right here."

She laughed. "You start that, Boots, and we'll never make it back to the party."

If it were up to him, they'd stay right there forever. He slid his hands around her soft summer dress and breathed in the fragrance he wanted to spend every morning waking up to.

"For the record." He notched his hat up. "Cotton's *definitely* not overrated."

Her lashes dipped, and the wind had to breathe for him.

Chase brought her hands down to her sides and took her in. Her hair in the sunlight, eyes more giving and compassionate than she knew. One look was all it had taken from the very beginning.

He ran his thumbs along her knuckles and inhaled slowly. "Liv, you're the girl I've been waiting for. Before we ever met, I prayed for you, for the family we'd raise together." He leaned back. "A family I want Tanner to be a part of, when he's ready."

Her chin started to tremble.

"I know it feels like life's had us stumbling from one challenge to the next. This summer's been the hardest I've ever walked through. I almost gave up on everything I knew." Chase brushed her bangs to the side, wanting full view of the eyes that held his heart. "But I wasn't acting the night I told you I can finally breathe again when I hear your voice. At the end of every crazy, grace-filled moment, this—us—reminds me why I'd choose it again and again." His hand drifted to the back of her neck, his forehead to hers. "Because I love you, Liv. Every awkward, rambling, animal-whispering inch of you."

Laughing through tears, she shoved him.

He cupped his hand over hers, ready to hold on forever.

"The promise I made you while camping hasn't changed. It doesn't matter whether we're in the middle of a woman's clothing shop or in the middle of a wide-open field, I want to spend every today of my life with you." He brought his hat to his heart, knelt to the wooden beams, and lifted a ring to the girl he'd never leave. "Livy Hensley, will you—?"

"Yes." All tears now, she tented her hands over her mouth. "Sorry." She reached for his cheeks and kissed him again. "Yes."

In love with everything about her, Chase laughed as he lifted her up by the waist and twirled her in the summer glow of the beginning to the someday he'd been waiting for.

Grace

One Year Later

The countdown on Livy's phone beeped at the zero mark. "Time." She looked up at her newest hire side by side with her most entertaining employee, a coffee war about to be put to the test.

Wesley held his hands out in a gangster pose. "Three skinny hazelnut macchiatos in under two minutes. Boom. That's what I'm talking about, girl. Lightning speed."

"Three's good." Sara eyed his lineup. "*Almost* as good as four." She swiped one of the drinks she'd just made, took a gloatingly long sip, and dished Wesley's pose back at him. "Boom."

"Ohh." Livy tossed Wes a fresh apron. "Looks like the coach just got schooled."

Sara beamed as Livy handed her her nametag. She'd been working hard all week to beat Wesley's speed.

"All right. All right." He fastened his own tag to the clean apron. "We'll see who's got game at tonight's open mic night."

Livy motioned them to the front of the café. "You just focus on bringing your A-game to the floor this morning. The breakfast crowd's about to hit."

"For the prettiest boss on the strip?" He waggled his bushy brows. "You got it."

She shook her head at him. Clearly, *some* things never changed.

As Wes led Sara out, Livy stayed in front of the drinks they'd prepared. Coffee wars might be an unconventional way to train, but it would always be her favorite. She laughed, picturing Chase's face covered in chocolate drizzle.

"Need me to show them how it's done?" he said from the doorway.

Half startled, and way more relieved, Livy turned and smiled. "You're home."

Chase sauntered over with a grin she been dying these last five days to kiss. She pulled her bottom lip in, waiting, eager. Eyes never leaving hers, he slid one hand around her waist and took his hat off with the other, owning that Jane Austen charm in all its maddeningly sexy glory. "I am now." He leaned in, stole her lip with his. And she sank a little deeper into the arms of a cowboy any Cinderella dreamer would gladly lose her slipper for.

A gagging noise sounded from the door, where Sophie stood trying to keep a straight face.

Livy turned toward her. "Hey. I thought you were heading out this morning."

"We are. Dad's waiting out front."

Dad. Despite how many times she heard Sophie call Mr. Miller that, it nearly broke her every time. She picked up one of the macchiatos and focused on the lid, lest she cry yet *again* at the thought of Sophie leaving for college.

Apparently, she wasn't the only one. Head down, Sophie crossed one foot over the other. "I just stopped by on our way out to see if, you know..." She raised a nonchalant shoulder. "You might need one more hug before I go."

More like twenty. The five Livy had given her during her final shift at the café two nights ago weren't anywhere near enough. She set her coffee down, met Sophie halfway, and drew her close. "Miss you already, love."

Sophie wiped away tears as she let go and slanted a loaded grin at her. "Enough to comp me a venti soy vanilla latte for the road?"

"Only if you make it yourself."

Sophie looked at her like she was completely mental for thinking that would ever be negotiable. "As if I'd let Wes anywhere near my drink."

Laughing, Livy slid her husband a glance. "Better him than Chase."

Two seconds, and those attractive freckles of his were already closing in on her. "Oh really?"

She eyed the caramel drizzle bottle on the table, so tempted, but backed into the door instead. At least out front, they had to act somewhat professional.

Then again, professional was relative when it came to Wesley. Behind the counter, he flipped the whipped cream bottle in the air like a performer before adding the final touch to a small hot chocolate he'd made for Tanner, who'd evidently just gotten there.

Livy leaned a shoulder into Chase's side. It only ever took one look at her son's face lighting up for her heart to melt. Ten months of getting to know him had filled her life with a kind of joy she'd never experienced before.

As soon as he saw Livy, Tanner handed his dad his drink and ran over to her.

She scooped him up off the floor and squeezed him tight. "There's the hug I've been waiting all morning for."

He leaned back. "Pawpaw Thompson says I give the bestest hugs ever."

Livy turned toward Chase, so grateful his dad was still a part of their lives. She set Tanner back on the floor and smoothed his hair to the side. "That's 'cause those Thompson boys know what they're talking about. You ready to stop by to visit him?"

"Yeah." Head down, Tanner twisted the rubber tip of his shoe on the floor as if something was on his mind.

Livy looked at Mr. Bradley, who raised his shoulders in reply. She squatted to Tanner's eye level. "Everything all right, buddy?"

He nodded. "Just thinking." After a moment, he lifted his blue eyes toward hers and tilted his head. "Would it be okay for me to start calling you Mom now?"

Tears. So many uncontrollable tears. Livy willed them back with a smile. "Yeah, sweetie. I'd like that."

"Okay." He raced back over to Mr. Bradley and the hot chocolate he was missing as if he hadn't just left Livy's heart in a giant puddle on the floor.

She rose and turned right into the arms waiting for her.

Chase kissed her forehead. "Have I told you lately how brave you are?" He turned her around so her back fit against his chest, slid his arms down hers, and crossed them over her torso. "All these lives touched because you were willing to take a chance on faith."

Livy looked from Sophie tucked under Mr. Miller's arm to Wesley zipping around the coffee bar like a lightning bolt and laughed. But when her gaze landed on Tanner slurping whipped cream off the top of his drink, she nearly melted all over again. With chocolate in the corners of his mouth, he gave her a smile she never thought could belong to her.

Blasted tears!

"Told ya we'd bring that confidence out in you."

Livy soaked in the gifts surrounding her, knowing confidence hadn't brought her here. Grace had.

"In fact…" Chase's grin grazed her ear. "I seem to recall a conversation about the proof of our coaching deal being in the results."

"Who said our deal was over?" Lips to the side, she turned toward him and circled her arms around his beltline. "*In fact,* I'm pretty sure you owe me a night out now that you're home."

"Is that right?"

"Mm. But fair warning, my coach might've taught me a thing or two about how to charm my date."

Chase nestled a Gumby-inducing kiss to her cheek. "You sure it wasn't the other way around?"

She swallowed, breathed. "Positive." Borrowing his charm, Livy stole his hat and winked. "Lesson number one, cowboy. It all starts with a little patience and persistence."

A WORD FROM THE AUTHOR

Thank you so much for reading *Chasing Someday*. One of the best parts about art is the way it connects with each of us differently. I'd love to hear your thoughts on this series. Email me anytime.

If you enjoyed this book, please take a moment to leave a review to help new readers discover Chase and Livy's story. Even if it's just one sentence. Reviews are a tremendous help to authors, which in turn allows us to keep writing more stories for you. I can't do it without you!

Enjoy all the books in the Home In You Series:
Still Falling: A Prequel
Write Me Home: Book One
Begin Again: Book Two
Just Maybe: Book Three
Chasing Someday: Book Four

Visit www.crystal-walton.com/new-release-mailing-list and be the first to hear about the next release.

ACKNOWLEDGEMENTS

Ryder, being your mom is the toughest, most rewarding experience of my life. I've never known a fiercer love, greater joy, or deeper exhaustion. Though this book took a year to finish, I wouldn't trade a moment of becoming a first-time mom. You hold my whole heart.

Erynn, girl. What would I do without my favorite meme-loving editor? Thank you for enduring an unpolished draft of this story, for forgiving me when I made you cry, and for correcting the atrocities I committed against southern food and beverages. If I come visit you, can I get my Southern Membership Card reinstated? :)

Shaela, thank you for working with me on this gorgeous cover. It's a joy to partner with you.

To each member of my launch team, thank you for the ways you've rallied behind this series. Your support, especially over this last year, has gotten me through. Huge hugs!

To each of my readers, thank you for giving this series a try, for letting these characters share in a small part of your life, and for joining me along one crazy ride of faith, courage, and grace. I hope each book has been a blessing to you in return.